Line of Blood

ALSO BY BALRAJ KHANNA

Nation of Fools
Sweet Chillies
The Mists of Simla
Indian Magic
Rajah: King of the Jungle

LINE OF BLOOD

Balraj Khanna

For
Sophy Thompson
Meeting of Minds — Great!
With affection,
Balraj

PALIMPSEST

Published by Palimpsest Publishers 2017
Palimpsest Publishing House Pvt. Ltd.
16 Community Centre, Panchsheel Park
New Delhi 110 017, India

ISBN 978-93-82622-21-5

Typeset by Nutan in Adobe Garamond Pro
Printed and bound in India by Thomson Press India Ltd.

For Francine

We were eighteen and had begun to love life and the world; and we had to shoot it to pieces.

Erich Maria Remarque

PROLOGUE

VISHNU HAD A feeling they were not going to make it. The five-carriage train lay stretched like a shadowy giant reptile across the dawn at the single-platform Puranapur station. Its steam engine huffed and puffed like a chained wild beast. Vishnu, too, was gasping, desperate to get onto the train. Out of breath after running along the village path, he was nervous about the uncertain trip. 'Hurry, Didi. We must not miss the train,' the boy said crossly, pulling his big sister Meenakshi's hand. It was all her fault. First, she wouldn't wake up, and now, she was walking like a tortoise. Although he knew that their father had sent word last night to stationmaster Nanda to expect them, Vishnu was sure that the train was about to chug out leaving them behind. This fear was eating into him. This was one train ride Vishnu was not going to miss at any cost. It was a birthday treat. He had turned ten today, and their father was taking them to Ambarsar for a visit to the famed Golden Temple.

'Didi…!' he groaned. Couldn't she walk a little faster? '… Did you eat opium last night?'

'Yes, Vishnu. That's what I do every night. Don't you know?' Meenakshi said irritably.

Aware of the turmoil in his son's mind, Jyoti Prasad took his children's hands in his and made them run. They sprinted the rest of the path – a good two hundred yards of darkness – and were panting by the time they arrived at the station. It was the last stop on the thirty-mile line from Amritsar.

Stationmaster Nanda presided over the deserted platform, his hands clasped behind his back. The vermillion mark on his creased forehead acknowledged Lord Krishna as his family deity. Vishnu noticed the tilak and then the sad look around his face. The stationmaster was unhappy; the train should have left seven minutes ago.

'Prasadji! I know it's now India, but still…'

'Sorry, Nandaji, sorry,' Jyoti intoned.

'You are going to get me the boot. Sure as day is day and night is night. Now get in. In, in, in…'

As the man and his two children clambered into the only second-class compartment, the guard appeared from nowhere. He folded his hands in a namaste to Jyoti Prasad and waved the green side of his lantern towards the engine. A shrill scream tore open the sweet and sleepy dawn, frightening the jackals into silence in the wheat fields on both sides of the track. A light jolt and… Phew! Vishnu began to breathe again.

The second-class compartment was roomy with long, padded and plastic-covered seats. The other coaches were all third-class; there was an Inter Class compartment too. Even though it was pitch dark inside, Vishnu knew the seat colour – moss-green; he knew that on each seat was embossed NWR. There were only two other passengers in the car, both wrapped up in cotton sheets spread out like crocodiles on the long seats. The couple greeted his father warmly. Vishnu noticed that the man had a heavy, tired voice, but his wife's was sharp and shrill. Soon, the man dozed off. His wife, however, went on talking.

She was not talking, really – just complaining about the 'murder in the market'. This was not actually about any blood spilling; she was pointing to the spikes of inflation. The sharp rise in prices was practically *slitting throats*. To make things worse, the woman complained, items had suddenly begun to disappear from the market. 'Hardly anything will be available anytime soon, given the present climate.' Couldn't she talk of something a little less mundane? Vishnu knew that the elderly chant God's name early in the morning. Not complain about prices. Put off, he huddled next to his sister and fell asleep.

There was light all around when Vishnu awoke – cool, diffused half-light. The train made a loud thudding noise, and the woman was still rabbiting on, now about the real mayhem going on all around. Put off again, Vishnu nearly went back to sleep, but decided to give her a glance; he could just about see. When he saw her, he was shocked, like the slap of an electric current: the woman had a bushy beard and was wearing a fez!

Vishnu nudged Meenakshi; she was fast asleep. Taking his mouth close to her ear, he whispered excitedly: 'Didi, do you know what happened? The woman sleeping on the berth last night has turned into a man! Really, a man with a flowing beard!' Unable to suppress his excitement, Vishnu shook his sister. They were near Vatala Junction. That meant the train had run a distance of seven miles.

Meenakshi, sixteen, older and more mature than her brother, heard his rasping voice. She rubbed her eyes and looked around. Giggling a little, she shut her eyes again. She knew who this woman with a beard was – Shaukat Ali, a prominent public figure and a Muslim League leader in Puranapur, a good old friend of both her father and Uncle Bhagwan. She wondered why

Vishnu was being so silly.

Vishnu hadn't recognized the man in the darkness. To take the local politician for a woman with a beard? Laughable. He laughed a little and called himself what he knew Meenakshi was already calling him under her breath – *gadha*, a donkey. He whispered into her ear again, 'Why does he talk so much?'

'Because…' Meenakshi was mumbling.

'Because what?'

'Er… he is a leader.'

'But so is Uncle Bhagwan. A Congress leader. He doesn't talk nonstop.'

Bhagwan was Jyoti's younger brother, almost the same age.

'Some leaders are like that. See, Gandhiji doesn't talk at all when he has something important to say. He observes *maun vrat*, refusing to talk. Now go back to sleep, *gadha*. I want to listen.'

'Anyway, how is your health, Shaukat?' Jyoti Prasad said, his voice relaxed. Once close friends, they were meeting after quite a while due to recent turmoil and the changing times.

'Not first class. That's why Missus and I are going to Ambarsar. To see a cardiologist, her cousin's nephew. Just qualified.'

'Nothing serious, I hope.'

'Not really. Only, I get a pain every now and then.'

'Still smoking a lot?'

'Try not to. My one vice.'

'But a man of many virtues, our Shaukat.'

'Don't know about that, Jyoti. In life, there are more important things to worry about than a man's health.'

'Nothing is more important than one's health.'

'Maybe you are right. But…'

The League leader had now moved on to the hot topic of the day – Partition.

'Inevitable now. Inn-Evvi-Tabble, I'm afraid. But there needn't be any bloodshed here like there was in Calcutta last year.'

'Why?'

'Because we are brothers, really.'

'Then why do you want to split away?' Jyoti said.

'Religion, Bhai. Religion. Beyond you and me.'

'We've lived together for generations. All sons of Mother India.'

'True. Sons of Mother India, blah blah… But things have changed. Open your eyes, Jyoti Prasad, and see the writing on the wall. There is only one word.'

'Yes, Shaukat Ali. It is Independence.'

'No. It is Partition as Quaid-e-Azam Jinnah has rightly demanded. Even Attlee grudgingly said yes to it in February. And it is to happen by June next year, at the latest.'

'Grudgingly means not really. Most other bigwigs in London don't want it either. Including Churchill.'

'Nobody in London really cares. Including your Churchill.'

'That is not true. Anyway…'

'Anyway, whatever happens, happens for the best. But nothing untoward must happen in our Puranapur. Personal guarantee given. Yours sincerely has worked it out with my dear old friend Bhagwan. We may have begun to think differently but…'

A long hysterical whistle shut him up. The train, now running at about twenty km an hour, lurched to a sudden halt, throwing everybody off their seats.

'Ohho!' the League leader cried.

Everybody was badly shaken.

'You alright, children?' Shaukat asked.

They were all okay. They collected themselves and stuck their necks out of the windows to see what the matter was. Fields of ripening golden wheat sprawled endlessly in the mellow light of the early morning. At the head of the train, close to Vatala station, was the scene of the ugly commotion. A clutch of rough-looking men surrounded the engine.

'An accident,' the politician said and stood up. Instinctively, he flung open the carriage door and leaped out. He wanted to be on the scene of public concern to offer immediate benefit of his leadership. Jyoti and other men from the train followed out of alarmed curiosity, some twenty of them. Headed by Shaukat Ali, the procession had gone a mere fifty yards when it was stopped in its tracks; a tall, thin man with death written all over his face was running towards the befuddled crowd. He sported a goatee and wore a fez like Shaukat Ali. A number of Jat peasants chased him, among them many swarthy Sikhs; Vatala was in Sikh territory. One of them pulled out the curved Sikh *kirpan* from the sheath by his left side. The blade glinted in the rising sun as he brandished it menacingly.

'Murderer! Cow slaughterer,' he shouted and all the Jats around him echoed: 'Murderer! Cow slaughterer!'

'Save me, Shaukat Ali Saab. SAVE me…' howled the frightened man.

MURDERER! COW SLAUGHTERER!

Scared by the metallic monster hurtling towards her, a stray cow grazing in the field by the railway line had suddenly veered around to go over to the other side. The fat cow mistimed it by just one split second. The monster, whistling deafeningly to avert a mishap, had to hit her, carrying a mound of flesh and bones in a stream of blood until it lurched to a shuddering halt.

The accident could not have happened at a worse time. There was anger in the air waiting only for a spark. Danger lurking around. The mood of the Hindu and Sikh peasants was murderous too. The cow, for them, was not just the giver of milk; she was Gomata, a goddess they worshipped. Now, before their eyes, the most revered animal had been slaughtered on the rail. The same animal that was slaughtered by Muslims for sumptuous meals. To add to the misfortune, the hapless train driver was a Muslim man, complete with a macho beard and skullcap.

By now, the train was empty of passengers – Hindus, Muslims and Sikhs. Meenakshi and Vishnu joined their father. Jyoti and Shaukat looked at each other, the sense of impending doom throbbing under their chests. It was touch and go.

'Do something, Jyoti. You are Bhagwan's brother.'

'Do what, Shaukat?'

'Save the poor driver Abdullah. He's a father of four. All girls. All unmarried. Save him from these fanatics.'

'Save me, Prasadji. Not my fault. Did my best to warn her. But she just walked right in front of the train. Swear by Allah. Swear by you…'

Jyoti moved fast. He placed himself between the blood-baying crowd and the engine driver.

'Brothers, it was an accident…' Jyoti shouted.

'Why didn't he use his eyes and brain and apply the brakes on time?' the armed man yelled.

'…A very tragic accident, brothers.'

'…Move aside, man. Or else…'

The man put the tip of his razor-sharp *kirpan* at Jyoti's chest. Jyoti tried to wrench it from the man's hand. He failed, and his hand received a long cut. Meenakshi and Vishnu screamed at the sight of blood.

'Good gentlemen, you all. This man is the elder brother of Puranapur District Congress leader Bhagwan Prasad. He is pleading with you to let the man go,' Shaukat cried, giving Jyoti a handkerchief.

'In the name of Mahatma Gandhi, I beg you.' Jyoti said.

After a long pause, which could have ended with cold-blooded murder on the mute railway line, the men went away. But despite his bloodied hand, Jyoti still wanted to go ahead with the planned visit to the Golden Temple. Shaukat forbade it. Vatala station was only a little walk away. There, Shaukat had Jyoti's hand dressed – it was a minor cut – at the station dispensary. In the end, Jyoti could not take his boy and girl to Ambarsar. Emergency braking by the train driver had caused some damage to the track. It would take hours to repair.

ONE

THE MULLAH ATOP the fifty-foot marble minaret of the Badami Mosque cast a long and pious glance all over the town and beyond it, the sprawling country. Then, in a matchless voice that was loud and sonorous and had won the rather young man, at just thirty-six, this important job and put him where he was – closer to Allah than any other living Muslim around – he began proclaiming repeatedly His greatness, 'ALLAH HOO AKBAR!' This message resonated far and wide. As he paused for breath, he surveyed the scene from his lofty perch. He saw a pleasantly familiar sight – men spilling out of Puranapur's streets to stroll in the lush fields surrounding the town as moving dots.

They did so almost every day at this hour to take the name of God in their own ways before sunrise, the best time of a long, hot summer day. It was a collective habit as old as Puranapur itself, which literally meant Old Town. In fact, it was a very old medieval town, the only one perhaps in all of Punjab with no beggars. People here never locked their doors, nor had a theft ever been reported in living memory. But its mixed population of twenty thousand retained no memory of its long past. At present, people had other things on their minds. Things more precious, such as their lives.

As the countryside echoed with the mullah's message, which was the Muslim call to prayer, the people, depending on their taste, snapped pencil-size twigs off an acacia or a neem tree – one sweet and the other bitter – and chewed them to brush their teeth and walked a mile or two in the morning dew. When the sun peeped out, some of them stopped to bathe at a well. On their way back home, they all bought freshly picked vegetables, mangoes and melons.

If this was time for the humans to quietly exercise their limbs and rinse their lungs with fresh air, it was also the hour for the birds to welcome the new day. They did so in their own matchless way. And there were so many of them – the peacock, crow, kite, parrot, dove, koel, bulbul and the turquoise-feathered neel kanth, the flying mount of the Hindu god Vishnu, Preserver of the Universe. All at once, they cooed and cried and cawed so loudly that they seemed involved in a bitter quarrel over something serious. Restlessly, they flew from tree to tree and grove to grove of mango, jamun and tahli trees. Only when the sun began to bite would they vanish from sight and colonize the same groves. There, their vocal chords exhausted, they would quieten down. And Puranapurias would go home.

These mornings were like little poems. And like them, they were over too soon. But their imprint on body and soul lingered well into the day. Their beneficiaries were men and young boys on weekends. Women, both Hindu and Muslim, were not to care for this delectation in dew at dawn. It would be immodest of them to be out and about, displaying themselves. They were doing what they were supposed to do – sweeping and mopping up homes, bathing children, washing clothes, cleaning utensils and tossing butter parathas for the walking poets' breakfast.

While men walked and talked, youngsters larked around looking for wild mushrooms. There weren't many to be found. To avoid fisticuffs, which often resulted when a couple of them came upon one at the same time, they sensibly allotted each other *jagirs*, or territories. The rest was a matter of luck.

Vishnu made a valuable discovery that mushrooms usually grew where he had found some before. But he did not tell his cousin Shashi. Nor did he know that Shashi, too, had made the same valuable discovery. So had their friends Ravi and Vijay. And like Vishnu and his cousin, they were keeping it to themselves.

That April morning, a Sunday, was like any other – just made for walking aimlessly on dewy grass as the birds bickered noisily overhead and on the ground. Vishnu, *jagirdar* of ten acres, was miserable today. He hadn't found a thing.

'Not one mush. Two inch or three.'

Vishnu had looked and looked.

'This stupid earth everyone wants to call theirs.' He didn't care for it. 'The fools can have it with my permission.'

A pair of low-flying peacocks fluttered past, a few feet above Vishnu's head. He chased them for fifty yards and found himself in his cousin's *jagir*. His face, round like an apple until now, became an inverted pear when he saw Shashi or, more specifically, his breast pocket. It was full of Vishnu's shame; it bulged.

'Shit arse,' Vishnu called his cousin who bore a striking likeness to him; the two could have passed as twins.

'Our lovely mother earth. She loves me.' Shashi laughed. That hurt Vishnu.

'Shit arse.' Vishnu spat at mother earth.

'Never mind, Vishnu boy. Mushrooms are only

mushrooms. Not pearls. Try again next Sunday,' Shashi quipped.

'Same story every time, yaar. Why does it happen only to me? What have I done?'

'Some people are born lucky. Some not. Got to take life as it comes. Try, try, try again. Like that Bruce.'

'Only someone as bright as you would think of that, brother.'

Shashi put an arm around Vishnu and led him to look for their friends. While passing through what was no-man's-land – not a fruit and veg field, but a large fallow thicket of thorny bushes known simply as the Jungle – they spotted a real jewel by a dung heap, a straight white four-inch thing sticking out of the yellow ochre mother earth majestically, like a mini-rocket. Vishnu's face lit up. It became apple-round again.

'It's mine,' he announced his claim.

'It's mine,' Shashi put in his at the same time – after all, this was no-man's-land – and freed himself from any obligations as the contender's cousin.

'I saw it first, greedy dog. Go rub your tail on that cactus plant there.'

'You rub your backside on it, Wasp Balls.'

For some reason, boys called Vishnu Wasp Balls. Nobody knew why. It was one of those things. Vishnu hated it. He had had many fights because of it. But boys didn't always call him that to his face. Anyone who did, did so because he 'no longer loved life'.

The mercury shot up. Vishnu caught his cousin by his throat. But there was a sudden change of heart. He decided to postpone killing him there and then. He would do so after he had pocketed that white beauty soaring out of the earth. Shashi was three months younger and a little smaller, so that wouldn't be a problem.

The two boys ran to it, pushing and pulling each other. Vishnu got there first. The mushroom was a good four-inch high, a rare find, the like of which they had never seen before. Jumping with joy, Vishnu threw himself at it to pluck it out. As he did so, it vanished.

'It's a snake, Wasp Balls. A white snake,' Shashi screamed pulling his cousin by his shirt and ripping it from the waist to the armpit.

It was common knowledge that white snakes were the last word when it came to death by snakebite. The face would swell up and become blue, the eyes bloodshot, followed by convulsions, leading to a horrible death.

Shashi felt terribly shaken; his cousin had been within inches of certain death. He put an arm around Vishnu warmly and swiftly dragged him away. Vishnu didn't seem to care; he was laughing. Hand in hand, the cousins sprinted away to join their friends. They were dying to tell the world the tale of the vanishing mushroom.

Running past the thorny berry bushes, they startled a large flock of tiny nameless birds. For a few seconds, the little birds hovered overhead like a rapidly moving cloud, before settling down in the same trees again. The boys marvelled at the spectacle but kept running. As they turned by the bushes, they came face to face with, of all people, Vishnu's father. Tall and fair-complexioned with a faraway look on his face, Jyoti Prasad wore a white see-through *mulmul* kurta and English-style white cotton trousers; white was the colour of summer. He was out for his Sunday constitutional with his old Muslim chums, Mohammed and Aziz, both clean-shaven like him and just as tall. As was their custom, the three walked hand in hand, just like Vishnu and Shashi.

'How many then, Vishnu?' asked Mohammed. He had a

boyish face with a permanent grin.

'Fourth rate earth this, Uncle Mommed. Mushrooms don't grow on it any more. Only snakes...' Vishnu stopped. He had made a mistake, and it was not the funny kind. It was a terrible mistake; he shouldn't have mentioned the word 'snake' before his father.

Jyoti knew instantly what had happened. In a flash, he saw it all – his boy bending down to... to hand his life to a white snake. Jyoti felt a jab in his chest. His cheeks coloured, and he gave his son a back-handed slap on his head.

'Only snakes what, oye?' Alarm, worry and anger made his temple throb.

Shashi answered for Vishnu.

'How many times have I told you not to go to the Jungle, you rascal? How many? Home. NOW. And no more mushroom charming or snake gathering.' A deeply-worried Jyoti growled, giving his son another slap.

'Not Vishnu's fault, Jyoti. What's the matter with you?' Mohammed exclaimed, saving Vishnu from yet another slap. Then, he hugged him and caressed his apple-round face.

'Of course not. It was the snake's fault for being in its hole,' Jyoti said. 'Home. This instant. On double hop. You too, Shashi. Wait till Bhagwan hears about it.'

'This instant, Chachaji, in a moment.' Shashi bowed to his uncle, turned and ran with Vishnu. Terrified, they sprinted along the dirt. A while later, Shashi slowed down knowing he was safe, at least for several hours. His father was away in Vatala. He had gone there early that morning, with his assistant Desraj, for something important, something 'hush-hush'. Everything Puranapur's Congress leader did these days was important and often 'hush-hush'. He was due back later this evening by the second – and the last – daily train to Puranapur.

Jyoti's friends, too, were quite shaken by his son's close brush with danger. Anything could have happened...

'Charmed life the boy has. Like his father,' said Aziz. He had a slight bald patch on top of his head, which he had learned to conceal by brushing the hair up from the back of his scalp.

'Aziz, you talk such charming nonsense. Worth admiring.' Although the *kirpan* cut had healed, Jyoti's hand still pulsated with the slaps he had given his son. He began to feel guilty. And sorry. Very sorry.

The conversation drifted. Or rather, it returned to what the three friends had been talking about earlier – the arrival in the Indian capital of its last Viceroy, three weeks ago. Handsome and self-assured, young Lord Mountbatten had come with orders from Prime Minister Attlee to sort out the intractable issue of Indian Independence.

'We do live in uncertain times,' Aziz said in English. 'Will he succeed where older and wiser heads have failed?'

'In uncertain times, the only thing you can be certain of is uncertainty itself. Whatever can go wrong, will go wrong,' Mohammed replied, also in English. This is how the friends usually talked – in English, like all educated Indians, switching mid-sentence to Punjabi.

'Your optimism is really admirable, Uncle Mohammed.' Jyoti made no attempt to hide the sarcasm. 'Why do you always worry? Rejoice. Mountbatten will deliver. He gives out that sure look of confidence, so unlike that Wavell he's replacing.'

'Till then, it is knife in the Muslim back in Lahore, axe on the Hindu head in Multan, and burning of Sikh houses in Amritsar...'

Besides affection, what united the three was their fundamental antipathy to religion, the root cause of all problems in India.

'Why so pessimistic?' Aziz stopped him.

Before Mohammed could respond, there was another interruption. A bunch of young men in their early twenties, eight or ten of them, came in front of them, paddling their bicycles; some had friends on carriers. Shiny brass tiffin boxes dangled from the handlebars of their bikes. They were singing Hindi-film songs and laughing. Suddenly, they stopped; they had spotted the town's respected flour-mill owner, Jyoti Prasad. Their silence was a mark of respect for the man who would often give a bag of flour to a needy family – Hindu, Muslim or Sikh. But Puranapur being Puranapur, even the needy were hesitant to accept such bounty.

'Jai Hind, Prasadji,' they greeted Jyoti. As a further sign of respect, they hopped off their bicycles.

'Good morning, boys. Good morning.' Jyoti avoided the term Jai Hind. It was a national slogan. Yet, it had a distinctly Hindu ring to it.

'Leadership seems to run in the family. Must hand you that, sir,' said one hefty fellow, referring to Bhagwan Prasad.

'Meaning what, Dilbagh Rai?'

'Meaning how you snatched train driver Abdullah from death's open jaws, sir.'

Jyoti held up a hand. He didn't even want to think about it. While saving the man's life, he had nearly lost his own. Such was the mood of the mad crowd at Vatala.

'Talk about something else. See how beautiful this morning is.'

'Absolute peacock condition, sir. Just the ideal time for walking on God's good earth.'

'Then why are you on your made-in-England Raleigh? And the tiffin-shiffin? Going somewhere special?'

Jyoti already knew the answer, as did Mohammed and

Aziz. Today, 13 April, was Baisakhi Day – an ancient Punjabi festival to welcome the start of wheat harvest. It was celebrated jointly by the Hindu, Muslim and Sikh peasantry, essentially wherever water was to be found in great quantities – rivers, lakes and canals. Everyone was welcome to join in. The young men were heading for the great Ravi Canal a couple of miles away. This was one of the many constructed by the British from the Punjab's five fabled rivers to make the land the granary of India. Swimming in its cool, soothing grey-blue waters coming from the Himalayas was heavenly, even more so because of the festive sweets that followed on Baisakhi Day.

'Only the Ravi Canal, sir,' Dilbagh said. Then he and his companions hopped on their cycles and pedalled away, shouting the farewell in one voice, 'Jai Hind!'

Jai Hind literally meant 'victory to Hindustan'. Hindustan – land of the Hindus from time immemorial. These young men were members of the RSS – Rashtriya Swayamsevak Sangh – a radical right-wing Hindu group strongly opposed to the idea of a separate country carved out of India for the Muslims. Dilbagh Rai was the leader of its Puranapur branch. They knew Jyoti's friends were Muslim. Were they making a point? Was it meant as a taunt? Jyoti felt apologetic. Mohammed and Aziz were more like brothers than just friends, and they never ever talked about religion, a strictly private matter.

Thankfully, both Mohammed and Aziz appeared less sensitive than Jyoti to the whole thing. To them, Jai Hind was just another slogan, one of so many being shouted from rooftops day and night. Their friendship was too old – since primary school – to be needled by this sort of thing. Or anything else for that matter.

'What was I going to say?' Jyoti said, steering the conversation away from the Jai Hind nonsense. 'Oh yes – nice to be young, Badshah.' Punjabi men often called each other 'Badshah', meaning 'king', a word with all the ingredients of good friendship – respect, affection and flattery.

'Thirty-five isn't exactly old,' Aziz said.

'It is when you have three kids from six to sixteen. No, Mohammed?'

'Never too late for a bit of joy. And Mohammed isn't a day younger, though with only two kiddies,' Mohammed said.

'Plenty of time for more. Keep trying. That's where the real joy is, if you ask me. The secret is in trying,' Aziz said with a wink of the eye.

'Constantly?' Mohammed asked.

'Well, as long as the begum doesn't mind.'

'The problem is the begum gets a headache the night yours truly gets…' Mohammed laughed.

'Then do it in the daytime,' Aziz chipped in.

'What poetry, yaar! Beats Ustad Imam Din's hands down. Do it in the daytime indeed,' Mohammed intoned.

'If a man can't do it under the cover of darkness, he must make bold and do it in broad daylight. This motion is passed ha ha,' Jyoti jibed good-humouredly. He was now enjoying this idiotic conversation. It brought back a bit of their youth.

'What, with a house full of all those aunts and uncles and he-cousins and she-cousins and nephews and nieces coming and going –morning, noon, and night – and my own two monkeys on top? Sure, sure. Wonder when we Indians manage to do it at all. We simply are never alone.'

'We don't do too badly. Nearly four hundred million damn fools,' Aziz laughed.

'Anyway, how about a Baisakhi picnic today at the canal, Jyoti? We can't be too old for that sort of thing at least.' Mohammed looked at him expectantly.

Jyoti shook his head. Gangaram, the family barber, was on his way; he and his two sons would have to sit before him. Gangaram did so every fifth Sunday.

'Don't say no, Badshah,' Aziz said. He liked the idea. 'In a month or so the sun will be glowering and then, the misery of the monsoon.'

'Monsoon or no monsoon, what with Congress and the League at each other's throats and that Sikh leader, Sant, waiting hawk-like in the wings; who knows when we'll get another chance, if ever?' Mohammed pleaded.

Sant, meaning 'saint', was the fiery and feared leader of the Sikhs in and around Puranapur.

'Mohammed. Prophet of doom. Why do you always worry? That Sant may have a private army under him, but he has no sense under his turban. He can't move without Congress' permission,' Jyoti said.

'And with Partition around the corner, Jyoti…'

'Why do you say Partition? Why not Independence?'

'My apology. I meant Independence. So, let's go have a bit of fun at the canal.'

Jyoti didn't feel like it – all that cycling just for a swim. It was not even that. It was… he just didn't want to go. He mentioned Gangaram again. But his friends put their arms around him. He could not say no anymore.

'Go home and get your haircut. We'll still beat the sun and have our Baisakhi picnic at the canal.'

At thirty-two and mother of three, Rakhi Rani, Jyoti's wife, was the envy of every woman in the neighbourhood, married or unmarried. She had eyes poets sang about – long, deep and angular, like those in a Kishangarh painting; they would have done Radha proud. Lord Krishna's favourite *gopi* would need such a pair of doe eyes to charm her lover. And her face? It could still launch a boat or two, though a decade ago, it could have seen off an entire fleet. Rakhi was five-foot-seven, which, for an Indian woman, was tall. And because she stood straight, she looked even taller. In her father's house in Sialkot, in the good old days when the world was sane and innocent and quite a lovely place, she was called Sweet Palm. In their letters, her equally lovely sisters, Laaj and Kesari, still called her that. 'Dearer than my life Sweet Palm', or 'Dearest, dearest Palm', they would address their youngest sister from letters they wrote from Lahore. The elegant capital of Punjab had a European flavour about it. Did the elder sisters feel sorry that their impeccably beautiful Sweet Palm did not live in that city? Rakhi, too, missed them and longed to be back in their company.

In their picturesque Sialkot home, they chirped all day under the sturdy chinar tree and nattered all evening until they dropped off. Ah, those were the days. Life was a song, an endless series of ripples in time – not seen but felt by all. Once, when she had just turned sixteen and just been betrothed to Jyoti – preparations for their marriage were on – there came to their street a man who could draw pictures with a needle and blue ink on your body. This created quite a sensation in the neighbourhood; young women were excited about this *blue art*. For a paisa, some had pretty flowers or their names tattooed on their forearms. Others decided on 'Hare Krishna' or a mere 'Om' in Hindi. Rakhi, shyly, opted for something secular. She had two English letters – JP – scratched on her right hand by the tattooist's expert needle. They looked blue – green.

On her wedding night, their presence on her hand, with the exquisite henna designs, caused her to almost die. For he whose initials they were held her hand and said with impish joy, 'Well, well, well, what do we have here?'

Draped in yards of flowing scarlet silk and gold ornaments, the baffled bride hid herself further and bit the pallu of her sari. This was her way of saying what she wanted to. But the nineteen-year old imp insisted on an answer.

'A man has the right to know what his wife prints on her arm,' Jyoti pressed further. 'Don't you think?'

He got his answer; his bride came out of hiding. She pulled down the scarlet bridal veil and looked straight at him. Two large, expressive eyes told him everything he wanted to know, answered all the questions he had. A few drops of tears hung around her kohl-rimmed eyes like pearls. Jyoti felt a deep ache in his heart and knew he was happy. First, he kissed her tears, then her hands; hesitantly, reluctantly she still let him do that.

The same pair of hands now prepared, more reluctantly, his picnic tiffin. Though she liked his friends, Mohammed and Aziz, who called her their 'little sister', she really did not want Jyoti to go to the forested canal bank. The trip to the desolate place… in such troubled times…

It was a glowingly warm morning. Out on the veranda, Jyoti sat cross-legged on a flat wooden bed-like *takht*. Next to him was his mother; his children called her Dadima. The old woman's skin was guava-pale and almost translucent. Her eyes closed, she turned a rosary, murmuring 'Ram, Ram, Ram' rhythmically. She had done half her work for the morning. She didn't have to do it, but Dadima loved doing the chore, for without it her morning was not complete. She had churned the yogurt she had set last night into *lassi* and snow-white butter. She did this every day at the crack of dawn. She finished just as the mullah in his marble tower a few hundred yards away was about to open his account with God in a ringing voice. He hadn't gone beyond a dozen 'Allah Hoo Akbar's when she, seated cross-legged on the *takht* in Chauri Galli, town's prime residential address, got ready to open her conversation with God, calling Him by a different name. The two stopped within minutes of each other. Then, Dadima busied herself with the other matter of the morning – milking Kunti, the family cow.

Today, however, she had a little problem – a mild pain in her right leg, now recurring every other day. *Let me ask Meenakshi, the girl is good with the cow*, Dadima thought. The old woman felt her right leg. The two of them would do it together. They loved the process of milking. Perhaps Kunti did too.

Kunti was tethered in the cowshed behind the house. It stood at the end of an unploughed, uncultivated plot of land that belonged to Jyoti.

Usually, Dadima did the morning chore fluently after a good night's sleep. But these days, she could not sleep well. A fear seized her. She knew everybody else was scared too – an inescapable symptom of the uncertain times. She heard voices. And distant noises. Like everybody else.

'Meenakshi, my tea,' Dadima addressed the kitchen door on the other side of which, she knew, sat her favourite granddaughter, making tea for her and Jyoti. Meenakshi was everybody's darling.

'Here, Dadima.' Meenakshi brought a glass of tea.

'Meenakshi *beti*, my leg,' the old woman said taking a loud sip. The granddaughter understood. She picked up the milking vessel. 'But I'll come with you and drink my tea there.'

Jyoti, left alone, sipped his tea, and shook his left leg. He got ready for his haircut but somehow looked worried. He knew his mother had had a bad night, as had his wife. He also knew why. She too heard voices and noises.

Barber Gangaram arrived. Old and small, toothless and hairless, with a shiny, well-oiled scalp, he was rather early today.

'Ram, Ram, Jyoti.'

Although Gangaram was only a barber and Jyoti the prosperous owner of a flour mill, he still called Jyoti by his first name. Gangaram had known him since his birth, performed the ritual of his first *mundan*, shaving the newborn's head, and was now here to give him his latest cut.

When Jyoti didn't respond, Gangaram continued, 'Going somewhere?'

A valid question. Jyoti always had his cut after his two boys, one of whom was still asleep. Gangaram placed a small mirror on a little stool on the *takht* itself, arranging his things around it. After some small talk, three of the country's most famous names came under his scrutiny.

'That fork-tongued Jinnah will have his Pakistan at any cost. He's too clever a *vakīl* for our *bhola-bhala*, naive Nehru and even our all-trusting Mahatmaji. Great men, both, but no match for the slimy lawyer.'

'It's not about who is a better *vakil,* Gangaram; it's about national unity. Pandit Nehru must stop him from destroying it. Only he can. And Mountbatten.'

'But Panditji is giving in at every point. Even more so our Mahatma. It's like watching a horror movie in which you know the villain will finally win.'

'But why are they giving in?'

'You tell me.'

This went on for a while. Jyoti was moved by the simple barber's reading of the situation, when most educated men had no inkling of it.

Another visitor arrived – Sher Singh, a sturdy young Sikh of twenty-two. He had joined Jyoti's workforce at the mill last year, but he also worked in his house when required, which was every day. He lived in a little mud house at the back of Chauri Galli with his mother, Chandri. Still looking sleepy, Shera folded his hands on his chest, waiting for orders.

'Sher Sigh, the cycle,' Jyoti said, turning his head towards where the bicycle stood, by a fragrant jasmine bush at the far end of the walled courtyard. There lay a wooden box of all-purpose tools from ages ago – wrenches, spanners, hammers, screwdrivers, varieties of nails and screws, and even an old broken bicycle chain dangling from a nail in the wall. Hardly any of them were ever used; Jyoti was no good at these things.

Shera understood. He knew all about bicycles, could take one apart and put it back together before the crow could fly from the Badami Mosque to the railway station. Before he came to the mill, he had worked at a cycle repair shop and had made a name for himself as the master puncture man of Puranapur. But Shera was quick-tempered. One day, he got into an argument with a difficult customer, who wanted proof of his being the best puncture man around. Shera gave it to him. He punched him in the face and kicked him in the groin and got himself sacked on the spot.

As Shera went to the bicycle, the back door of the courtyard opened and in walked Meenakshi to get something. This had an arresting effect on Gangaram's scissors.

'Arrey *bhai*?' Jyoti said. Why had the barber stopped?

'I am looking,' the barber said.

'What's the matter?'

'The matter is your girl. She is growing up.'

'Girls grow fast these days, Gangaram.'

'So, you should be worrying about her. Soon, soon.'

'I already am. Much, much.' Jyoti was lying. He had never given the matter a thought. She was only sixteen.

Gangaram started scissoring again.

'Got a boy in sight?'

'That's the thing, Gangaram. Boys from good families don't grow on trees.'

'I know, I know. But what would you say if I came up with one? A first-class boy number one.' Gangaram stopped again and then continued in a whisper, 'The Sunar boy. Right caste. Right age – nineteen. In the third year of college. B.A. pass next year.'

Jyoti turned uncomfortably on the flat wooden surface.

'The Sunars? Too big, no?' As the flour mill owner, he was not badly off. But the Sunars were 'top, top' jewellers. They handled gold, diamonds and pearls. He only sifted grain.

'Not for the girl, though, Jyoti Prasad. A rare gem.'

'The Sunars are a mountain of gold. The Prasads only a heap of flour.'

'Not true at all. Anyway, leave it in my safe hands.'

These things were always arranged by barbers. On behalf of the girl's parents, the barber would approach the boy's family. It was one of those age-old customs with a logic of its own. The beauty of it was it never failed. The barber knew best. And was trusted.

As Meenakshi was going back, Jyoti took another look. She was a gem all right. *His gem.* He felt a flutter in his chest when he realized what he had been talking about – about the preparations to part with her. Until that moment, he had not known what she meant for him.

'Meenakshi,' Jyoti called out to her. He had nothing to say to her, really. He took his eyes off the little mirror and looked at her. He realized another thing: until that moment, he hadn't known how beautiful she was, with her mother's Kishangarh eyes, and how grown-up she really was. Just then, at the other end of the courtyard, Shera, fixing the bicycle, slipped on a wet leaf and fell. Meenakshi saw and burst out laughing with a hand on her mouth, and it rained rose petals inside Jyoti's heart. She looked just like her mother when she was sixteen.

'Aren't you milking Kunti, *beta*?' Jyoti called her '*beta*' – son. Indian parents often call their daughters '*beta*'. This elevation from girl to boy captured the great love for their daughters, equal to their love for their sons.

'Dadima is doing it after all.' Meenakshi had a feeling her father hadn't called her for that. She was right. Jyoti had called her because he wanted to hear her voice. It was soft and brittle, and it broke his heart to hear it, and he felt what a sudden gust of cool monsoon breeze brings to an oppressed body on a hot, hot day.

'Cycle done, Bauji. Polished from the rims to the handlebar,' Shera spoke.

At the same time, Rakhi came with a tall, shiny brass tiffin carrier, emitting mouth-watering aroma, and placed it on the *takht*. This coincided with two bicycle bells ringing out loudly in the street. Mohammed and Aziz had arrived. Picnic boxes dangled from their handlebars and folded mats were strapped to their bicycle carriers. Jyoti's younger son Mindi woke up hearing all the noise. He saw and guessed what was happening, and wanted to be taken along. When the father said no, the son rolled on the floor and howled.

'Never been to a picnic in all my life!' The six-year-old howled and howled.

'Take Mindi along,' Mohammed said.

It was either that or…

'All right, you brat. Get off the floor.'

Jyoti rolled a towel a few times around the horizontal top tube of his bicycle to make a comfortable seat for Mindi. All the neighbours came out to see the men ready to take to their bikes. No one else was celebrating this Baisakhi. What was there to celebrate, with their ears ringing with those warning voices and distant noises? Rakhi had prepared her husband's tiffin box, but she really didn't want him to go. The three men were about to ride out when appeared in the doorway three visitors. One look at them and Rakhi's eyes sparkled; a smile crept all over her face.

Two gorgeous-looking women in star-spangled saris and a girl of fifteen from Lahore. Rakhi's sisters, Laaj and Kesari, with Laaj's daughter Sharda. The three sisters hadn't met for months. They had come from the railway station in a horse-driven tonga, laden with gifts for everyone from the princely city once patronized by the Mughals. The residents of Lahore were proud of their heritage. The seat of power for some of the Mughal rulers, it was also a major city of the British Empire. And for many, Lahore was simply the *Paris of the Punjab*. The city of commerce, art and glamour. Owned and driven by the popular Muslim poet Mam Din, the wooden vehicle creaked loudly to a halt outside the Prasads' solid, straight-grained walnut-timber door adorned with a rash of brass knobs. The news of arrival raised a hubbub inside the *haveli*, with the family members busily rushing to the front door, their faces beaming with welcome smiles. The neighbours came out only to be stunned at the sight of the two glamorous sisters who surpassed in beauty and grace Noor Jahan, the queen of the silver screen. The post being what it was due to the times the world was living through, Laaj and Kesari had sent three unanswered postcards, and finally, and without waiting any further, had simply taken the train. They changed at Ambarsar and had come for a surprise family reunion, because they missed their little sister just as much as she missed them.

First the sisters cried and cried as they hugged and hugged. Then they laughed and laughed and laughed as the presents were handed over and opened. But all that mirth posed a serious problem for the equally delighted Jyoti: What to do? Go for the picnic with his friends, or…?

A teary-eyed Mindi solved his father's dilemma.

'I have never been to a picnic in all my life.'

'Go, go, go, Mindi *beta*,' his aunts said, crushing him in their arms one after the other.

'But I will love you so much when I come back.'

The men bought the early-season *choopa* mangoes from an orchard and were on their way. The tracks in the fields were rough, making cycling an effort. But the three friends were used to them. As boys, they had ridden there in dust and mire many times, often on a single bike, all three of them. It was still quite early, but the sun was up and hot when they arrived at the red-painted railway bridge on the wide canal. The canal was now mostly dry with the water level quite low, due to the lack of rain in the far-off Himalayas during the winter months. After cycling in the glaring sun, they were now sweating. Their faces flushed and shirts wet in patches. The men longed to get out of them and dive into the grey-blue cool water below.

Usually, for Baisakhi, the canal banks would see a big gathering of revellers. The festive mood catching up, the place would have the look of a *mela* with food stalls lining up the dirt track and vendors moving around with their fares. Not today. No families were to be seen there – only a handful of young men from the nearby villages frolicking in the water. The only townsfolk here today were young RSS men, Dilbagh Rai and his second-in-command Singhara among them, swimming under the bridge in the barely waist-deep water. Surprised to see Jyoti, they waved at him. He waved back and then, with his friends, chose a shady jamun tree some fifty-sixty yards away, to make camp. They spread out their mats and put down their tiffin boxes. Then, they stripped to their underwear to dive in.

'Mindi, you are the boss now,' Mohammed said. 'Dip the bags of mangoes in the water to cool them while your papa and uncles have a dip. Then we'll take you for a long swim. And that's a deal. Okay?'

'Okay, Chachaji.'

The three men leaped into the water and swam away. Mindi did what he was told. In fact, he overdid it. Anxious to please, he dipped the brass tiffin carriers as well. He let them remain immersed until he thought the job was well done.

He was pleased with himself. 'Mindi *munda*, good *munda,*' he intoned. The little boy then stripped and walked off naked towards the bridge to be close to where all the fun was happening – boys leaping into the water. The sandy earth under his bare feet began to burn, but he didn't care. He had never been to a picnic before. At the bridge, he struck a friendship immediately.

'What's your name, son,' said a perky Sikh boy sitting idly on a steel girder, his legs dangling.

'Mindi.'

'You come here often?'

'No. First time.'

'And how old are you?'

'Six. And you?"

'Double. Whose son are you?'

'My father's?'

'What a coincidence! So am I. Put it here.'

The boys had a hearty handshake.

'One usually is one's father's son. Unless…'

'Unless what?'

'Unless one is a bastard, like a Muslim,' the Sikh laughed.

On the other side of the steel girder stood a sixteen-year-old, with bulging biceps and the Muslim crescent of the moon tattooed on them. He was listening. He caught hold of the Sikh by his throat and the *jura*.

'Son of a bitch. What did you say?' He pulled the young Sikh by his topknot.

'Nothing.'

'Nothing, you stupid Sardar?' The youth with the tattoo pushed him off the bridge into the water below. He did the same to Mindi with his foot. 'You dogs! Have a good drink, both of you.'

While the Sikh boy swam away expertly, Mindi bobbed up and down, drowning. People saw. Among them, Dilbagh Rai and Singhara, who were right there. They made a mad dash and caught Mindi by his hair, bringing him up to the bank. Many young men gathered around. They held Mindi upside down, pressing his stomach and back. Mindi had swallowed quite a bit of water; other than that, he was all right. But a minute longer in water and…

Now, several Hindu and Sikh boys ran up to the bridge and beat up the tattooed fellow. Muslim youths came running from all directions and a real fight broke out. It had to be seen to be believed. The canal-side festive air turned into a marauding mood within minutes, and the place became a veritable battlefield. Jyoti, Mohammed and Aziz saw the unfolding scene of violence and climbed back to the bank and came running. Before the brawl became too serious, they managed to stop it. Luckily none of the brawlers were carrying knives or rods.

Mindi cried and cried. He cried louder on seeing his father and clung to his neck. Jyoti was stunned. So were his two friends.

'All right, all right…' Jyoti said, hugging and kissing his son. He said that again and again, and that was all he could say. Mohammed and Aziz kept shaking their heads. The culprit was a Muslim. They felt responsible for what he had done to little Mindi.

Although Mindi had recovered, the picnic had turned sour. It could have been tragic had Dilbagh not been there. Jyoti thought of the picnic, the food packed by his wife for this outing. *I should not have come.* He reprimanded himself silently. *Jyoti Prasad, you* bewakoof*! What if…?* He could not think any further. *What is Rakhi going to say?* He wished he had that bicycle chain.

The food in the tiffin boxes was soaked with water, now only good for the stray dogs. But the mangoes had survived, cool and luscious – two bagfuls of them. Mohammed took matters in his hands.

'I say, you did a fine cooling job, boss,' he said, and Mindi smiled. The men felt a little better.

'A smart boy is one who does what he's told. The smarter one does more than double.' Aziz laughed.

Mindi giggled forgetting the tears drying on his cheeks. The men felt grateful. Mohammed took Jyoti's hand in his and pressed it.

'The coolest mango I ever ate in all my life, boss,' Mohammed said, sucking one noisily.

They left as soon as the last mango was eaten.

Jyoti made Mindi promise not to cry when they got home. But the boy broke his promise the moment he saw his mother, which was a hundred yards from their house. Rakhi stood inside the doorway with her sisters watering the jasmine bush. When the child came in, he wrapped himself around her legs and sobbed bitterly.

'Oh my God! Hai, hai, hai!' Rakhi wailed hearing what had happened.

'But thank God, *meri jaan*,' Jyoti said to her.

'Yes, Sweet Palm,' Laaj said, looking both shaken and relieved. 'Let's thank Him who saved our darling Mindi,' she said, holding her earlobes in gratitude to Lord Krishna.

'You said you would love us when you returned from the picnic. Where is that love, Mindi?' Kesari said, taking him in her arms.

Mindi planted big wet kisses on both her cheeks.

'What about me?' Laaj said, offering her cheeks.

Mindi put his arms around her head and kissed and kissed and kissed.

'I will never forget this day in all my life. For going to the canal and for coming back home,' Mindi said, shaking his head.

'Today, I ate the coolest mangoes of my life,' Mohammed said to his Little Sister Rakhi. Mindi grinned when Mohammed told his mother of the cooling job he had done. The story made everybody laugh. It meant that the men had not eaten. It also meant that the lady of the house had to do something about it. Suddenly, the Prasads had two extra guests among them. And guests were like gods, more important than family members. The tradition obliged them to treat guests as best as they could. Rakhi looked at her husband with those eyes of hers and went away with her sisters to make a meal. The menu suddenly had to be changed from the Sunday goat-meat curry to something strictly vegetarian, in thanksgiving to Krishna.

Jyoti, his eyes unfocused, took his friends to the *baithak* on the first floor, which overlooked the hot empty street of

Chauri Galli. It was the most beautiful in all of Puranapur with pink and green balconies jutting out like decks. Jyoti spread a white sheet on the carpet, and they sat crossed-legged around it. The aroma of the food the women were cooking wafted in. When the food was ready, Shera served, and the children turned up to watch. The crockery used today was rarely used – Royal Doulton, which had come as part of Rakhi's dowry. It came out of a tall glass cupboard where other family valuables were kept. It was opened only when very important guests came. Or these old friends of Jyoti's.

'I always get the same plate in your house, Jyoti. Royal Doulton. What an honour,' Mohammed said, smiling.

'Nothing but the best for you, your Little Sister says.'

'Kingly karela. Wah wah!' Aziz licked his fingers as he munched the crispy bitter gourd slices.

'And the bhindi?' Vishnu asked about this other summer favourite, the okra.

'The bhindi? Nobel Prize, Vishnu. No one should be given it except Mohammed Chacha and Mindi,' Mohammed said.

It sounded like a verse. Everybody laughed. But not Jyoti. His mind was elsewhere; good food did not interest him right now. Mohammed noticed his friend's indifference and changed the subject.

He picked up a week-old magazine lying about. Away in Delhi, the new Viceroy had been doing his PR bit, being photographed with leaders such as Gandhi and Nehru. On the cover of this magazine, Mountbatten and his wife were seen with Jinnah in the middle. It was a photograph that had made India laugh. The Muslim leader had rehearsed a line for the press – 'A Thorn Between Two Roses'. When the moment came, the gent said to the world press, 'A rose between two thorns.'

'Our dear Quaid, can't get anything right,' Mohammed laughed.

'Our Quaid Jinnah wants Pakistan to express faith in Allah. But I am doing fine here; I pray five times daily. No thank you, sir. Nothing personal, but your League doesn't represent me,' Aziz said.

He voiced what most Muslims felt – a disapproval of the idea of Pakistan – chief among them being two great pillars of the Congress. They were the respected Abul Kalam Azad and, the Pathan Chief of the North-West Frontier, Khan Abdul Ghaffar Khan. The latter was better known as the Frontier Gandhi, being a devoted disciple of the Mahatma and strictly against the division of the country like his revered mentor.

'Me neither,' Mohammed said, agreeing with Aziz. Aziz, too, noticed Jyoti was not really with them. He was looking at them but actually was somewhere else.

Although Jyoti's mind was far away from his friends, he felt they said that to please him. He was touched.

'But how can there be a Pakistan without Partition? And what will it mean?' Aziz said.

The men did not know. But Shera, serving, did.

'It will mean, Sirji, that Punjab will stink like our *ganda nala*.' The flunkey's mention of the town's open sewer made them flinch. It meant squalor and bad odour. Jyoti looked disgusted. He waved Shera away cursorily.

There was a moment of irksome silence.

'Can't happen to our peaceful Puranapur,' Aziz said.

'Perhaps nothing will. But what about the dangerous Sant roaming around the villages?' Mohammed looked worried.

The periphery of the bustling market town was dotted with villages. They were Sikh villages where Muslims were a minority, just about a third of the population – Puranapur just the reverse. The martial Sant – massive, menacing – held complete sway over the countryside. A volatile man, the medieval chieftain was a fiery speaker. He invariably delivered the same message in all his *gun-powder* speeches: 'O Hindus and Sikhs, stand together and fight the tyranny…' Tyranny, not of the British whom he loved, like many others, but of Islam.

Suspecting that Jyoti wanted to be with his visiting in-laws, his friends hurried through lunch; and he walked them downstairs to say goodbye. The guests fed and gone, the women got busy with their own lunch. With Dadima and the children in the kitchen, the three sisters settled down on low stools whose six-inch legs were wrapped in silver. Jyoti joined them and made small talk; but they knew he was lost, not the usual, ebullient man. Rakhi and her sisters talked only of one thing – how gracious Krishna was and how grateful they all were.

The afternoon sun grew fierce, making them all lethargic. The Lahore ladies, usually known for their refinement, started yawning.

'You must be very tired after the train journey.' Jyoti turned to his sisters-in-law. 'Time for a little siesta, ji? No?'

'We don't feel tired at all,' Laaj lied.

'But *you* look tired, Jyoti Bhai,' Kesari said.

The sisters realized he needed to be with his thoughts. They all went up to the drawing room to lie on the thick carpet under the electric ceiling fan.

When everybody was fast asleep, Jyoti slipped out. He took the bicycle chain from the wall, went out to the cowshed, and began lashing himself mercilessly. He made sure that he didn't make any noise. Yet, led by her wifely instinct, Rakhi rushed to the cowshed, hissing 'No, No, No.'

'It was an accident. It was not your fault, my Nath.' She placed herself between her Nath – her Lord – and the next lash.

Then, the two clasped each other and cried bitterly.

Before the day was over, outside the brass-knobbed walnut door was an unusual visitor – Deputy Police Inspector Partap Singh. A tall and handsome Sikh, he was the same age as Jyoti Prasad. He too lived in Chauri Galli. His beard was always well-gelled, as was his imposing moustache. He came in the local poet Mam Din's tonga, the one that had brought Rakhi's sisters in the morning. His face framed in a white beard, the tongawalla was a small, delicate man. Even though he was a lightly-built man, his social standing was high. No one knew how old he was. He was 'young with the young and old with the old' – magical. His magic lay in his verses, which was often enigmatic and which people thought was sublime. In elegant Urdu, Mam Din often composed and recited his poems while driving his tonga, standing upright. He held the reins of Aftab, a white stallion, like an ancient charioteer charging into battle. His verses, combined with the ride in his carriage, was like a double treat.

The policeman and the poet embraced the harassed-looking flour-mill owner. Children from the neighbourhood came and surrounded them. Shera also turned up, thinking his boss might have an errand for him.

'He found us divided, he kept us divided, he wants to leave us divided – the Angrez,' Mam Din versed. He picked up Mindi in his arms and gave him a packet of mouth-watering barfi, the sweetmeat everybody so loved.

'Not the Angrez's fault. Our fault,' Jyoti said. Rakhi had cleaned up his lacerated back and covered it with talcum powder, but it still hurt.

'So gutsy Mindi, our new hero. Wasn't the bad boy afraid

of you?'

'He ruined my first ever picnic, Mam Din.'

'I'm banning the canal,' the policeman laughed.

'Can't do that, Inspector Sahib. Air and water – God's gift to mankind,' Jyoti made a quick repartee.

'God? What is God? God is a marvellous gift like gravity, which the earth sucks,' Mam Din intoned philosophically.

Mam Din was all set to compose and recite, but a bicycle bell interrupted him. It brought Jyoti's brother Bhagwan and Shashi. Bhagwan looked almost exactly like Jyoti and was just as tall. He wore the trademark white khadi of the Congress and a Gandhi cap. He took Mindi from Mam Din and rubbed his unshaven ticklish cheeks against the boy's. Mindi laughed and struggled happily in his uncle's arms. It was an old uncle-nephew sport.

'Unheard of, such a thing happening here. What are we witnessing, Mam Din?' Bhagwan said. He was due back later, but he got a lift home in a PWD truck. 'Which way do you think will Puranapur go?'

'I asked Aftab the same question. My horse neighed and looked up at the sky.'

'What will you do if it goes to Pakistan?'

'I'll whip Aftab and drive into the clouds.'

The children loved that. They giggled heartily.

'The question is, what will we do if Puranapur goes to Pakistan? We have neither Mam Din's tongue nor his tonga,' Partap Singh said to Bhagwan in English.

Being the Congress leader, Bhagwan was expected to give an answer. But he kept quiet. He flicked sweat off his brow and let Mindi down.

'Wait and see what the new Viceroy does,' he said.

'Unlike the wavering, old Wavell, Mountbatten is a

decisive man. He will keep us all united, the handsome man will,' Jyoti said.

'A man is known by his deeds. We will see if he plays with a straight hand or produces a rabbit by some incredible sleight of hand,' Bhagwan said and went upstairs to see his mother and the guests from Lahore.

'Bhagwanji looks worried,' Mam Din said.

Everybody was worried, for nobody knew the answer. The talk turned to the 'Predictor of Puranapur', a Hindu astrologer by the name of Kanhaiya Lal.

'Rumour has it that Kanhaiya Lal knows the answer. But the Owl Face won't open his mouth,' Shera said. It was bold of him, a servant, to have an opinion in the presence of his boss and the police inspector.

'Blast that Kanhaiya. Don't want to hear his name,' Jyoti scowled.

The 'Predictor of Puranapur' had forecast all kinds of things for the city and its inhabitants in the past, most of which were bad. The worst was his prediction of an earthquake fifteen years ago. He called himself a messiah, but people called the unpopular man 'Owl Face' after the ugly bird of night. Thus far, he had neither said yes nor no about Partition.

'Someone should shoot that mad dog,' Partap Singh said. 'Or put him in a mental hospital.'

Just then, Mam Din remembered that he had to take a passenger to the hospital next to the police station.

'Come on, Sardarji,' Mam Din said to the policeman. Given his higher social status as the local poet, the tongawalla could call him 'Sardarji', a chief, a common term used to address Sikhs. Anyone else in his position would have addressed the policeman more reverentially. 'I'll drop you at the *thana*.'

By now, everybody knew of the ugly incident and the

fight at the canal side. A new fear struck people, as if something more terrible was going to happen. Was that a foretaste of things to come?

It was tea time for the family. Rakhi and her sisters were busy making pakoras, as Shera and Balla, another young servant, served hot tea in tall glasses. The most in-demand were the potato and brinjal pakoras; a close second was the bhindi pakora made with okra coated in gram batter and spices and deep fried. This was a Kesari masterpiece. Frying them to perfection was Laaj's speciality. Seated comfortably on a stool with silver legs, she fried the battered vegetables over glowering coal fire in the backyard. With strong, sweet tea, these pakoras were fit for gods, Prime Ministers, and Viceroys.

Jyoti made Bhagwan eat in a hurry because he wanted to take him out for a walk in Saddar Bazaar, the town's commercial hub, when the light was still good.

As soon as they had finished munching pakoras with tea, they left. Outside Dr Gupta's shop, they ran into Shaukat Ali.

'I heard everything. I'm very sorry, Jyoti. Can't believe such a thing happening here in Puranapur. The boy okay?'

'He's fine. It was a silly but dangerous thing. Mindless and silly.'

'Allah be thanked. Heartiest congratulations, Jyoti.

Dr Gupta, fifty, with respectable salt-and-pepper hair, came out to greet them with an effulgent look. He embraced the two brothers and Shaukat Ali. A brief review of the incident followed with all four agreeing it was a freak incident.

'A godsend, this meeting of you two,' Jyoti said to Shaukat and Bhagwan. 'People should see you two together.' He suggested the two leaders take a joint walk in the town centre.

'But my people won't like it,' Shaukat said.

'Nor mine,' Bhagwan said.

'Rise above it, yaar. It will be good for the locals; they can sleep peacefully. You two being seen together is good news for Puranapur. Take a long walk,' Dr Gupta cajoled them, taking their hands in his.

Shaukat and Bhagwan looked at each other; leaders of two rival political parties, but otherwise friends of well over two decades, smiled like they had always done. Shaukat looked back at the doctor's clinic. What he saw made him laugh a little. Ten yards on the left of the clinic sat, cross-legged, a street dentist facing a heap of teeth he had pulled out of people's mouths. On the other side of the shop sat on his haunches an ear-cleaner with the tools of his trade – little metallic chisels and tiny spoons, tucked neatly in a roll of his red headgear. Both men were scanning the passers-by for potential clients.

'Half the medical profession is here within twenty yards. Now isn't that something?' Shaukat said, and all four of them laughed cheerily.

'I, too, have to wait for patients sometimes,' Dr Gupta said. 'A bit cool now. Have a nice walk,' he added as the leaders of the Congress and the League carried on with their walk, down the busy bazaar, looking casual and relaxed. And hand in hand, Jyoti and Dr Gupta went back to his clinic. Inside, DAV High School headmaster Rama Kant was sitting alone. Vishnu had just joined that school. Rama Kant put aside *The Tribune* he was reading and slapped his forehead in disgust.

'Why is our Bhagwan walking with that snake?' he said.

'The right thing to do. To reassure everyone, to tell Hindus and Muslims and Sikhs they are brothers,' Dr Gupta said pleasantly.

'How can you say something like that, Doctor Sahib? I don't believe my ears.'

'There's an ear-cleaner outside my shop if you need your

ears cleaned, Headmaster Sahib.'

'But Shaukat is a snake. What do you do with a snake?'

'You charm it,' Jyoti said.

'You have an answer for everything, Jyoti Prasadji,' Rama Kant said. 'A man for all seasons, isn't he, Doctor Sahib?'

'Jyoti is a man of reason, and he has said the right thing, you must admit. But Shaukat was never a snake.'

'A good man who has strayed into wrong politics,' Jyoti smiled.

'True, too true, sadly, Jyoti. But what's the matter with your back? You are sitting straight as a ramrod.'

'Prickly heat, Doctor Sahib.'

'Walk shirtless in the rain when it rains.'

'I shall when it rains.'

There had never been a day like this for Jyoti. It was not over yet. The family was going to gather on the roof for a secret session tonight. Those to attend were Dadima, her two sons, their wives, and Rakhi's sisters. The matriarch would be the chair. There was only one item on the agenda – barber Gangaram's proposal. Until Bhagwan's third child arrived, the Prasads lived as an extended family. The habit remained. Every now and then, they came together again. Like tonight. Tonight, everybody would sleep on Jyoti's roof, two to a charpoy as usual. With three extra guests, the roof pulsated with joy and turned into a playhouse of fun it had never been before. Vishnu and Shashi began somersaulting in the happiness of being part of such a big group, but sharp shouts from their mothers put an end to it. Their sisters and cousin Sharda from Lahore were given a string cot to share. A foot wider than an ordinary charpoy, it was quite comfortable. But the girls had more important things to do than falling asleep. Meenakshi and Mona wanted to know all about the *Paris of the Punjab*. They were keen to pick up every bit from Sharda about the glittering Anarkali Bazaar that resonated with the jingling of gold jewellery, tinkling glass bangles. The comforting warmth of pashmina and the smooth sensation of silk, and nameless other items every girl would die for; they wanted to know about all that from their cousin. Besides, they had a hundred and one stories of their own to tell her for at least a hundred and one times.

The starry night stories ceased only when stern warnings came from their mothers.

The young folk finally did succumb to pressure and the conference began. It proved to be a short-lived one with a decision taken swiftly. There was no other business – just one more thing, but that was for the two brothers alone.

Gangaram's proposal dealt with and plans made, the brothers walked off to the far end of the roof. Bhagwan did all the talking. It was about his visit to Vatala.

Bhagwan and his deputy Desraj were picked up at Vatala station at dawn that morning by a lorry and driven to a village in a bend in the Ravi, one of the five great rivers of the Punjab. The journey was rough and bumpy, but the village, Patti Khem Karan, turned out to be one of immense charm. It was hidden behind clumps of tall chinar trees wilting in the sun. Mud houses coated with a paste of cow dung and earth, had an air of cleanliness about them. Above their doors were signs of the swastika in white, while above the windows were floral designs in red, yellow and blue. The lorry came to a halt in the village common where people sat cross-legged – about five hundred men, women and children. They faced a dais from which spoke the fiery Sikh leader Sant, a self-styled 'saint', a yellow-and-blue robed Sikh. He had an intense look, sparkling snow-white teeth, flowing black bushy beard, and a bright blue turban.

A couple of years older than Bhagwan, the Sant held a long gold-tipped arrow in his right hand, and a revolver in an upholster slung from his left shoulder. By his side stood his Hindu deputy Gautam, a six-foot giant of Bhagwan's age, armed to the teeth.

The Sant sprang to his feet and embraced Bhagwan.

'Congress Secretaryji, we are honoured,' the Sant murmured and waved at his captive audience. Then he turned to Gautam. 'Rejoice, my son, rejoice. We have a special guest in our midst. A VVIP.' He beamed a smile at Bhagwan, fixed him with his hypnotic eyes and began a monologue about what the Islamist rulers had done to Hindus and Sikhs in the past.

'Converted millions by the sword… Beheaded those who wouldn't convert… Emperor Aurangzeb the Cruel had our Ninth Guru Teg Bahadur beheaded in 1675 in Delhi, because he refused to become a Muslim…'

Bhagwan had not come here for a lesson in history. 'But, Santji, that was hundreds of years ago. Things are different now. Independence is round the corner. Now, it is time for brotherhood.'

'You can't talk brotherhood with Islam; you can't.'

'Mahatma Gandhi has been trying hard to talk to Mr Jinnah for unity.'

'Jinnah drinks Scotch whisky daily, eats pork sausage himself, and demands a homeland for Muslims to live as pure Muslims.'

'Sant, Bhagwanji hasn't come here for your lectures. Where is your hospitality?' Gautam admonished the Sant.

The Sant mellowed. Refreshments arrived – hot samosas, sizzling jalebis and piping hot tea in an exquisite bone china teapot. Bhagwan admired its elegance.

'Yours,' the Sant said grandly.

'I haven't come here for your tea and teapots. I have come all this way to talk.'

'Plenty of time for that. First…' The Sant put an arm around Puranapur's Congress Secretary and led him away from the village. Desraj and Gautam followed. They went up a hillock with an awesome view of the Ravi. Even more breathtaking was what Bhagwan saw on the sandy riverbank – over two hundred armed, mounted Sikhs in a spectacular uniform of blue, yellow and black drilling under the supervision of a man in an army colonel's uniform.

'My hungry lions. Hungry for revenge and what they were born to do – defending our dharma.'

A dazzling display of horsemanship came next, followed by the bloodcurdling Sikh battle cry:

WAHE GURU JI KA KHALSA!
WAHE GURU JI KI FATEH!

'Bhagwan, I thought it would reassure you to see all this. All this is to frighten the shit out of them Muzzies.'

'Frightens the shit out of me too.' Bhagwan knew the existence of scores of such private armies in the Punjab – Sikh and Muslim.

'But by the Guru, if they do anything to you in Puranapur. They are three to one there…'

'I have Shaukat Ali's word they won't.'

'What about their AHAA, their so-called Allah Hoo Akbar Army? It's more a HAHA army, if you ask me. Its soldiers will scamper away with their tails between their legs at first sight of my lions.'

'Shaukat says he has their word.'

'Only a naïve Congressman will believe a habitually deceitful League-walla's word. The best thing to happen to India was the coming of the Angrez. He milked the Indian Cow, he did, of course. But he got rid of seven hundred years of murderous Muslim rule, gave India the rule of law, justice, fair play – things unknown to brainwashed Islam. The *gora* gave us modern education, science, technology…'

'But Santji…'

'I know, I know. I know you haven't come all the way to hear my lecture.'

'…Just promise you won't start anything, Santji.'

'You want more words. I give you mine. Happy?'

In farewell, Sant handed him a sackcloth bag with something round and big in it. 'Don't look into it until you are out of Patti Khem Karan.'

'Looks like there's someone's head in it.'

'Wish it were Jinnah's.'

It was the beautiful Made-in-England teapot.

'How did it go with that turbaned nutter, Bhagwan?' Jyoti did not like the fake saint with a gold tipped arrow.

'I got what we wanted from him – his word not to start any mischief.'

'What else did you get from him?'

'A Made-in-England teapot,' Bhagwan laughed. 'We'll use it when someone important comes.'

'What did you see there?'

'His private army, navy and air force.' Bhagwan laughed again. 'Frightening!'

'Foolish boy, you know he is another Hitler. Instead of the Fuehrer's toothbrush moustache, he has a flowing beard. He is sworn to a final solution of the Muslims.'

'It's typical Sikh talk, meaningless hot air.'

'Dangerous hot air.'

'But the Sant can't make a move without my permission.'

It was well past 11, an intense blue-black sky perforated by glowing pinholes making it a delectably pleasant night. The brothers went off to their charpoys by their wives' sides to sleep. But Jyoti could not sleep.

Something was shadowing him – a phantom.

If I see a shooting star now, my family and Bhagwan's will be saved.

A pinpoint of light darted from the star-filled blue-black void above. It travelled six inches and vanished in the same void.

But what about Mohammed and his family?

Half a mile away in Moti Bagh, Mohammed turned to his wife on the roof.

'Begum...' Mohammed whispered, pulling her into his bed. The rest of the family was fast asleep. His chance. 'Begum...' he wanted to ask if she had a headache.

The begum smiled. If Mohammed had been able to see her face, he would have said instead, 'I love you. Very much.'

Salma, knowing what was on her husband's mind, had smiled. It was the smile of someone who wanted nothing else in the world but that moment. She was loved and desired by the man she loved more than life itself.

'Ji, you said something?' Salma whispered back, laughing inaudibly. Suddenly, a wave of yearning crept into her limbs. But at the same time, she heard the charging horses – *daddum, daddum, daddum...* The galloping hooves wiped out her smile sending a chill into her heart.

'Ji, do you think it's going to be all right?'

'Yes, it is. Pretty boy Mountbatten is here.'

'His wife is very beautiful.'

'Not as beautiful as mine.'

That brought her smile back. From then on, Mohammed let his hands do the talking inside her shirt and leggings. Salma became breathless.

'Begum, have you been running or something?'

'Yes, to get her quick, quick.'

Mohammed looked up at the sky above. 'Thank you, Sir.'

The two-year old Seema gave a piercing yell from Salma's bed. Salma slipped out of Mohammed's arms with the same ease and grace with which she had gone into them, leaving him hard, huge and bursting. Bursting!

'Sir, couldn't you do a little babysitting for half an hour for your very humble servant?' Mohammed said to the sky. 'Spoilsport.'

On Wednesday, after lunch, Jyoti turned up at Aziz's shop in Saddar Bazaar – ENGLISH BOOK DEPOT – for their mid-weekly game of *shatranj*. It was hot, so hot a thin layer of moisture gathered inside Jyoti's sunglasses.

'In heat, water evaporates. It doesn't condense.'

'What?'

'This heat, yaar. It's melting my goggles. And it's only

April.' Jyoti took off his sunglasses.

Mohammed arrived holding a black umbrella and with an even darker piece of news. The headless body of a man had been found early that morning in a pond under the railway bridge at Vatala. No one knew who he was. All they knew was that he had come from Puranapur. The corpse had a return ticket on it. This was disturbing and mysterious. It's disturbing because murders, which had so far been occurring in places far away from Puranapur, were now casting their shadow over this peaceful place. And mysterious because no one was reported missing from this small town, where everybody knew everybody else.

'The Hindus are saying it was a Muslim spy. The Muslims are saying it was a Sikh. The missing head is hindering identification,' Mohammed added.

'They are all barking mad. A spy here? In this little place where time does not move, everyone tells you everything even before a question is asked?' Aziz was incredulous.

Jyoti shuddered. Bhagwan had been to Vatala only the other day. What if...? He was Number One on the Allah Hoo Akbar Army's hit list. What if he went there next time and...? Jyoti saw a decapitated head lying in the moss-green pond under the railway bridge – a hairy watermelon, its juicy redness scattered around it. Instead of its black seeds, bits of white curd peeped through the foul-smelling pond.

'What if our Puranapur goes to Pakistan, Badshah?' Jyoti said.'What if Puranapur goes to Pakistan?'

There was a long-standing agreement between the three that whatever happened, they would stay put. For, like most Muslims up and down the country, Mohammed and Aziz did not believe there could be another country by another name.

Jyoti did not know what to say. He felt helpless and miserable by his inability to understand what he felt.

'Will you kill us?'

'Jyoti, it's true the world is going mad. But you've gone madder. What nonsense is this?'

TWO

AS A RULE, young unmarried girls were told by the elders at home to look plain and austere. Their parents reacted strongly if they tried to look attractive and wore flashy clothes. Any girl who dabbed kohl too prominently around her eyes, applied rouge on the cheeks, or tinted her lips red was in for trouble; the mother or an aunt would pull her up: 'Foolish girl, don't let your head spin just because you think you have great looks.'

As a rule, young unmarried Punjabi girls wore cotton – salwar kameez along with the all-important dupatta, a long scarf draped over the chest and thrown back around the shoulders. It was meant to conceal the alluring womanly contours beneath it, an essential symbol of female modesty. No self-respecting young woman would knowingly let her dupatta dip below a certain line. If she did, then she was a slut.

Like most of her friends, Meenakshi had a good wardrobe – a few colourful shirts, muslin dupattas, and three pairs of salwar kameez. Meenakshi was happy with what she had, though she would have loved to have another thing – a garara.

The garara was the rage of the day. It had come from the

Paris of the Punjab. As legwear, it was quite like the salwar, but with a crucial difference. It was generously flared at the bottom, giving the girl a doll-like look. Once Meenakshi had borrowed her friend Shanti's exotic new acquisition, just to see how she looked in it. Her mother was sharp in her disapproval: 'Shameless hussy, go give it back.'

So it came as a shock to Meenakshi when Rakhi changed her tone the very next day. 'Meenakshi, I think you should have a garara of your own after all, *beti*. And a new kameez.'

Rakhi went with Laaj and Kesari to choose the cloth from Taj Silk Store. After a struggle with rolls of cloth, they picked out a very special kind of silk. Very expensive too. The sisters quarrelled over paying for it. No way was Rakhi going to let them pick up the bill. Nor did her sisters relent. After some serious haggling, the charmers from Lahore won.

'Something special from us for our very special niece. It has nothing to do with you, Palm Tree.'

Back home, they sent for the family tailor Gulab Chand. He was given one of Meenakshi's salwars to take his measurements from. He spread the garment on a charpoy and jotted down the measurements in a notebook. Meenakshi, her cousin Sharda and her brothers looked on. Then, Rakhi handed the tailor the material from Taj Silk Store. It took everyone's breath away. It was a scintillating two-tone silk, pink and sky-blue all at once. Everyone felt it between their fingers exclaiming 'ooh' and 'aah' in admiration and surprise.

'New kameez for the girl,' Rakhi said, giving the tailor one of Meenakshi's old shirts to copy.

The tailor took the fabled silk, then shook his head. 'Rakhi *bibi*, I made the shirt two years ago. The girl has grown since. Just look how much,' Gulab Chand said.

But Rakhi wasn't going to let the man put his measuring

tape around her daughter. It would be like the tailor touching her. She told him to put an extra inch here and there.

'Is it a lie that you are the best tailor in town?'

'What do you think, Rakhi Bibi?'

'Well, then.'

The town's best tailor did what he was told. He came back two days later with the new clothes. Meenakshi tried them on. Perfect.

'A perfect Princess Royale, my niece.' Aunt Kesari hugged her.

'A Maharajah's daughter,' Laaj said.

Everybody beamed with pride, more so the Maharajah. But all Meenakshi wanted to do was run and hide; so utterly happy was she that she felt ashamed of herself for being so.

Gulab Chand was paid and dismissed. Then Rakhi did something that made everybody gawk. She asked her daughter to change so the new clothes did not get crushed.

'Fold them up neatly, and put them in the trunk.'

'Mother!' Vishnu and Mindi cried.

'What do you have against the girl looking like you used to?' Kesari protested.

'What do you mean by *like she used to*? She still does. Every inch her daughter's mother,' Laaj countered. She pulled out a five-rupee note from inside her blouse and waved it around Meenakshi's head three times. It would be changed into coins and distributed among beggars back in Lahore.

'I agree. Totally,' Kesari said, hugging the confused girl, and proceeded to do exactly what her sister had just done. With a big smile, she said to her other niece Sharda, 'Your time in a year or so. And ours to take the train back home.'

'Oh, don't go now, Mausi, not so soon," Mindi pleaded with tears in his eyes. 'You've just come. And I am loving it so much.'

'We'll be right back for the engagement soon, Mindi *beta*.'

It was time. Mam Din was waiting outside with his tonga. Jyoti accompanied them on his bike.

The house suddenly seemed so empty.

'Go put your clothes in the trunk, *beti*,' Rakhi said to her daughter.

'Mother's best policy: if you want your clothes to last longer, wear them only sometimes. If you want them to last forever, don't wear them ever.' Vishnu laughed.

'Another day. When someone comes calling.'

That day came soon. A few days after visiting the Prasads', Gangaram received a call from the Sunars. In their grand, high-walled *haveli*, he had to work on their boy first, as always. In the third year of college, Gulshan – tall and handsome – was all set to graduate soon. Strongly built, he looked more like an army officer on probation or a budding cricketer than a jeweller's son. In fact, he was still in white flannels since he had played cricket in the morning on the town's maidan right behind their sprawling house. His side had just started batting so he had rushed back for a 'quick, quick' cut. Understandably, he was in a hurry and told the barber to make it snappy for him to get back to bat fifth.

'Gulshan Bau, even when you were a very young lad, you were always in a hurry.'

'My side has just started to bat. I have to get back.'

'An English game at a time like this?'

'Why not? Anyway, what do you think of the new Englishman.'

'First it was Divide and Rule. Now, that they can't rule, so it is Divide and Quit,' the barber said.

'Mountbatten won't let it happen. He loves India.'

'But like our Nehru, he can't stand up to Jinnah.'

'Gangaram, Nehru and Mountbatten are men of vision. Unlike the narrow-minded Jinnah.'

Gulshan's mother, Dulari, came and put an end to their pointless discussion. Tall, huge and wide, Dulari was in her mid-forties. As was her slightly younger sister, Piyari, who came with her. Both were widows. They sat down on a sturdy charpoy, which groaned under their combined weight. A few minutes later, their younger brother, Bhushan, of similar dimensions, turned up for his haircut. Gulshan dashed away as soon as his was over and Bhushan took his chair.

'Dulari *bibi*, where are your eyes?' the barber said.

'Where all eyes should be. On the future, Gangaram. Where else?' The gem in Dulari's *nath* glistened as she looked up at the sky. She put her hand on her nose to mildly press it.

'They should be on the present, Dulari Bibi.'

'You are talking of Mountbatten? Of his how and when?'

'No, no, no. I am talking of the boy who's become a man. I am talking…'

Dulari understood even before Gangaram could finish.

'…of a first-class gem for him.'

'Girl from Puranapur?'

The barber lowered his voice to a whisper. This made Dulari's *nath* move and her left eyebrow rise.

'That mill owner's daughter?' Dulari said, fixing her *nath* again. This caused a little irritation in her nose, leading to a loud sneeze. She sneezed three times. Not a good omen.

'Don't you think the boy needs a family with more… what shall I say?'

'Best boy, our Gulshan. What he needs is best girl. God has given him the rest.'

'Then God will give him whatever else he needs.'

'That's why He made you send for me.'

'But Gangaram, I sneezed.'

The fact that the woman had sneezed worried Gangaram too, the general belief being that someone sneezing over an important decision boded ill. But he knew his way around. '*Bibi*, the times we are living through should make the whole of India sneeze all day, every day. Think of it, and do what I say.'

'And what do you say, Gangaram?'

'I say no harm in just taking a look at the girl.'

'I agree,' Bhushan spoke. 'What harm?'

The decision was taken. The brother and the sisters would go to the Hanuman temple on Tuesday. Gangaram would make sure that the girl was there. Tuesday was the day of Lord Hanuman, the monkey god, god of strength, the god most sought after these days. Everybody went to the temple on Tuesdays. It was a ritual everybody observed. The three looked at Meenakshi through the crowd. Then at each other. Without a word, they stood up to go, causing a stir and drawing attention. They had just arrived. 'Who do they think they are, these gold-and-silver widows?'

So it was agreed. The barber did the rest.

This was how it came about. And Rakhi's sisters came back for the occasion, looking like Bombay film stars. The street, gaping from doorways and craning from windows and those quaint balconies, was wowed again as they got down from Mam Din's tonga. They displayed glamour that filled the Prasads with pride, boosting their *shaan* and status tremendously. They brought more presents for everyone. For their special niece, Aunt Laaj had gold earrings and Kesari two lengths of sky-blue and mustard-coloured *fabrique en France* chiffon from Lahore's famous Anarkali Bazaar for alluring dupatta scarves.

11May, another crisp Sunday morning – sharp bright light and prickly heat promising a scorching day ahead. The mullah up there and Dadima down here in Chauri Galli had said their prayers to God. Well, two different gods – his and hers. Yogurt had been churned, Kunti milked, and Jyoti was hurrying home from his walk.

In a buoyant mood, Jyoti was stopped by the paan-and-cigarette seller Chandu, as he passed by his booth at the street corner. Chandu always had his radio on to attract customers. Today being a Sunday, people had stayed at home, and there was no one at Chandu's shop.

'Prasadji, news just came that Nehru is with the Viceroy in Simla. Having *private talks* without the pesky Jinnah around.'

'That's wonderful news, Chandu.'

'Of course, Sirji. And the radio says he is staying with the Mountbattens in their palace.'

Scenic Simla at seven thousand feet in the Himalayas was the Raj's summer capital. No Indian politician had ever stayed at the palace as a houseguest of the Viceroy. It was a rare honour given to Nehru.

'That's even better, Chandu.'

'What does it mean, Prasadji?'

'It means Pandit Nehru will have the Viceroy's ear. It means a kick in Jinnah's arse. It means our leader will be able to talk Mountbatten out of Partition.'

Jyoti ordered a sweet paan and had it wrapped up.

At home, he found Rakhi and her sisters in a tizzy. He told them the good news.

'Now there won't be Partition, Lady JP.'

But today, Rakhi was not interested in the world.

'Go bathe, Meenakshi *beti*, with perfumed Yardley soap. And wash your hair with English shampoo. Sharda *beti*, you lend this girl a hand.' Rakhi shouted at Meenakshi and Sharda.

'You hear, ji? Nehru is with Mountbatten in Simla. ALONE,' Jyoti turned to his sisters-in-law, who were just as interested in the world today as their sister Palm Tree.

'And make two ponytails today. Sharda *beti*, you make sure the tails are straight and braided well…'

'Now, there will only be Independence and no Partition. Are you listening, Lady JP? NO PARTITION.'

Rakhi was not listening.

'…You are going to wear your new clothes.'

Her mother's last words filled Meenakshi with maddening delight. She bathed, washed her hair, and had it turned into twin ponytails in such haste, it made Vishnu raise his eyebrows.

'Catching a train, are we?'

Meenakshi was dying to get into those clothes. She was afraid that if she didn't hurry, her mother might change her mind about it.

'I say!' Vishnu whistled when she was dressed. Then, he addressed their mother, 'Ma, she is your carbon copy. True. Just look at her.'

Their mother came, took Meenakshi and Sharda by their hands, and led them to a room, bolting the door. She stood her daughter before a mirror, put kohl in her eyes, lightly brushed her cheeks with rouge, and did something that killed the girl three-quarters. Rakhi added a hint of lipstick to the girl's lips.

'Ma!' Meenakshi had guessed. Her heart began to beat

faster. Her joy of a minute ago flew out of her like a bird in a cage with the door left open. Now, she didn't care for the garara, the two-tone silk shirt, or the diaphanous chiffon dupatta.

'Who is coming, Ma?'

'Aunt Dulari.'

'Who is she?' Meenakshi had never heard of her.

'She owns a mountain of gold.'

'But what is she to us?'

'Don't eat my head with your silly questions. Aunt Dulari is Aunt Dulari. Sharda *beti*, look after your cousin. I have a hundred things to do.'

Then Vishnu and Mindi were bathed and made to wear their best clothes. An unusual excitement gripped the house. It multiplied when Bhagwan and his wife Maya arrived with their children similarly spruced up. Their sixteen-year old daughter Mona took her doll of a cousin and Sharda away to a distant room and plied Meenakshi with bits of information that had come her way, adding a little spice here and a dash of lemon there to make it hot and mouthwatering.

Suddenly, a roar went up among the children.

Puranapur's best sweet vendor was at the door, a huge basket on his head. By his side was Shera. Behind them were Jyoti's three other mill hands – Balla, Judge and Shambhu – all of Shera's age. They also carried baskets on their heads. The baskets were full of sweets – mouthwatering barfi, royal balushai, irresistible chum-chum and heavenly kalakand. While the drooling children watched hungrily, the women carefully arranged the sweets in seven large brass *thal*s and decked them up with thin silver foil. They had them put out of sight upstairs under Shera's vigilance, with orders to strangle anyone who neared them with the intent of poaching.

'Balla, Shambhu, Judge!' Rakhi shouted. 'Mop all the

floors, sprinkle water on the courtyard and flower bushes. Remove every speck of dust from sight.'

Orders given, Rakhi and her sisters went away to change and dress up.

The guests were to arrive at eight. By seven, everybody and everything was ready. The floors glistened. As did the children's faces. Dadima's too. She had washed it with the yogurt she had set last night. She had rubbed on it a blob of butter she had made that morning. Her usually guava-pale skin looked semi-transparent.

By half past seven, everybody was at their place. The children were on the balcony and looked out curiously. The servants sat idly on their haunches in the courtyard. The two brothers and their wives waited anxiously in the drawing room on the first floor with Laaj, Kesari, and Dadima. Meenakshi was where she was supposed to be – out of sight with look-alike cousins Mona and Sharda. In attendance were Vishnu and Shashi. Just after eight, a tonga passed by the house. It was Mam Din's. It did not stop. Half a dozen other tongas passed by the Prasad house in the next forty minutes or so. But where was this Aunt Dulari? The children got tired looking out for the elusive guests and eyeing those fabulous sweets.

'Next tonga, surely,' they said.

It was. Tota's carriage stopped outside the Prasad home. Tota was the family's favourite tongawalla after Mam Din. His delicate two-wheeled wooden carriage shuddered, heaving up and down as Dulari and Piyari stepped down from its rear seat. It did the same when Bhushan and family servant Hansraj emerged from the front. Chauri Galli came out to peep at the rarely seen *gold-and-silver widows*.

Entering the house, the widows were visibly stunned by the apparitions from Lahore. Bhushan couldn't stop staring.

'I say, why so much trouble, sister?' Dulari said familiarly, looking at the great feast laid out in her honour. 'All I have come for is to see the girl. Where is she?' Dulari hitched up her white muslin sari and spread herself on the divan with two long sausage-shaped cushions.

'Sweeten your mouth first, sister. Plenty of time,' Rakhi said expectedly.

'But where is she?'

'Must be playing with friends,' Rakhi replied. Then she gave her son a loud shout. 'Vishnu, go see where your sister is.'

Vishnu sat in the room next door with Meenakshi, Mona, Sharda and Shashi. Vishnu knew his mother was aware where they all were. He also knew it was part of a game. He laughed and pulled out his tongue at his sister.

'No idea where she is, Mummy. Was here a minute ago.'

'Go find her. Why did she slip out?'

'Children these days. Do they do what they are told?' Dulari played along though she also knew the game.

'But our Meenakshi is not like that,' Bhagwan said.

'Very obedient and adoring,' Maya added.

'I hear from Gangaram she has a sweet face, and I have come to see her and give her my blessings.'

'Best barber, Gangaram,' Bhagwan said.

'Gave me my first and last haircut. And all those in between,' Jyoti said with a little laugh to blunt the edge of nervousness that filled the room. Bhagwan too.

'We hear that Mountbatten has gone to Simla and that Nehru is with him there without the ogre Jinnah. Surely, it is a good thing for us. No, Secretary Sahib?

'A very good thing, indeed.'

'Mountbatten is a good man and close friend of our Jawaharlal, unlike Wavell. But can he talk the new Viceroy out of making Pakistan?

'Over Jinnah's dead body, his henchmen say. And I say, then give us his body,' Bhushan laughed. 'And why does he always look as if he hasn't been to the loo for days?'

'How very observant of you, Bhushanji,' Bhagwan said.

'I have a solution. Give the man a sleeping pill and a strong laxative every night. That'll sort him out.'

This made everybody laugh.

'Food for thought. The League should take your advice, Bhushanji,' Bhagwan said.

'He might get his "moth-eaten Pakistan", West and East Pakistan. But it won't last six months. How can it, separated by a thousand miles of Indian territory?' Bhushan went on.

Tea arrived in the Sant's teapot.

'What a beautiful teapot! Never seen one like it,' the chief guest remarked.

'Bet it's made in England like everything else. Why can't we make beautiful things?' Bhushan said.

'We do better, Bhaisahab. We make beautiful people,' Laaj said with a sparkling smile.

'We also make beautiful things. Of gold and silver and ivory. Our Anarkali Bazaar is full of them,' Kesari said.

'That's correct. We went there once, and my sisters saw and they bought. We came back with a camel-load of stuff from there,' Bhushan said, smiling at Kesari. The way he looked at her made it clear he was a man smitten. Jyoti and Bhagwan said to each other with their eyes, 'Lecher'. They dismissed him from their minds, knowing Kesari was totally oblivious of 'the fat fool'.

'Surprisingly, the people of Lahore seldom go to Anarkali Bazaar. But it seems we'll be going there a lot, soon,' she said, a subtle but a meaningful statement.

In an attempt to change the topic, Jyoti said, "Our only

daughter, followed by two sons."

Dulari cleared her throat and turned to Jyoti. She had done a lightning calculation in her head about the size of the dowry most of which would have to come from the *Paris of the Punjab*, from this famous bazaar itself. 'Just the right size for a family. Wish I had a few more. But God called Gulshan's father back.'

A sad look came over Dulari.

One didn't talk of the dead on such occasions nor of God calling people back. Jyoti's forehead furrowed.

'Drink your tea, sister. Or it'll get cold,' he said.

'When we've seen the girl.'

Had they overplayed the game? Jyoti stood up and went next door to fetch her.

Mona put an arm around her cousin and led her in. Frightened Meenakshi almost fell over an invisible obstacle.

'Come here, young lady. Let me behold your face. Do you go dressed up like this to play with your friends?' Dulari held Meenakshi by her arm and let her yellow chiffon dupatta covering her head and face fall to the shoulders. 'Smile for me.'

Meenakshi managed a smile.

'Why, sister Rakhi...?'

'Why what, sister Dulari?'

'Why have you hidden her in these awful clothes?'

Meenakshi was alive no more. Perhaps dying would be preferable to this ordeal.

'Meaning what?' Rakhi breathed nervously.

'Meaning... does she need shiny shiny silk and a doll's garara to look... what shall I say?' Dulari didn't finish. She pulled Meenakshi and embraced her.

There were sighs of relief all around.

'A laddu to sweeten the mouth of this Anarkali. No, give

it to me. Let me sweeten those rosebud lips.'

Dulari took a laddu from Maya and placed a bit of it between Meenakshi's reluctant lips.

It was time for sweets for everyone. The children – Vishnu, Mindi, Shashi and the others – were given plates heaped with them. They polished them off quickly. Mindi, thinking nobody was looking, licked his plate with his tongue. But he was seen.

'It will rain on your wedding night if you do that. It will rain cats and dogs when you go on your horse to get your bride,' Aunt Dulari said.

'True? I'm having a party in my mouth.'

'We can see that. But it always rains on your wedding night if you lick your plate.'

'I'll ask Papa to buy me an umbrella.'

There was laughter, the laughter of a happy family. But there was someone who was anything but happy – Meenakshi, the source of everyone else's happiness. She wanted to run from the bulky woman with a nose ring and hide somewhere where she could not be found. But she knew what she was supposed to do – sit through it all and look bashful. She didn't have to try. She simply looked that, feeling bewildered when Auntie Dulari called her Anarkali or the pomegranate blossom, 'rosebud', even 'a piece of the moon'. When Dulari announced she was leaving, Meenakshi sighed deeply, in relief. Dulari dipped a hand in hervast cleavage and brought out an exquisite diamond ring.

'On the occasion of seeing your moon face,' Dulari said and slipped the ring through Meenakshi's finger. 'No matter if Puranapur goes to India, Pakistan or Japan, you come to us. Right?'

'Right,' the children chorused.

Dulari gave Jyoti a little jewel box for the safekeeping of the ring.

It was time for the Prasads to bring out what they had in readiness for the Sunars. Jyoti had put aside cash to buy the expensive Telefunken radio and a second-hand Morris Minor he had seen at the Texaco petrol pump. That went instead towards paying for what he had to give his future son-in-law and his family. It consisted of a thick gold ring to be worn by the boy at the proper engagement ceremony later, English woollen cloth for two suits, white and blue poplin for two shirts, and two Tootal ties. There were hundred and one rupees in cash for him and the other three, along with Banarasi silk saris for the sisters and an embroidered silk kurta for Bhushan. And finally, a bulbous something wrapped in silk cloth – the teapot! It was customary that if a guest lauded something, it must be given to them at parting. Also customary was to ignore the guests' protests, as it happened that morning.

Bhushan took the clothes from Jyoti's arms into his own. He held them with care, as if he held a sleeping baby. It was a precious bundle. It marked the *sagan* of their golden boy Gulshan to the Prasad gem Meenakshi.

As everybody assembled downstairs, seven *thal*s of sweets made their appearance. Beside the teapot, there was room only for two *thal*s in the tonga. Shera, Balla, Shambhu, Judge and the Sunar servant Hansraj carried the other five on their heads and walked single file on the hot May evening. Dulari now pressed something into Rakhi's hand – a passport-size photo. Neighbours watched. In the rush, Meenakshi was forgotten. This was her moment.

Meenakshi ran to an unused room, where winter bed clothes – blankets, *razais* and *tulai*s – were kept piled up on charpoys. She threw herself onto one such mountain and burst out crying. A minute later, Mona and Sharda turned up next to her.

'Why are you crying?' Mona said.

Meenakshi did not say anything. Actually she had no answer.

'Silly girl, why do you cry? You should be happy.'

Meenakshi clung to her cousin's neck and cried and cried. Wedding trumpets deafened. When she shut her eyes, she saw the *doli* waiting outside the house, ready to take her away from Mother and Father and Vishnu and Mindi and... It was unbearable.

Vishnu tiptoed in with the photograph.

'Look how handsome he is,' Mona said, pushing the photo under Meenakshi's runny nose.

Meenakshi wouldn't look. Mona pleaded. After a while, Meenakshi succumbed. She had a quick look. It was an attractive, youthful face. Meenakshi fell in love with it at first sight.

'Stop crying and wipe your tears. Good thing no one took *your* photo. You look like a circus clown with all that kohl running down your rosy cheeks. God is quite thoughtless sometimes. Why does He make some people beautiful when all they want is to look ugly?'

Mona took Meenakshi downstairs to the hand pump in the courtyard. She washed off all the kohl and rouge and lipstick.

'There. You look like a human being again. All those tears! My God! Anyone would have thought Auntie Dulari was a witch who came to gobble you up,' Mona said. 'Mind you, she looks the type. Man-eating type. You for breakfast, me for lunch, and Shashi and Vishnu for dinner.'

Suddenly, the house filled up with people. The neighbours had come to congratulate the Prasads. Mona steered her cousins back to the room with the blankets, so that they wouldn't be disturbed. But they were invaded – by all their brothers and sisters. They came with lipstick thick on their lips, reddened cheeks, and bumble-bee eyes with too much of kohl. They had come to make Meenakshi laugh.

Meenakshi laughed.

'Donkeys.' She thumped them and hugged them.

There was a big celebratory family dinner. Shera and Balla were sent to buy four legs of goat and two live chickens. An expensive delicacy, chickens were eaten on special days only. Back home, Balla held the chickens down one by one on a wooden board. Sher Singh unsheathed his Sikh *kirpan* from his left side. Holding the shiny curved blade aloft, he emitted the fierce Sikh battle cry and chopped off their heads with one blow each. The children standing around him clapped. To give their sister a little break from work, Laaj and Kesari took charge of the kitchen. But they let Palm Tree make her masterpiece, the universally loved phirni dessert.

Next morning, the Lahoris went back home. The entire Prasad clan walked them to the station and waited until the train came. Mindi was in tears. 'Mausiji,'he said, clutching at the clothes of Laaj and Kesari in turn, 'come back soon, soon.'

Meenakshi was happy. It was a constant pain that she loved. She longed to tell Mona about it. But courage flew out of her each time she tried. With it, the words. Anyhow, Mona knew.

'He really is handsome, you know, Meenakshi?'

'No, I don't, and I don't care.'

The cousins were returning from school one afternoon.

'Not even a little bit?'

'Not even a little bit.'

'Shame. But then what can one expect from a silly thing

like you?'

'Mona, I know you. You want me to talk.'

'Rubbish. You don't care, you don't care. Your business. None of mine, handsome or ugly.'

'Anyway, cameras never tell the real truth.'

'But your eyes can. If you keep them open, that is.'

Because of the troubled times, attendance had declined at the Hindu school. Only half the girls still came for the classes. But the Prasad girls were regular – it was their last year of high school. Escorted by Balla, Judge or Shambhu, they walked down to school every morning, for Bhagwan insisted they do. It was good politics. Otherwise, people would think Congress had panicked.

They were walking through Saddar Bazaar, past Uncle Aziz's bookshop, looking at the cluster of jewellery shops, one of which was run by the Sunars.

'What do you mean – keep your eyes open? They are. I always keep them open, especially when I am with my crafty, star-pulling cousin.'

'Keep them open, but don't look around.'

Meenakshi couldn't help it. She swung her eyes around full ninety degrees, and her eyes locked with those of a young man fifteen feet away, standing on the plinth of a shop front above the open sewer. He beamed a lighthouse smile, and Meenakshi almost fell. She wished she had listened to Mona. She wanted the earth under her feet to open up, as it had done for Sita, Lord Rama's wife, and swallow her.

Now, Meenakshi was more in love than ever.

'Told you not to look. But do you ever listen? Now walk straight. What's happened to you? And hurry.'

The girls ran and were soon out of the danger zone.

'Handsome. Or not, Cousinji?' Mona said. 'What do you

think, Cousinji?'

'Uglier than the photo, if you want to know.'

They saw him again that evening. It was a Tuesday and the Hanuman temple was crammed. They had never seen him at the temple before. He was helping Pandit Shri Ram carry the life-size wooden statue of the monkey god out of the temple to the large rectangular courtyard outside. The bystanders were looking admiringly at the idol – painted red, yellow and green – the very symbol of strength and dour devotion. A full moon shimmered and the rising evening was scented with the fragrance of the blossoming jasmine from bushes lining the courtyard. In the melee, the cousins got separated. Mona looked this way and that. Suddenly, she found herself staring at Gulshan.

'I say…' Gulshan whispered.

'What do you say?' Mona said defiantly. The cheek! How dare he speak to her!

'Lovely moon.'

'So?'

'Lovely stars and…'

'And what?'

'And jasmine perfume.'

'What are you taking about?'

'A short walk under the moon and the stars.'

'What's stopping you? Moon and stars are for everybody.'

'Then… please…' Gulshan begged.

Mona understood. She managed to find and extricate Meenakshi from the throng. She brought her behind the temple wall. Beyond it were fields and endless nothingness of dust.

'Why bring me here, crazy girl?' But Meenakshi knew. Mona then vanished and Gulshan appeared.

They stood face to face, Meenakshi trembling. His being

so close made her mind go blank; her legs went limp. But in a distant corner of her dysfunctional mind she knew what she wanted to do – run back.

'Everybody is right.'

'What?'

'They are right – you are out of this world.'

'What?'

'You are beautiful. How much? I can't tell you.'

'Don't tell me then.'

'But I must.'

'Why?'

'Because if I don't, I'll die.'

'You lie.'

'I don't. Ask my heart. Listen to it.'

Gulshan took Meenakshi's hand and placed it on his throbbing chest.

'What does it say?'

'Nothing. Absolutely nothing.'

'You lie. Because it says something truer than the moon, the stars and the jasmine's fragrance. It says I…'

'I must go. I must.'

'Listen. Listen to the beat of love. Closer. Please.'

'No. I must go.'

Gulshan took her hand to his lips. Then he pulled her to him. Suddenly overwhelmed by a strangely beautiful languor, Meenakshi yielded. Once in his arms, she went totally limp. For how long? She did not know. All she knew was she had to go. But she did not want to go. Startled for no reason, she disengaged herself and ran. Burning with shame, she ran and ran. She ran straight into Mona.

'Your face, Meenakshi. It's lit up. Have you been to the moon or something?'

The calendar with a flute-playing Krishna print said it was the18th of May. Nearly one in the afternoon and hot, hot, hot beyond bearing. In his office, Jyoti sat under the divine whirring ceiling fan, his sticky white muslin shirt clinging to his back. It was time to go home for lunch, but he was waiting for Shambhu. Shambhu was to bring some cash from Dr Gupta. Jyoti had sent him there to deliver a one-maund sack of flour, the third this month and three times more than the Guptas ate in normal times. Jyoti knew why. He thought it a bad idea. People would notice.

Shambhu was not the fastest of workers. But he could carry a sack of flour on his head to any place in town. Once, his friends lionized him for his strength. But now, Shambhu wanted to be acknowledged for something else, for being what he was, a Brahmin.

'I'm a Brahmin, you fools. Respect me,' he demanded.

Shera, Balla and Judge would tell him to go do what Brahmins were famous for, freeloading at religious ceremonies only Brahmins could perform – births, marriages, deaths.

'Go load rice pudding from one end, unload it from the other,' they joked and did what was done to Brahmin boys everywhere – give tormenting tugs to his distinctive Brahminical topknot.

But ever since they had entered their twenties, there had come a change in Shambhu's tormentors. Shambhu was a top-caste Brahmin and they were not. One was born a Brahmin, not made. No amount of money could make one a Brahmin – the Brahmins had come out of the mouth of Brahma, the Creator. The next lot of Kshatriya warriors had emerged from His arms. The traders came from his torso, and from His feet, the Untouchables. This was Divine Law – unchangeable.

Now, Balla and Judge felt privileged to be his closest friends, and even the Sikh Shera was aware that Sikhism was born out of Hinduism. They began calling him 'Pandit ji', the 'learned one'.

'Why's your mug red like a monkey's arse, Panditji?'

Shera, Balla and Judge knew it was because of the heat and Shambhu's running.

'Mountbatten is gone.'

From the boss's perch in his office, Jyoti overheard the banter of his workers. *Mountbatten gone? Where?* He had been in India only two months, even less. *Is he dead? Shot?* Jyoti hoped not; he was India's last hope.

'Gone where?' a worried Jyoti asked, coming out.

'London, Bauji.'

'How do you know?' Jyoti was relieved.

'Just heard on Aziz Sahib's radio. I was passing by his shop, Bauji.'

'Cycle, Shera,' Jyoti shouted.

Jyoti pedalled off in haste. Bhagwan had told him what he had learnt from the grapevine. The buzz was Nehru and Mountbatten had got on swimmingly well during their Simla tête-à-tête. The talk was meaningful and substantial. The two had first met in Singapore two years ago, after the Japanese surrender, and developed high regard for each other ever since.

Instead of going home, Jyoti raced to Aziz's English Book Depot in Saddar Bazaar. A knot of men – Hindus, Muslims and Sikhs – stood at the door for the 1 o'clock news as they did every day. But something had just gone wrong with Aziz's radio.

'True?' Jyoti asked the people with puzzled looks.

'He's chickened out,' said someone in a fez – Mullah Jaffar, the muezzin of the Badami Mosque. 'Well known fact, that's what rats do when the ship starts to sink.' It was an ungenerous remark. But then, Muslims did not hide their dislike of their last Viceroy because of his friendship with Nehru.

Jyoti side-stepped the issue by making just a general comment about it: 'Don't say that, Mullahji. Mountbatten is a great man, a brave man. He made the Japs surrender.'

Mohammed was there too, inspecting the radio with an angry Aziz.

'Made in England, would you believe? Just when you want it to deliver, it fails,' Aziz said and thumped the set. As he did so, the radio came back to life, but the news was over.

'Why do you think he's gone to London, Aziz?'

'My guess is as good as yours, Jyoti.'

'Nehru probably had his way in Simla, and Mountbatten has gone to London for new orders from Attlee,' Mohammed said, convinced he was right.

It made sense. Jyoti liked Attlee. Everybody liked Attlee, the opposite of Churchill, who had called Gandhi 'a half-naked fakir'. Jyoti had a hunch that Attlee would never agree to Partition, whatever he was supposed to have said about setting a deadline for deciding India's fate. But there were many guesses.

Back home, Jyoti found Bhagwan with his wife and children. They cherished the occasional family meal over which two brothers with their families met. Then several bicycle bells rang outside Jyoti's walnut-timber door. A whole brigade of cyclists had turned up. Among them were Dr Gupta, headmaster Rama Kant, soap-manufacturer Hirdey and Bhagwan's own assistant Desraj. They had come looking for the Congress leader. That they all arrived together was a mere coincidence.

The doctor wore a tie, a white cotton suit and a khaki sola topi. Rama Kant was in plain white shirt and trousers, Desraj in homespun khadi and the Gandhi cap, typical Congress wear, and Hirdey had just a *banyan* on. They presented quite a sight, drawing looks from the passers-by: *what the hell are those well-to-do gentlemen doing there in the smouldering heat*?

'Where to in this infernal sun, all suited-booted like that Jinnah fellow always is, Doctor Sahib?' Jyoti said, opening his door and taking them upstairs.

'I was on my way to see a patient, when I saw this delegation outside your house. Thinking it must be something important, I stopped. What's it?'

'Must be something to bring them here in 110ºF.'

'I'll stay just for a moment and hear what you all have to say,' the doctor said. He was sweating profusely.

'Is Bhagwan with you? Want to know why Mountbatten has flown off and left the ship rudderless. Rumours floating around that AHHA will take advantage and attack while he's away,' headmaster Rama Kant said, wiping big drops of sweat from his eyebrows.

'Frankly, the Viceroy didn't seek my permission, nor did he bother to tell me why he was going to London, Headmaster Sahib,' Bhagwan laughed, as he walked into Jyoti's drawing room. His son and nephew followed him in.

'Maybe he has gone there to buy new clothes,' Rama Kant giggled appreciating his own wisecrack. 'Likes to look tiptop, Dickie does. You know. Never leaves the palace or the Rolls Royce without razor-sharp creases on his trousers.'

Down in the kitchen, Rakhi had quickly made a jug of iced nimbu pani. Shera brought it up on a tray with glasses, spreading relief.

'Obviously, he's gone there to talk to Attlee. Obviously. Common sense,' Jyoti said. 'He was sweet-talking the decadent Indian princes at length the other day, licking the difficult League arse at an even greater length a day later, but paying Congress only lip service just yesterday. Without any results, might I add? He ought to know that you don't learn much when your own lips are moving all the time…' Headmaster Rama Kant lectured.

'But he has to talk to everybody in the land,' Jyoti and Bhagwan spoke at the same time.

'…The man talks too much – loves his own voice. Should be called *Mouthbatten*. Why, for heaven's sake, doesn't he talk some sense into the man who really matters – Jinnah? Why doesn't he knock into his thick skull that this is India, one country for everyone?'

'Hindus and Sikhs here are scared, Bhagwanji. Very scared. I have been hearing it in every street,' Bhagwan's deputy Desraj said.

'What have you heard, Desraj?'

'That an attack by Allah Hoo Army is coming any time any day or night. People are peeing in their pants.'

Vishnu and Shashi perked up.

'We haven't seen anyone peeing in their pants, have we, Shashi?'

'Not yet.'

While the gentlemen laughed, Desraj went on: 'Sir Sahib, people need to be talked to. Must give a speech today, Bhagwanji, to reassure them. That everything will be all right soon, soon, when the Viceroy returns.'

'Mountbatten has to come back soon. Hopefully, he'll come back with some good news for us all. My guess is he will,' Jyoti said.

'That remains to be seen, man of all seasons and reasons,' the headmaster laughed.

'Right you are about our dear Jyoti at least, Rama Kant. On both counts,' Dr Gupta said, finishing his drink and rising.

With a number of Congress activists, Desraj and Hirdey hastily made arrangements for a *jalsa* to be held after sunset when the air would be a little cooler. In no time, the place took on the look of a village fair. A sizable crowd had already turned up, nearly a thousand, half of them Muslims. The venue, as usual, was the large dusty clearing opposite the post office. Knowing that the Congress boss was No.1 on the League hit list, Jyoti told Bhagwan where to stand for his speech.

'There you're shielded by the trunk of the peepul tree.'

But Bhagwan ignored the warning and stood in the open, in full view of a would-be assassin. Jyoti, regarded by everyone as his right-hand man and No.2 on the same hit list, came and stood behind him.

Like all leaders, Bhagwan was fond of making long speeches. The audiences would lap up every bit of the politicians' pyrotechnics, listening intently to them, the longer the better. In a small town, political rhetoric was good entertainment. Long after the *neta* made the *bhashan*, townsfolk would be talking animatedly about the points he had made. But today the local Congress leader spoke for only thirty minutes.

'...Dark clouds of division hang over Mother India. But in our hearts, we know we are not really divided. Only temporarily separated from each other in our ways of thinking. The issue is Indian Independence. And we are well on our way to achieving it. With dignity. With honour. With peace. Where there is a will, there is a way. We have the will, and we know the way. It is with Mahatma Gandhi and Pandit Nehru. It is with Frontier Gandhi Khan Abdul Gaffar Khan and Maulana Azad...'

People had heard all that before. Today, they wanted to

know why the Viceroy had buggered off from Delhi.

'Bad timing to run away with the fire crackling, isn't it, Bhagwanji?' a shopkeeper summed up the general mood.

'Every overseer goes from his station to the headquarters from time to time for further instructions. Mountbatten Sahib wouldn't have gone if he thought the fire was turning into a blaze. He probably thinks June next year is a bit too far, though I personally don't think so. After having governed India for so long, England must take its time and make sure it leaves us united and in peace. The Viceroy has gone to London to talk it over with Prime Minister Attlee. That's all. No need to worry… Jai Hind!'

An hour later, exactly at the same venue, another *jalsa* took place. Organized by the Muslim League, it was addressed by Shaukat Ali. Shaukat had not been advised by his aides where to stand or where not to – the Hindus had no hit lists. He stood with his aide Mullah Jaffar, just where Bhagwan and Jyoti had. His audience was much larger. A telling feature of Congress and League meetings was that while the former were attended by one and all – Hindus, Sikhs and Muslims – at the latter, only Muslims came. Others were not welcome. But the mill owner and his friends went anyway.

'I do not agree with Mahatma Prasad that the issue is Indian Independence. Indian Independence is a Hindu–Muslim issue. The fact is, India is not one, but two nations – Hindu and Muslim. Professor Bhagwan lectures us about democracy and boasts that Congress represents every Indian. The fact is Congress is a Hindu-dominated organization. The time has come for us to part ways.

'However, there is something my worthy opponent and I agree on: where there is a will, there is a way. We too have the will, and we too know the way. Pakistan. It lies with our great leader Mohammed Ali Jinnah…'

Shaukat Ali's audience, too, had heard all this before. Today, like Bhagwan's, it wanted to know about the Viceroy's sudden flight from this country.

'...To get confirmation for what he has agreed with Mr Nehru in secret, surely. The fact is, he is eating out of Mr Nehru's hands. The fact also is Nehru has both the Mountbattens in his pockets, one in one, the other in the other. So, we can expect nothing from him. We must row our own boat. Yet, we must try not to tangle our oars with the other boat's. Puranapur has always been peaceful. And so it shall remain. My personal guarantee. Pakistan Zindabad!'

In parts of the Punjab more than anywhere else, however, the 'crackling fire' began to spread like wildfire. Stabbings occurred in almost every area and more houses were set on fire. The shroud of fear thickened. People knew the invisible assassin was just lurking around.

'Hear it, hear it,' Rakhi said every night.

Daddum, daddum, daddum.

Salma heard that every night too.

'Bhagwan said the right thing about the will and the way,' Aziz said to his friends across the chessboard, a pawn held in his hand.

'But so did Shaukat,' Jyoti said.

'When everybody is right, it means trouble,' Mohammed chuckled.

There was no trouble in Puranapur unlike elsewhere in the Punjab. Only like the heat, tension rose. It rippled in the bustling Saddar Bazaar – the business nerve-centre, traditionally controlled mostly by Hindus – where Hindu and Muslim shops jostled one another. An uneasy calm hung nervously over the tenements, which looked and smelled like rotten teeth and reeked of over-ripe mangoes and melons, of smouldering cow-dung fires, of cooking fat, frying garlic and nameless spices. It resided in every home, where people slept fretfully at night.

It seemed to be a wise move to shut down the town's institutions – the Government College for men, and its two high schools, Rama Kant's DAV and the madrassa. But soon, it dawned upon them that it was not such a good thing after all. The shutting down of schools and colleges ended in too many idle young men roaming the streets and the alleys.

Nobody knew how, but it had started. People started hoarding – wheat, flour, corn, pulses, ghee, sugar, salt, spices… even onions and garlic. They also began to move from one part of the town to another. Hindus and Sikhs living along the wide avenues of the affluent Muslim neighbourhoods moved to the narrow streets where these communities were the majority in the congested heart of Puranapur, also the oldest part of this medieval city. Muslims made a reverse movement. Some – Hindus, Sikhs, Muslims – took their valuables, put a padlock on their doors, and took the train. They went north, east, west and south to find safety with relatives. They would return when this madness was over.

Jyoti saw all this. So did Mohammed and Aziz. They understood. But they did not understand really. They were baffled. They were pained. There was a great deal to say. There was nothing to say. Whatever was happening was beyond anyone's control.

'All our great leader Jinnah's doing. For what? Kindly educate me and oblige,' Aziz said.

'What about the old Inqilab Zindabad then?' Jyoti said.

That was once the slogan – Long Live the Revolution – raising which Indians for long had fought for Independence.

'Dead as a dodo. Back then, Indians were fighting the British,' Aziz said, swallowing to push down a rising lump.

'Now, Indians are killing each other,' Mohammed said with a similar lump. 'But pray for what? For my Quran or your Gita? Jinnah Saab, this is not intelligent behaviour.'

'Jinnah Sahib, you say you have tested the depth of the water, but you haven't wetted your toes. You may be a brilliant lawyer, but you are narrow-minded and for a leader, being narrow-minded is a dangerous thing. I rest my case.' Aziz looked away.

Jyoti also looked away; his silence spoke for itself. The three felt helpless, as if they had no power to reverse the rising tides rushing to engulf them. It was unbearable.

Rumours. More rumours. They carried with them the foul smell that could be coming from the *ganda nala*, which carried the town's refuse.

The three friends had even less to say to each other about the state of their world. They took to walking in the fields every other morning and to playing more games of chess in the afternoons. While rooftops sizzled under a scorching sun and the rest of Puranapur laid its weary bones for an uneasy siesta, they stared at each other's infantries, kings and queens with vacant eyes. Something sinister was headed their way. They feared for their families. In their homes, the same feeling prevailed. Mohammed and Aziz's aged fathers took solace in prayer; they prayed longer than usual. In Chauri Galli, Dadima lamented the fact that hardly any Muslim families were left in the area now. She had so many friends among them, whom she loved and who loved her.

'When neighbours fly away, something from your heart also flies away,' the old woman mumbled. 'But what has to happen will happen. And whatever happens, happens for the best; our forefathers said that a long time back.'

'Whatever happens, happens for the best,' Aziz echoed the old woman over the chessboard the next afternoon in his bookshop.

'That which has to happen, has to happen. And whatever happens in the end is which would have happened in any case,' Mohammed said, pressing his short supple fingers against each other.

'That's old Hindu shit,' Jyoti growled.

'If it is your Hindu thinking, it is also ours. Because our forefathers were Hindu. Muslims like to deny it. But it is a fact. So why do you always argue?'

'I was not arguing.'

'Anyway, the point is, the fire is crackling.'

'Whatever happens, happens for the best,' Jyoti Prasad was talking to himself. 'What shit! Everything turns out right in the end. What total, utter and absolute shit! We Hindus love to deceive ourselves.' He was taking a stroll around his house that evening. It made him think of something he had not thought of in a long time – the earthquake of fifteen years ago. He then twenty-one, Rakhi eighteen. They had been married for a few years. Baby Meenakshi was a year old. One night, as Puranapur slept, Jyoti, full of love for Rakhi's full breasts, had lain with her on the roof when mother earth became angry. It rumbled, and houses, made of the very substance they stood on, crumbled.

Much of Puranapur was made of raw earth and wood. It fell apart amid shrieks of the dying and buried alive. Even brick houses fell. Many didn't. Those who lived in them survived. Next day and the days and months and years after, those who survived echoed Mohammed's words – whatever happens, happens for the best.

Then, Jyoti had agreed because he and his family had survived. Then, Jyoti still didn't really know what it meant having a wife and a child. Then, Jyoti just lived. The wife had come along because it was time for his parents to find him a mate. The child followed because of what Jyoti did with Rakhi every night.

Now, Jyoti had been married for many years. Now, Jyoti knew what his family meant to him. Rakhi and the children and Bhagwan with his family formed the sum total of his life. It was complete. If another child came along, it would still be complete. There was nothing more he wanted for himself. A three-storey house, a piece of land, a mill, enough to eat, enough to cover his back with. He had his own cow, servants, bicycle and hand pump.

'Having been born a human, one has to work. So much better if one enjoys one's work.'

Jyoti loved his work – grinding grain into flour. It fed people. Jyoti was a happy man, despite occasionally feeling miserable lying awake in the dark of night, thinking.

Jyoti also knew another earthquake was on its way. Would the bricks of his happiness withstand it? He had deciphered the real meaning of the writing on the wall. He knew Mohammed and Aziz, too, had. It was that either he or they had to go despite what they said to each other. Then how could it be right? Jyoti sat down on the stump of a dead babul tree. He looked back at his house. It looked reassuringly solid.

A slight noise on his left made him look up. His mill boys, all four of them, were taking a short cut through his plot.

'What are you doing here, boys?'

'Going to see Balla's grandma, Bauji,' Shera replied.

Balla lived with his grandma at the edge of what had now become a mud-walled, mostly Muslim area. It lay beyond the wheat fields behind Chauri Galli. The old woman had refused to leave for the safety of the Hindu-Sikh area. The boys were going to talk her out of it.

'What, again?' Jyoti knew the whole story. 'Maybe I should talk to her,' he said walking with the boys.

Balla's grandmother, Amar Dai, worked a street *bhatti*, on which she roasted people's grain and turned their yellow corn into fluffy white popcorn. Her *bhatti* was an eighteen-inch wide hole in the ground with a two-foot wide iron wok covering its mouth. The wok was a quarter full of grey sand from the Ravi Canal. Logs of fire underneath it, from another hole, heated up the sand and the hot sand turned corn into popcorn in a matter of seconds. A large sieve did the rest. The likeable old woman was popular. Her fee was one anna, one sixteenth of a rupee, or a good two handfuls of wheat or corn that people brought. On a good day, she made anything from twelve annas to a rupee in cash. This, and what her grandson earned at the mill, kept them in lack of want. At the moment, she sat idly with her neighbour Khanum, a Muslim widow, who was telling her what the men had talked about in the morning.

'Stubborn Amar Dai, you must listen and go…'

The old woman shook her head. She knew all there was to know about Hindus, Muslims and Sikhs.

'Didn't Guru Nanak have two main disciples – one Hindu and one Muslim, Bala and Mardana? Then?' she said.

'That was four hundred years ago, Amar Dai. Things are different now.'

'Maybe. But once brothers, always brothers. Khanum, what you say makes no sense.'

'Listen, Grandma. In those days, they didn't have the League or the Congress. Nor politicians.'

'What about Gandhi? He is a good man for all.'

'But no one listens to him anymore. Now they think of him as a useless old crank. India has become a mad house; the patients have become their own doctors, our Jinnah and your Nehru. So go if you want to live and work your *bhatti* for many more years.'

The old woman was honoured that her grandson's boss himself had called on her. But she refused to budge. Her home was not only the four walls she lived in. It was where all her friends of fifty years were, friends she loved and who loved her. Then why should she go to live elsewhere?

'Because it has become dangerous,' Jyoti said.

'Who would want to harm a harmless old hag?'

'Come live with me and my mother,' Shera said.

'Or with me, both of you. I live alone. Balla will bring your charpoy. And his own,' Shambhu said.

'You have become more stubborn than a mule, Grandma,' Balla said. He was embarrassed.

So was Jyoti – he had failed to make the old woman change her mind. But he admired her for her faith in what she believed in. He thought about it every day.

Exactly two weeks later, on the 31st of May, Mountbatten came back. Habitually of a pleasantly determined countenance, the former Supreme Commander of Southeast Asia exuded that bit of extra confidence as he emerged from his old war-time York aircraft. In the blazing sun, his immaculate white naval uniform with medals gleaming had an electric sheen to it. And he had a glint in his eye. Those who saw him on the sizzling tarmac of Palam Airport in the merciless Loo – the hot, dry summer wind typical to India – could tell he had come back with something up his sleeve. Never less than conscious of his public image and his natural ability to impress and get things done, he was oozing a new-found energy. Popular at home after his Second World War triumph, and now even more so in India, he seemed ready and anxious to fulfil his self-determined role and place in world history. Ever in a hurry to get things done, he appeared to be in a much greater haste now. King Emperor George VI's cousin had come with a new plan for his Indian Empire… and a new date.

On the following Tuesday, 3 June 1947, Mountbatten, Nehru, Jinnah and the Sikh leader Baldev Singh made their way to the rotund, red-painted All India Radio building in the heart of New Delhi, throbbing with life, commerce and colour. They were there to speak to the Indian people about India's future, about their future. It was early evening, laced with a hot June breeze that blew in their anxious faces as they got down from their British cars to enter the famous pot-bellied edifice.

Two hundred and fifty miles away in dusty Puranapur in the north, Dr Gupta had invited a few friends – the Prasad brothers, headmaster Rama Kant, Mohammed, Aziz and Inspector Partap Singh – to come and listen to the words that would change the map of India and decide their fate. The same hot breath of an early June evening blew in the faces of these men when they arrived at the doctor's house, behind his shop, riding their Raleigh and Hercules bicycles. As usual, they spoke to each other in English.

'Come in, come in,' the doctor greeted them warmly, even though most of them were already in his drawing room. 'How are you, Mohammed?' he asked his friend and then inquired after Mohammed's expectant sister's health.

'Thank you, Doctor Sahib. She is well. Baby due soon. In good health, inshallah.'

'Not to worry. Everything will be all right. Bhagwan, any new gold nuggets of Congress news?'

The men settled down under an electric fan whirring overhead. A servant brought well-cooled bottles of Vimto with straws sticking out. 'Everyone knows it is Partition, Doctor Sahib. But no one knows when and where the borders will be drawn.'

'Mountbatten has fifteen months. So there is no hurry. He is a man of good judgement. Beat the Japs,' Aziz said.

'Good judgement usually comes from bad experience. And that often comes from bad judgement, as the Chinese say.'

'That's being very cynical, Rama Kantji. Fifteen months is long enough for him to sort out the Independence issue. It can be done calmly, if dealt with intelligently by us Indians,' said an irritated Jyoti.

'Tall order that, for us Indians, Prasadji, doing things intelligently,' Rama Kant laughed.

'Question is, how are they going to divide the big cake? It is effectively history's greatest divorce ever. No, Jyoti?' Dr Gupta flashed a wry smile.

Jyoti sat up, looking ill at ease.

'No, Doctor Sahib, it is not divorce. It is demolition. The demolition of India by one man with our leaders as willing accomplices. Mainly Nehru, whom we all have revered. Including Gandhi, whom we have adored, not to mention Mountbatten whose hands we are eating out of.' Jyoti looked personally betrayed.

'Rather violent, Jyoti.'

'Real violence is yet to come, Doctor Sahib. Mother India's breasts are being carved off to become West Pakistan and East Pakistan with our great leaders as bystanders, which makes them accomplices.'

'Too true, too true,' Mohammed said.

'What on earth do you mean, Mohammed?'

'I mean our Quaid was determined to get his Pakistan at any cost, and our Congress didn't do enough to stop him. It could have. Especially Pandit Nehru.'

'Is that what you too really think, Jyoti?'

'What does it matter what I think or what we all think? Pandit Nehru should have never agreed to the division of the country.' Jyoti raised his voice. 'NEVER. Whatever reasons and justifications put forward by the crafty Jinnah. You are dealing with millions of lives, HUMAN LIVES, damn you. Not playing legal games like point-scoring junior lawyers.'

'Panditji did everything he could to stop Partition. But…' Partap Singh said.

Jyoti went on in the same anguished voice, only more heightened now: 'But not enough. However complex the issue of greedy Maharajahs, grasping politicians and their arse-licking lackeys, Nehru should have said NO. However complicated and however difficult Jinnah is as a man, Nehru simply should have said no to him. NO. NO, NO. Anything else, but NO to Partition. Ditto the great Englishman.'

'Anyway, why didn't they ask the Indian people what they want? Why hasn't there been a referendum? Why is everything being decided by this self-serving triad of Nehru, Jinnah and Mountbatten?' Rama Kant gasped having raised his pitch a little too much.

'Our Quaid wants to be the President of his Pakistan,' Mohammed said, looking dejected. 'Like most Muslims of India, I do not want our country to be divided.'

'Well said, Mohammed Bhai.' Partap Singh was disgusted. 'Why didn't Pandit Nehru let him become Prime Minster of India as Mahatma Gandhi had suggested?'

'Because our dear Jawaharlal wants the plum job for himself, doesn't he? Loves to shine on the world stage. Ambition. Ego. Vanity. Simple as that,' Rama Kant could not hide his bitterness.

Dr Gupta turned to Bhagwan who had so far been lost in thought.

'You seem to be with them in Delhi, not with us here, Bhagwan. And where is our Mahatmaji in all this?'

'Walking the Bengal countryside to prevent another outburst of violence,' Bhagwan said.

'Our Mahatma should have been in Delhi at this moment. He fought for it for thirty years. This should have been his day. TODAY. Now it's like a wedding without the groom.' Carried away by emotions, Jyoti was almost shouting. 'We have a wedding cake all right. But guess who is eating it, and having it too, by courtesy of – guess who?'

The radio presenter put an end to this bitter discussion. Mountbatten spoke first. The new plan was Divide and Quit. The new date was Friday, 15 August, ten weeks away! The boundary line would be completed shortly. It would be published soon after the 15th of August to avoid violence.

Stiff-collared and suited-booted, Jinnah was unable to believe his luck and therefore, had little to say. Turban-wearing Baldev Singh even less. The rose-in-buttonhole Nehru, never short of the right words that often moved his doting audiences to tears, spoke last.

'...We are little men serving great causes. But because the cause is great, something of greatness falls on us...'

'Wah wah, wah wah,' interrupted Rama Kant in mock admiration. 'Little men indeed!'

Not a word was said after that. Stunned, Dr Gupta's guests looked at each other in puzzled and pained silence. To be told that they were going to be free in a few weeks brought no joy to anyone.

Painfully disillusioned, Jyoti finally spoke. 'So, it is not fifteen, not twelve, nor even ten months. Ten weeks. What's the bloody hurry? What's the matter with these men?'

Mohammed answered: 'The matter is, please-all *Mouthbatten* has gone mad letting it happen. The matter is, spineless top-jobseeker Nehru has gone mad letting it happen...'

'Not so fast, Mohammed, not so fast,' Dr Gupta said.

But Mohammed continued. '...The matter is Attlee too has gone mad leaving the country they ruled for two centuries in such a fucking hurry. The matter is our Scotch-drinking, pork-eating Muslim wannabe President Quaid... I see rivers of blood.' He could have cried.

'But...?' Jyoti too could have. Jyoti could not utter another word.

They were all lost for words.

The whole world was lost for words. The question that haunted the little group was where the dividing line would be drawn. The question was what would happen once it was drawn. Would millions of people have to move from one country to the other? Could that happen peacefully?

There were too many questions. But no answers.

Next afternoon, the three friends met for their weekly game of chess. While Aziz was setting up the board, Mohammed, with a strange look on his face, handed Jyoti a thick, cloth-lined envelop. It was the sort one bought from the post office to send registered letters.

'Oye! What's this?' Jyoti was nonplussed.

'For reading at home. Not here,' Mohammed said.

Why did he look strange saying that? Jyoti ignored Mohammed and tore open the envelope. Inside it there was a *parcha*, an official-looking document.

'You serving me a writ or something, Uncle Mohammed?'

The document was in elegant Urdu with exquisite calligraphy:

> "I, Mohammed Salman Haidar, appoint Jyoti Prasad of Chauri Galli, Puranapur, sole custodian of my factory, Haidar Furniture Factory, of 100 Sikandar Road, in the event of Puranapur becoming a part of the new state of India, until such time as it might take me to require him to restore it to me. In the unforeseen circumstance of my death and that of, God forbid, my only son and heir, Maqbool, the aforementioned shall become its lawful owner. If Puranapur becomes a part of Pakistan, this document shall automatically become null and void."
>
> Signed: Mohammed Salman Haidar.

The *parcha* was witnessed by two people, one of them Aziz, the other the Hindu soap-maker Hirdey.

Jyoti hit the roof. 'What shit is this, Mohammed?' he almost shouted, banging the table with his fist so hard all the chessmen went flying. One ricocheted off the blades of the GEC fan overhead like a stray bullet. 'WHAT SHIT?'

'Foolish boy, shut up and listen...'

'I am not shutting up nor listening!'

'...There's been a change since yesterday. The elders insist we quit Puranapur while there's still time.'

'And go where, Mohammed?'

'Karachi, which is to be Pakistan's capital and where we have relatives, as soon as my sister's baby arrives. Nothing I can do about it. Elders are elders.'

'But you've said all along that you'd stay put.'

'Things are moving fast. Though the trains are hardly running. We'll walk if we have to one night, to Vatala Junction, and take the west-bound line towards Karachi next day.'

'But you said...'

'I know. But now I'm saying we are going.'

'Then take your *parcha* with you. Stick it where you like. Your back side I suggest. I don't want it.'

'Think, you idiot, think.'

'I have, and I think you are raving mad.'

'If Puranapur goes to India, they might spare our lives, but they'll burn our property. My factory first.'

Jyoti folded up the *parcha* and was about to tear it up in two then four, when Mohammed snatched it away.

'Same old foolish boy Jyoti as you were at fifteen. Listen. I know what I'm doing.' Mohammed slipped the *parcha* in the envelope and shoved it in Jyoti's pocket.

Flabbergasted, Jyoti looked around. He saw a pen standing idly in an inkpot on Aziz's wooden cashbox. He picked it up and wrote out a similar document, passing his mill to Mohammed. Jyoti signed it and stopped Mam Din driving past in his one-horse carriage.

'Mam Din.' Jyoti handed the paper and the pen to the poet.

Mam Din read the paper. A sudden change came over his usually cheerful face. It got distorted as if he had been hit physically when he put his signature under Jyoti's. 'I wish I had never lived to see this day,' he said to no one, looking devastated. Jyoti stopped another passer-by, headmaster Rama Kant, of all people, as usual with an unopened umbrella despite a blazing sun. He handed him the pen. Jyoti would have preferred someone else, but he wanted the second witness to be a Hindu.

'This is what I call friendship. Others may have other names for it, such as madness. Mine is friendship.' Rama Kant gave Jyoti a look one gives to an imbecile. 'What do you say, Mam Din?' he said to the poet.

For once, words failed the poet. Misty-eyed, he looked to be in pain. As if he had seen a tragedy foretold.

'Whatever has to happen will happen, but Mam Din doesn't want to be around when it does.' He drove on.

The Big Countdown to Tuesday, the 15th of August, had begun. Jyoti made a tear-off calendar. Every morning, he pulled off a leaf. The leaves fell slowly. There was a huge hump in the heart of this old town, known as the Belly of Puranapur because it was shaped like a hugely expectant mother's belly. This mound was also called Simla Hill; it had thrown up a luxuriant growth of wild flower bushes earning it that name. The breezes of times past had whispered that underneath that mound lay the homesteads of a lost civilization, four-walled structures of fired bricks, among the first made by man. The streets around this hillock were the oldest and the narrowest. Hindu, Muslim and Sikh families had lived side by side there for generations. The remainder of Puranapur surrounding this part of the town was largely Muslim and much larger, being full of wide open spaces.

As more leaves of Jyoti's calendar fell, a change occurred that made Hindus and Sikhs tremble. Muslims from the surrounding villages started pouring in and occupying those open spaces, living under bamboo poles holding bed sheets for cover. They came with their cows and buffaloes and goats. They carried immense bundles on their heads. Living in their villages had now become too dangerous. They significantly raised the number of Muslims in Puranapur, frightening the families around Simla Hill. But reassurance came, and it came from the very villages the Muslims had vacated – from the Sikhs there.

'I am here. Don't worry,' the Sant sent word.

Life carried on, if uneasily. Then one evening, Puranapur began to buzz. Kanhayia Lal, the Seer, had 'grounded' himself. He had had a deep trench – six feet by two feet – dug by his followers. Lying flat in it, he had buried himself up to his neck for a whole night with a squad of twenty keeping a *laltain* vigil. While the young men kept looking on in the dim light of the lanterns, the Seer meditated. Puranapur held its breath. Whatever might the hated but feared bastard predict – Puranapur for India or Pakistan?

Hindus and Sikhs loathed the shaven-headed and dreaded charlatan. Muslims called him a blackmailing *kafir* dog. They spat at his mumbo jumbo as occult Hindu practices. The Muslims detested his gurus, the self-appointed torch-bearers of an illusory past greatness. And what did the Hindus think of the custodians of Islam, the mullahs and the imams? Nothing but preachers of hate, brainwashing children from the cradle to become indoctrinated soldiers of faith. Convert, or kill if you can't convert. Kill, kill, kill – their own kind too, Sunnis vs.

Shiites and so on.

But everybody waited for the next morning when the Predictor would come over ground. Would he then take off? The Prasad brothers refused to watch the pathetic stunt. But their sons went with their friends to see the fun. Hundreds of men – Hindus, Muslims and Sikhs – gathered around the Owl Face's living grave and asked, 'Which way, Predictorji?'

But the Predictor maintained an enigmatic silence, looking up at the sky meaningfully. Hindus and Sikhs thought that the outlook was positive. And so did the Muslims in the crowd. Saying nothing and looking at no one, the Predictor KL went straight to his door and Mrs KL shut it on the world.

'Put him back in his grave,' Vishnu shouted.

'And cover it with earth,' Shashi burst out laughing.

There was laughter all around.

The morning Jyoti peeled a page of his calendar to reveal the number 29, Friday, the 18th of July, a few hours later across the seven seas in London, the Indian Independence Bill received the royal assent. Coincidentally, an Indian sun scorched Buckingham Palace with the mercury at 97°F – 'the hottest day of the century', BBC Radio informed its audiences. It said nothing of the royal signature. Nor of the fact that in the royal despatch box in which the Bill had arrived, there were two more bills for the King to sign – South Metropolitan Gas Bill and the Felixtowe Pier Bill. Anyway, most BBC listeners tuned into something far more interesting – the running commentary of the Test match at Lord's between England and South Africa, in which the home side was doing swimmingly well. It had bowled out SA for 339, and the King was well pleased by it. But he stared at the Indian Bill for a long two minutes before signing it, a tear welling up. King George VI was signing away the Jewel in his Crown for no fault of his!

Back in Puranapur, a bullock cart sluggishly made its way up the charmed Chauri Galli. A number of barefoot street urchins walked around it and a while later, trailed it. Not because it was an unusual sight but because the bullock cart carried strange cargo. It was piled up with black trunks and expensive furniture. Aziz accompanied the cart on his bike, holding its wooden frame with one hand. The vehicle came to a halt outside Jyoti's house.

'Jyoti Prasad. Jyoti Prasad,' Aziz shouted the same way he would have twenty-five years ago to ask his friend to come out to play.

Jyoti came running out followed by Vishnu. One look and he knew.

'Your brains, Aziz. Have you completely lost your mind?'

'I too have decided. We are going with Mohammed…'

'You too have gone mad.'

'…And we can't take any of this heavy stuff with us. So?'

Aziz was sweating profusely in the 110°F heat.

'So, grow some sense in your head. Why have you done this? What's the matter with you?'

'The matter is our Quaid. The matter is your Nehru. The matter is *Mouthbatten*. The matter is religion. So look after all these things until it is all over.'

The whole street gathered around the bullock cart. People embraced Aziz with affection. Then Jyoti put an arm around his friend and took him inside for a glass of iced sherbet. Shera, Balla, Judge and Shambhu unloaded the cart. People outside hung on, bewildered by what the kind and gentle English Book Depot owner had done. A question mark was etched on every face: *what next?*

People waited. The city's commercial heart, Saddar Bazaar, was nervous. Life and business carried on, but uneasily. Many Muslim shops didn't open anymore. With the exception of government offices, most other establishments remained closed… even the town's Government Hospital shut down, its few doctors and nurses had just disappeared to *safety*. People went out only if it was absolutely necessary. They seldom ventured far. If they did, they did so at their own peril. Mullah Jaffar in the Minaret of the Badami Mosque called out to Allah every morning, but he no longer saw fields around Puranapur filled with moving dots. July this year had set a new record, the mercury soaring higher than ever before. Yet there was no sign of monsoon. The blue sky remained empty.

Jyoti shut his mill down with many open sacks of wheat, but hardly any of flour. Thankfully, it was in the Hindu-Sikh area. Mohammed too had shut his factory, also in the same area. His workers – mostly Hindus and Sikhs – had fled without notice or pay. Aziz opened his shop now and then, and the three friends still met there. Something was now missing in their games of chess. Yet, they never talked about it. They knew they were sitting on the edge of a cliff. One or two of them would have to go.

Late one afternoon, after a delightful bath under the hand pump worked by Vishnu, Jyoti wrapped a lungi around his waist, and put on his shoes to go out.

'Don't go out, Nathji, I am frying some pakoras,' Rakhi said from the kitchen. Soon it would be time for the daily family snack; children were already hungry. And everyone loved pakoras.

'Back soon, Lady JPji.'

For days, Jyoti had been thinking of Balla's grandmother. Suddenly, he knew what he should have said to the stubborn old woman to change her mind: 'Grandma, it is for Balla's safety. For his life.'

Jyoti walked across his plot, past the fields into the neighbouring, mostly Muslim, area.

'Jyoti Prasad, you know what you are? A fool. You shouldn't be here,' Jyoti told himself what everyone would have said. But he never listened to anyone.

Balla's street was empty. Jyoti saw Balla come in from the other side and go into his house. Then he saw him run to where his Grandma's *bhatti* was. Something was wrong. Jyoti hurried after him.

'Balla!' Jyoti shouted.

Balla didn't hear. He ran on. Jyoti ran after him. Passing by Balla's little house, he noticed its wooden door and windows were charred; there had been a fire. He saw four young boys by the old woman's *bhatti* with her tied up and lying flat beside it. They were laughing and pushing her around in a circular motion. Jyoti saw Balla go mad and become Bajrang Bali, Lord Hanuman of strength. He lifted a boy not older than twelve, and hurled him against the wall of a house. Two bicycles were parked there. The boy fell on them, hitting his head on the brick wall. His head split and blood trickled down his face. The boy screamed. The other boys howled. Balla roared. The boys then turned and ran away.

By the time Jyoti arrived on the scene, Balla had untied his grandma. He was arranging the frail old lady on a bike's carrier by the wall.

'Bauji!' Balla was dumbfounded to see Jyoti there.

'Run, Balla. Run before the boys return with men.' Jyoti hopped on the other bike and they cycled away furiously. They stopped only when they reached Shera's house.

'Shera. Shera,' Balla cried.

'Gone to a Sangh meeting,' said Shera's mother.

Though not a member of the RSS, Shera often attended their meetings. Dilbagh Rai and his second-in-command, Singhara, welcomed him. Shera was strong and fearless. They hoped to use him when the time came.

The old woman was semi-conscious. Her eyes were half-closed and her mouth frothed. Balla and his master laid her down on a charpoy. Chandri, Shera's mother, brought water. But the old woman could not drink it.

'Them Muslims done it to her?' Chandri asked. She was in her mid-forties, but looked years older.

Balla didn't answer. He was trying to make his grandma drink from the brass glass he held to her mouth.

'Drink, Grandma. Drink,' Balla pleaded.

By now, a crowd had gathered at Shera's door. People had seen the mill owner and his servant cycle like a hurricane with the old woman clinging to Balla's back.

'Drink, Grandma. DRINK,' people pleaded.

The old woman tried to shake her head. She couldn't. She tried to raise a hand. She couldn't. She put a finger at her flat chest. Jyoti bent over to check. Her heart was hardly beating. It stopped completely early next morning. Balla raised a piercing long wail. Alarmed, people came running, among them Judge and Shambhu. The two embraced their distressed friend. Shambhu wanted to say something, but he choked and burst into tears.

Some women from the neighbourhood washed Balla's dead grandma following the Hindu custom. The men were bothered by a question: *money*. Where was it to come from for the firewood and the cremation shroud? Nobody had any. Neighbour Durgadas, Vishnu's English teacher, pulled out a pink two-rupee note from his shirt pocket, as did Hirdey. Not enough, not at all. Even before anyone looked at Jyoti, the mill owner opened his wallet and gave two five-rupee notes to Shera and Shambhu to go and buy the red *kafan* and a bundle of firewood. The Muslim cloth merchant, moved by the situation, refused to accept the money. He too was very fond of the old woman selling popcorn sitting by her *bhatti*. Even the firewood seller, another Muslim, waved the lads away without taking a rupee. It touched the hearts of Hindus and Sikhs when Shera and Shambhu reported back. But Puranapur had always been like this, the entire town coming together to stand by a man in trouble. The town had a large heart; so no one was surprised by such gestures. About an hour later, when they were ready to take the body to the cremation ground, a policeman turned up. Though most of his men were Muslim, the town's police chief, Ashraf, thought it only proper to send a Hindu constable to the mourners to inquire about the case, first of its kind in Puranapur.

'You have come to arrest someone, Ganesh?' the RSS leader Dilbagh Rai asked.

'Yes, him, Balla. For breaking a young citizen's head and for stealing two bicycles with an accomplice.'

'Yes, arrest him and me. I was the accomplice,' Jyoti said.

'I have to do my duty,' the policeman said, colour flooding his face when he realized who the man was.

'And duty is duty. So put your handcuffs on Balla and me.'

Dilbagh Rai handed the 'stolen' bicycles over to constable Ganesh. But the policeman was still in a fix. He scratched his balls and wrote something in his Report Book. He showed it to Dilbagh Rai, scratched his balls again and went away.

'What did he write?' others asked Dilbagh.

'"Cycles found. But the breaker of a citizen's head untraceable. Reason: Country in deep shit."'

That pleased everyone. Another question arose: where was Balla going to live?

'With me,' Judge said. He had a room of his own.

'No. With us,' said Shera's mother warmly.

The cremation went ahead smoothly. Getting back home, Jyoti had a bath, as was the custom after a cremation under the hand pump, worked by Rakhi. Jyoti had a nagging sense of guilt. He should have gone to see the old woman earlier.

'She might be alive today if I had,' he said loudly.

'Dadima, what is your son talking about?'

'His father used to do the same, mutter to himself.'

Word spread about the incident. Rumours flew around. Fear seeped into hearts. The pulse of Puranapur began to run abnormally fast. To put it in check, and against heavy opposition, League leader Shaukat Ali wisely suggested that the young culprits be punished, even if nominally. They were given six light cane smacks, barely touching their out-stretched palms, by the headmaster of their madrasa, in public. Good diplomacy to bad effect. It enraged the AHAA. The brothers of the 'murderer' boys took an oath over the Quran to…

Meanwhile, the Prasad brothers agreed that something had to be done to control it all. Jyoti felt that Bhagwan should have a meeting with his opposite number before the situation got out of control. His old friend Shaukat Ali in the Muslim area was thinking the same. Bhagwan dispatched the trusted intermediary Hirdey to arrange a meeting. Hirdey made soap in his backyard and sold the bars sliced with a steel wire from his front room. Wrapping a soap bar perfumed with English oil, his best, as a present for Shaukat, he set up a meeting for the two leaders at a strange venue – a remote spot tucked away in the fields, screened off from all eyes.

They embraced – the once close friends meeting after quite some time. Shaukat offered Bhagwan a Gold Flake who held up a hand; he didn't smoke.

'Still smoking a lot, Shaukat? How many a day now?'

'Cut down from forty to twenty, yaar.'

'Still too, too many. Settle for half of that.'

'I keep trying, but…'

'How's the family?'

'Fine, fine. And yours?'

'They are well. And you yourself, Shaukat?'

'The same as ever, Bhagwan. Plus, wear and tear.'

Bhawan remembered that Shaukat always had a bad back besides a heart condition. And because of that, he always stood straight like a ram rod.

'Remember what we used to say back in college?' he said.

'That I stood straight because I had something stuck up my arse. Boy, you were bad. You can say the same again today. I really do have something stuck up my backside.'

'Haven't we all?'

'Now coming to the point.'

'A joint Congress – League public meeting.'

A bombshell.

'You are mad, Bhagwan. Headquarters will kick me in the ass for it. Some bastard may even shoot me.'

'Nonsense. It's for peace. We agreed that whatever happens, no violence in Puranapur. None. Use your statesmanship, my old friend Shaukat.'

Shaukat used his statesmanship. And it worked. The HQ agreed, strangely. The clearing opposite the Post Office was jam-packed. Men climbed up trees lining the sides of the square to look and listen. Shaukat spoke stirringly for twenty minutes. Bhagwan spoke movingly for twenty minutes. They ended their speeches by saying the same thing: no one from either side should, for any reason and under any provocation, say or do anything to hurt the other side.

To each other, they whispered, 'Future not looking good. Must keep meeting.'

THREE

EVERY YEAR DURING the monsoon months, it sometimes rained for days on end. The streets of Puranapur would become little rivers and the countryside around it one vast lake guarded by trees. The town folk dreaded this annual dose of misery.

But for the very young, it was a bonanza. They joined logs of wood together and made *ships*. They navigated the streets with long bamboo poles normally used to uphold mosquito nets at night. Sometimes, the boys took their crafts to the countryside to hunt for frogs and snakes. Frogs were difficult to catch – they leaped away – and the snakes rare to come by. But if the boys saw one, usually a harmless grass snake rippling away in the muddy water for its life, they bashed its head with bamboo poles. When the creature was 'dead double dead', they dangled it from a pole. Back in the streets, they waved it in their friends' faces to frighten them. That had them in stitches. Fun over, they gave the dead snake to Sham Sapera, the snake charmer who doubled as a hakim. Sham Sapera cut it up in small pieces and bottled them in foot-high glass jars with some special oil and let them marinate for weeks. He sold the oil to people with certain ailments ordinary medicine could not cure, such as joint pain. Of the snake skins, he made a powder to rub on the eyes to make people see more clearly. It worked.

In the summer of 1947, it seemed monsoon would never come. A severe drought had set in. The parched Punjab earth cracked up. The countryside became a graveyard dotted with dead cattle. Long-necked vultures feasted on them. At least twenty vultures popped around every carcass pecking on raw rotting flesh. Vishnu, Shashi, and friends Ravi and Vijay fired stones at them from their catapults. The long-necked birds flapped their wide wings as they took off, making the boys laugh.

Far away in Delhi, Nehru was reportedly head over heels in love with Lady Mountbatten and vice versa. Another fourteen-hundred kilometres away, Mahatma Gandhi was still treading the dirt tracks of Noakhali, the scene of a recent communal carnage, persuading Hindus and Muslims to keep peace.

Mid-July, there arrived in Delhi an English barrister called Justice Radcliffe. Attlee gave Radcliffe one of the strangest jobs in history. It was to create the dividing line between the two would-be nations. The gentleman had never set foot on this troubled land before. He had exactly four weeks to complete this task. Arming himself with all kinds of maps – territorial, demographic and others, he locked himself in a grand red stone house in the grounds of the Viceroy's Palace.

In Puranapur, Muslims in the more exposed, poorer parts of the town, were erecting five-foot high mud walls. It gave them a sense of extra security. Cocooned by fear, they did not realize that when the chips were really down, the mud walls held no promise at all.

Still, while murders, rapes, looting and arson occurred every day in the rest of Punjab, Puranapur was peaceful, thanks mainly to two wise men – League leader Shaukat Ali ably backed by his right-hand man Mullah Jaffar, and Bhagwan Prasad of Congress advised by his brother Jyoti.

In spite of the unbearable white heat and long spell of drought, no one wanted the monsoon that summer. No one except cousins Vishnu and Shashi. Then, just like that, the waters came from the skies. It rained non-stop for two whole days and two whole nights. The streets turned into rivers and the countryside a wide lake. With friends Vijay and Ravi, they had already prepared their 'ship' in anticipation. When the rain stopped, they navigated it up and down Chauri Galli. This was monotonous without much thrill, but the countryside this year was strictly forbidden. But there were plenty of open spaces behind the Hanuman Mandir; on the high walls of the temple sat a group of young men whiling away their time. There, the four sailors spotted a wiggly black line. What incredible luck!

While the boys were busy boating around the flooded town, there turned up at Jyoti's door Bhagwan's assistant Desraj, asking to see his boss. Bhagwan knew instantly. It must be some very urgent tiding that had made Desraj come braving the floods.

'A word in private, Bhgawan Sirji.'

The two walked out in the knee-deep River Chauri Galli.

'Bhagwanji, a large cache of arms arrived last night at Vatala Junction, deadly things under tightly roped tarpaulins – guns, bombs, swords, spears.'

'Who told you?'

'Sirji, our Hindu chaiwalla. His job is to keep a watch on the station and know what is happening. We pay him to spy.'

'Who else knows about it?'

'Shaukat. Naturally. The arms are for Allah Hoo Army.'

Nearby, the young sailors were jubilant at their find. A snake was making rounds of the pit now flooded with roiled water. It was just there, going round and round crazily. As the boys arrived, tense and excited, Vishnu's mosquito-net pole did not prove long enough for the deep pit and the inevitable happened. He lost his balance and fell overboard, finding himself almost face to face with a five-foot cobra. His friends instantly went into action and killed it. The men sitting on the temple wall saw and ran and carried Vishnu to the temple compound, convinced he had been bitten. Gently, they laid him down on the floor in a deathly hush.

'What are you doing?' Vishnu laughed, leaping up. The snake hadn't got anywhere near him. But it could have.

'Wasp Balls!' Shashi shouted giving him a kick up his backside. All present guffawed.

When Vishnu and Shashi got back home with the story, the momentary sense of relief was replaced by anger. Jyoti went mad. He smashed up the 'ship' outside and the poles. Then his fury turned to his son. 'You foolish brat,' he screamed and slapped and kicked him.

Rakhi also screamed rushing to the boy's rescue, 'STOP. DO YOU WANT TO KILL YOUR SON?' She held his hand.

Before things could take a turn for the worse, Bhagwan came back.

'What are you doing to my nephew, Jyoti?'

'Giving him a lesson in sailing.'

The other boys had thoughtfully brought the dead cobra along, dangling it from a bamboo pole. When Bhagwan saw the five-foot killer, he too went berserk. He caught Shashi by the hair and did exactly what Jyoti had done to Vishnu.

Dadima shouted, 'Have you brothers gone mad or what? Isn't there enough madness going on in the world?'

'Ma, you keep out of it. Let me sort out the good-for-nothing child,' Bhagwan said.

'Call yourself a leader? Who made you leader? Congress Committee? Committee should resign.'

This would have gone on and on, but a loud and alarming shout from the street put an end to it.

'Bhagwanji! Bhagwanji…'

It was Desraj again. He ran into the house like a maniac.

'Bhagwanji. Bhagwanji…'

Desraj's nostrils flared, his eyes bulged, and his mouth was wide open. The brothers knew. Either Radcliffe had drawn the line giving Puranapur to Pakistan, or Mahatma Gandhi or Nehru or *Mouthbatten* had been shot.

'The Sant…' He raised a finger to speak.

'Gone? There?' the brothers said in disbelief and relief, pointing to the monsoon sky.

'No, sir, he's here. With his army. To attack.'

'What nonsense are you talking about?'

'Get onto the roof and see with your own eyes.'

The men raced up to Jyoti's roof, followed by the tearful Vishnu and Shashi. Being the tallest house around, they had a commanding view of the flat countryside turned into a lake of rainwater, on the left of a mud-walled enclave of mud houses of poorer Muslim families five hundred yards away. A little further on stood the railway station in total isolation. It was calm out there, but there was something sinister about the place. There was a throng at the mud wall of scores of men on horses. They carried lances, which glinted when the horses shuffled. As the horsemen got closer, the men on Jyoti's roof could see their yellow and blue turbans and tunics. They could clearly make out the Sant on a white charger, his talisman in hand, the long gold-tipped arrow.

'What is the damn fool doing here, Desraj? He's gone

nuts, the stupid Sikh,' Jyoti said.

'He's come to attack this unguarded area of the poor.'

'He can't do that. He gave me his word he wouldn't,' a shocked Bhagwan said.

Meanwhile Sant's *jatha* kept advancing towards the Hindu area. Suddenly, Bhagwan knew. The Sant had come to see him, the damn fool had. They all raced down to the street. The Sant had been told where to find Bhagwan.

The two men had a big bear hug.

'Bhagwan, you're worked up. Just look at your face.'

'Good to see you, Santji. But how come you are here?'

'This is how you welcome me – *how come*? Take me in for tea. My word, how lovely are these boys. Your names, sons?'

'Vishnu.'

'Shashi.'

'You been crying? Were you being naughty?'

'Only a little, Santji,' Vishnu said.

'I haven't brought you anything. But I have my horse. Do you fancy a ride on it?'

'Oh, yes please, Santji. I've never ridden a horse before. Neither has Shashi.'

'Well then.' The Sant lifted the boys onto the horse's back. He sat behind them astride the beautiful animal and cantered away, watched by all the families around now out in the street. Then he half-galloped, to the boys' thrill, for a hundred yards. When he turned back, there was clapping by his soldiers and the onlookers.

'You see, Bhagwan, my brave lions are like children. All they want is your love and they are happy. See?'

Sant's more than two hundred soldiers in high blue turbans, yellow-and-black tunics, and armed to the teeth, presented a magnificent if frightening sight. This little display of his warmth for the children went down well. It meant the Sant had come in peace. Bhagwan put an arm around his shoulder and led him into Jyoti's house for refreshments.

'What about your army? I am afraid we can't provide for two-hundred at such short notice,' Jyoti said.

There was laughter: who the hell could give tea to two-hundred and counting?

'Not to worry. It's all arranged. They will go to the big Puranapur Gurdwara where a *langar* awaits them.' *Langar* at a Sikh shrine was free *welcome* food, only dal and roti, for anyone at any time of the day or night, irrespective of their caste or creed. The Sant had already sent fifty rupees as donation to the gurdwara. That would be more than enough for his men's dal roti.

Refreshments were relished over small talk, with Dadima present. *But what is the Sant doing here?* Bhagwan worried.

'Clean hearts are good for the garden of friendship, Santji. So come clean.'

'My boys had become restless. Delhi's wait-and-see nonsense irritates them. I thought a ride out in the countryside would do them good.'

This was not clean enough. Bhagwan pressed on. 'You chose the right day for it all right. Your boys must have liked the flooded roads and water-logged bazaar a lot on their way here.'

'Well, my boys wanted the fez-capped pigs to shiver a little. They will, after they have seen my braves.'

'Every Muslim here must have seen them by now, Santji. Your boys are highly visible.'

'And they feel deeply injured, what with their mothers, sisters and daughters being raped in west Punjab. Their houses looted and burnt down.'

'But you promised you wouldn't start anything.'

'And a promise is a Sikh's word. But I cannot say what my

boys might get up to without telling me.'

Bhagwan tried hard to get a firm commitment. All he got was: 'Yes, yes, yes, Bhagwan Bhai. You know me. The garden of our friendship will ever remain rosy. I will never do anything without my brother's permission…'

From not far was heard the fearsome Sikh war cry, indicating that the *langar* at the gurdwara was over:

WAHE GURU JI KA KHALSA!
WAHE GURU JI KI FATEH!

'But brother Bhagwan, tell Shaukat Ali to go and take his people out while there's still time. Puranapur will be ours, the birthplace of Guru Gobind's youngest son; buried alive here.'

The ten score ferociously attired *boys* were back in the Chauri Galli broad street, which in fact was only fifteen feet wide as opposed to all the other streets that were no more than seven or eight feet, running cramped between walls and doors. People hung on in doorways. They looked from windows, feeling reassured. The mood became that of guarded rejoicing after some male banter and laughter. The Sant stood up; it was time to go.

'Thank you for the tea. My respects to Mother and Sister Rakhiji,' he said at the door.

'Santji,' Jyoti called.

'Yes, brother Jyoti?'

'You love India?'

'India is my mother.'

'Do you love Indians?'

'They are my brothers.'

'Then disband your army to save your brothers in Puranapur.'

The Sant stopped in his tracks, as if struck by a lightning.

'Now that is a thought that had never occurred to me.'

'I wonder why it had not,' Jyoti insisted. Although he gave Jyoti a good big-brotherly hug, the Sikh 'General' thought the Congress leader's brother was not just raving mad, he was plain stupid.

August, a notoriously weather-beaten month, was rising. India was edgy. The land of the five fabled rivers was in a state far worse than that. Independence was just a few days away. Everyone knew what it would bring, even the simplest peasant who couldn't write his own name in any of the three languages he spoke – Punjabi, Urdu and Hindi.

Through Hirdey, Bhagwan asked Shaukat for another urgent meeting. It took place at the same spot two days later. Immediately after the deluge had come a scorcher, drying up the countryside, making the world look chaste in the blinding white light of the sun.

Looking distinctly unwell, Shaukat Ali was worryingly late today. Bhagwan had almost given up and turned back. Shaukat Ali had come on the carrier of Mullah Jaffar's bicycle. The deputy held an umbrella over his head to shield him from the sun. Bhagwan also had come cycling, but he was alone. The League leader apologized profusely in the manner of Muslim nawabs of Lucknow for being late. Then the two embraced as usual.

'Does that lunatic with a golden arrow think we are scared of his blue-and-yellow Nihangi turbaners? We are not. Neither of your armed RSS loonies.'

'I have the Sant's word, but his Nihangis are very unpredictable, Shaukat. And the RSS men are just waiting for their chance. They hate you like you hate them.'

'I know. But we are not afraid of their swords and guns of 1857 Mutiny vintage. Our boys have much superior arms. Much, much.'

'I know they have just received guns and bombs...'

'How the hell do you know, Bhagwan?'

'Never mind how. The point is never to let any one of them use their weapons of 1857 or 1947 vintage. Or we are all finished... finished off by each other. You take my point?'

'I take your point. But how to stop this mutual self-destruction, Bhagwan?'

'Where there is a will, there is a way; we agreed. You keep your Allah Hoo Army baying for our blood under control – they'll obey you. I'll keep the lid on the mad Sant and his Nihangis.'

'What about the RSS? Their blood-thirsty utter nutters?'

'Blood-thirsty utter nutters of both sides should never be allowed to confront each other. That's what we have to ensure.'

'Easier said than done.'

'But this is what we have to do to save Puranapur, Shaukat.'

'This is what I tell our boys every day, Bhagwan.'

'With your commanding presence, they will listen.'

'I'm doing my best. You do yours. You have the right personality plus charisma.'

'I don't know about the charisma-shrisma, but I am doing what I have to.'

They embraced before parting company, Shaukat to go home to lie down for an hour or two; he badly needed to. And Bhagwan hurried off, cycling madly, to Dr Gupta's, not to miss completely an important live broadcast. Today, Monday the 11th of August 1947 was another day to remember. Today, the Governor-General-to-be of Pakistan in three days, Jinnah, was addressing the new country's Constituent Assembly from the port city of Karachi, his capital.

With the exception of Inspector Partap Singh, the same set of men sat around the radio in Dr Gupta's drawing room when Bhagwan arrived more than halfway through the broadcast, flushed and panting. The men's faces were blank and their foreheads furrowed with confusion as if they were in mourning. Jinnah was in full flow, the veteran speaker. He was saying: 'You are free to go to your temples, to your mosques, to any other place of worship in this state of Pakistan. You may belong to any religion, caste or creed – that has nothing to do with the business of the state…' Jinnah paused.

It made Dr Gupta's guests clench their fists with anger. If the lanky League leader stood before them at that moment, he would have got a few in the face.

'What the fuck is our great leader saying exactly three days before the birth of Pakistan?' Mohammed screamed. 'The only reason for its creation was bloody religion. Islam.'

'He demanded a Pakistan on religious grounds for years. Doesn't this speech make his demand redundant? It's too pathetic for words. Not to say dangerous,' Jyoti said.

'Very dangerous. How dangerous? He'll find out,' Mohammed went on.

'He has been clamouring for a separate homeland for the Muslims of India. So what does he mean now, this selfish psychopath?' Rama Kant said.

'I can't believe my ears. It makes a mockery of everything the "great gent" had stood for all this time and still does,' Aziz said. He felt demolished.

They all felt demolished. Jinnah had refuted everything he was known to passionately believe in. Baffled, sorrowful, and incredulous, they were numbed into mournful silence. But only briefly. For it was shattered by the sudden appearance of Bhagwan's deputy, Desraj, the harbinger of alarming news. He barged unannounced into Dr Gupta's well-appointed drawing room, looking highly agitated.

'Sorry to interrupt, sir, gentlemenji, but I had to. It's begun,' Desraj said, holding his chest.

'What has, Desraj?' Bhagwan said, eyes popping.

'Body found in the *ganda nala*.'

'Whose? A Hindu's? A Sikh's? A Muslim's?'

Why was Desraj looking at Jyoti and not him?

'It is Shambhu's, Prasadji.'

Something hit Jyoti, and a cloud of darkness engulfed him. Brahmin Shambhu was the gentlest of the human race. Jyoti saw a white shirt puffed up with air floating in black slime. He saw Inspector Partap Singh giving orders.

Suddenly, anger evaporated from the room. Fear filled it, and thoughts of Pakistan sank into Puranapur's *ganda nala* of death.

'Run long on double hop, and tell Partap Singh not to let it out it's a Hindu. I'm coming right behind you.'

'But everyone knows, Prasadji. Your Shambhu was a Brahmin. He had a topknot seven inches long. And Inspector Partap Singh has not turned up there yet.'

'Go make up a story. Say anything. GO. We're coming.'

They had hardly set foot in the street, when he-who-had-just-been-named called them out – Partap Singh, looking just as agitated as Desraj had been.

'Have you heard, Bhagwanji?'

'Just now. Bad. Very bad. Poor Shambhu,' Bhagwan said.

'Poor Shambhu, yes. But also poor Mam Din.'

'WHAT!!! Mam Din, the noble poet, a seer and beloved of all? WHEN AND WHERE?'

'Last night. Also in the *ganda nala*.'

This was ugly news, only four days before the BIG DAY. Ugly and horrible. It could lead to things unimaginably more horrendous. Who did Shambhu in was obvious and clear, as was who did Mam Din in.

In the resounding silence, the men ambled out into the street. Nobody knew what to say after Jinnah's shattering speech and the devastating news of the two deaths. Their silence meant they knew something awful was on its way.

Waking up a little earlier than usual, tongawalla Mam Din heard Mullah Jaffar croon sonorously – Allah Hoo Akbar – from his marble tower five hundred yards away. He had to pick up a sack of wheat flour from the now-closed Prasad mill to deliver to stationmaster Nanda. Cockerels far and near, and all the early birds also heard as the pre-dawn penumbra began to lift. They agreed with the revered gentleman with a bird's nest on his handsome face. The poet hurried, aware that Jyoti Prasad was making a special effort to open his mill. He didn't want to make the mill owner wait on a glorious morning.

But something was amiss. Mam Din's left eye twitched – a bad omen. In the present state of affairs, it meant bad things were coming. But bad things were coming anyway, weren't they? Mam Din knew like everybody else that the unknown Angrez, Radcliffe, with a butcher's knife in hand, had already been here for three weeks. He was sitting in a large room with a high ceiling in the shadow of Mountbatten's grand red-sandstone palace. The room's main white-washed wall was dominated by an immense map of a country he knew not a thing about. Smaller maps festooned other walls. The gentleman was peering at them, putting pins here and there, drawing pencil lines elsewhere. He was cutting up Mother India's breasts, Britain's farewell gift to the country it had ruled for two centuries.

A creature of habit, Mam Din did what he did on getting up every morning. He had a customary wash – hands, face, and the elbows. He rolled out his prayer mat and knelt on it, facing west in the direction of Mecca, the birth place of the Prophet – peace be upon him – fifteen hundred miles away in the sizzling sands of Arabia.

A little later, as Mam Din groomed his horse Aftab, he saw another omen. Ulfat the parrot, and Baggu the mongrel, who with Aftab made up his family, had vanished from their room-size wire-mesh enclosure. Mam Din had done the door last night as usual.

'Bird is bird and it loves the air…' It was understandable that Ulfat should fly off to freedom if the cage door had been left open somehow. 'Aren't we all trying to? But the dog…?' Mam Din felt devastated. Little Baggu loved his master. It was inconceivable that he would run away even if the door was left open.

After a small paratha and a glass of lassi, Mam Din drove to the flour mill, where Jyoti Prasad was indeed waiting. Behind him stood Shera who helped load up.

'Drop me home on your way to the station, Mam Din?'

'My pleasure, Janab.'

In Chauri Galli, Jyoti found he did not have four annas in loose change – the fare. He only had a five-rupee note.

'Forget it, Janab.'

'Don't be silly. You want to go out of business?'

'Pay me next time, sir,' Mam Din said, taking off. After the station, he rode to all the four corners of the town. He asked everybody if they had seen a solitary brown puppy. Puranapur was full of stray puppies – brown, black and white. He looked and looked and asked and asked.

'Our very dear Mam Din. If you miss your dog so much, he must miss you too. He'll come back to you.'

Just before sunset, Mam Din decided to call on Dei Amma, the old Muslim midwife, for a word of comfort. Dei Amma always had a kind word for everyone. Mam Din was half in love with her, but her late husband had been a close friend of his. So, out of respect for him, he had never allowed his emotions to come to surface. She lived with her young daughter who ran a school for very small children under a tree by their one-room mud house. The house stood a few yards after the wooden bridge over the *ganda nala*, where it emptied itself into a deep pool. The young woman was very fond of the tongawalla. She came out for a good chat with Mam Din Chacha and told him that her mother was out on a call. After inquiring about the mother and daughter's welfare, Mam Din reversed and rode away, saying 'Khuda Hafiz, God Bless'. He wanted to go looking for his dog.

At the lonesome bridge stood four teenage boys in turbans, bamboo sticks in their hands. They had killed a long snake with cowrie shells of white and brown markings. One of them dangled it from his bamboo stick. Laughing loudly, he waved it in the horse's face as the tonga came to them. Alarmed and terrified, the horse raised his front feet sky high, throwing Mam Din out of his driver's seat over the bridge and into the *ganda nala*, where the mud water was at its deepest.

Mam Din could not swim. He struggled to reach the bank, but failed. The boys extended the bamboo pole to him. It proved too short. The girl saw. She thought the boys had pushed him further into the slime. She screamed. Some men came running from the Muslim neighbourhood around. Fearing for their lives, the boys sprinted away.

The same night, the sky opened up with a delightful ferocity. Like the other young men, Shera, Balla, Judge and Shambhu stripped down to their underwear and treated themselves to a long rain-bath. Had it been last year, they would have danced the Bhangra. But such rejoicing this year would have looked out of place, even grotesque. Besides, the death of Balla's grandmother had cast a shadow over their lives. Balla was now living with Shambhu, a bachelor like him. After the evening meal, the four friends came and sat on the temple wall to while away the time yapping with other young men, who too had nothing else to do. It was fun. It was more – rain pelting down on their prickly-heat inflicted backs. It was comforting.

At ten or so, Shambhu yawned loudly and said he must turn in. Balla said he would join him later. Rubbing himself all over, Shambhu drifted away to his one-room mud hut, a few hundred yards away. He hummed a popular KL Saigal number from a Hindi movie, imitating the great singer's uniquely soulful delivery. Nobody in Puranapur locked their doors, leaving them simply latched when they went out. As soon as Shambhu stepped into his yard, he knew he had walked into a trap; thieves or robbers hid there. But Shambhu owned nothing a thief or a robber would want. Shambhu did an instinctive about-turn and ran.

Barefoot as he was, Shambhu slipped in the mud and fell. Three pairs of 'army surplus' boots pinned him down; he knew they were 'army surplus' because they were heavy and studded. A hand pulled at his topknot so hard, some of it came off his scalp. Although Shambhu cried out in pain, the pelting rain drowned out his voice.

Shambhu was strong. He broke free. But he was unlucky.

He fell again as he made a run for it. This time, the robbers – three of them, all soldier-types – tied his hands behind his back and stuffed his mouth with a cloth. They kicked him up his backside and made him walk along the bank of the *ganda nala* in ink-black wilderness. The muddy bank was not made for walking. But the robbers dragged him along for another hundred yards or so. There, they ungagged him, placing a knife at his throat.

'What do you want?'

'Revenge.'

'Revenge for what?

'For what was done to my brother by his headmaster.'

'What was done to your brother by his headmaster?'

'Do you want to live?'

'Yes, I do. Spare me. I beg you.'

'We will spare you but on one condition.'

'Name it, name it, name it.'

'Become one of us.'

'What, a robber? I will. I will.'

'No, a Muslim. Repeat after me: La Illah Illillah, Mohammed-un-Rasul-Ullah.'

This was the Muslim *kalima*, the oath. Uttering it made someone a Muslim. Shambhu, a Hindu and a Brahmin, couldn't do that.

'Repeat, you bastard: La Illah Illillah…'

'I won't. I can't.' Shambhu was a Brahmin, the highest of the high. If he recited the *kalima*, he would become a Muslim, an Untouchable, the lowest of the low.

'You won't? You can't?' The robber pressed the naked blade against Shambhu's throat. But he couldn't go through with it. He couldn't push the knife in him.

'NO. BECAUSE I AM A…'

The robber just kicked him fifteen feet below into the

swollen *ganda nala*. Shambhu could utter just one word before drowning: '...BRAHMIN!'

He was exactly half a mile from where lay Mam Din.

'He said he was a Brahmin,' the knife-wielder sneered. 'But Balla wasn't a Brahmin. Or isn't one.'

There had been a mistake.

The Prasad brothers and Partap Singh raced to Chauri Galli on their bicycles. They found Hirdey at Jyoti's door, as if he knew he would be needed. Lunch was ready, but the brothers had no appetite.

'The end then? Or the beginning of an end? Or the end of a beginning?' Bhagwan said, checking himself; his ironic rhetoric was uncalled for. It was time for action.

Jyoti also thought the same.

'All right, Churchill. Go do something about it.'

But what?

Mam Din had been to most Hindus and Sikhs of Puranapur what Mahatma Gandhi was to many Muslims in India – a frail and an ugly little old man they held in grudging affection. The brothers knew how most Hindus and Sikhs would respond to his death – with genuine sorrow. What they did not know was how the Muslims would react to what for them was Mam Din's murder. They shuddered.

'Where is the body?' Bhagwan asked.

'At the police station. And there are a hundred Muslims demanding it,' Partap Singh said.

'Where is Shambhu's body?'

'Also at the station, where else? And a hundred Hindus and Sikhs are demanding it. You've never seen anything like it.

Fourth Battle of Panipat any minute.'

'Where is your boss Ashraf?'

'Out of station on leave, Bhagwanji.'

'Good time to go on leave. That means you are the acting police chief now.'

'Not many Muslim policemen are left now anyway.'

'As acting police chief, what are you going to do, Sardar Partap Singh? You have to be seen to be doing something.'

'What, Bhagwanji? You tell me. You are the head of the Congress. You are my boss now.' The policeman scratched his groin. He was at his wits' end. So was Bhagwan. The same question haunted them both: what to do? Neither of them had an answer.

But Jyoti did, his brother's right-hand man and counsellor-adviser. Bhagwan never took an important decision without his approval, decided everything only after Jyoti recommended it.

'Shaukat Ali,' Jyoti said quietly.

'Shaukat Ali?' Partap Singh's jaw fell to the ground. He wasn't aware that the Congress and the League leaders, arch enemies, were on speaking terms. 'What has he got to do with it?'

Jyoti explained. What he said was simple but mad. Totally mad. Yet, given a chance, it could work. And if it did, it would save a lot of trouble, prevent a great deal of bloodshed, even the very destruction of the city.

'And why shouldn't it work? It's for the mutual good of us all,' Jyoti added.

Bhagwan dispatched Hirdey on his life's most important mission – to seek out Shaukat Ali for a 'sooner than ASAP' meeting, with the message, 'Our lives and those of thousands depended on its success. Or failure.'

The two leaders met again as soon as was possible. This time, both of them felt they were drawn to each other with special warmth, being pulled by a sense of imminent doom. A co-feeling emerged, reminding them of old times when Indians were one people. The two had played marbles together on the ground of their primary school, hockey in high school, cricket at college, and had marched together under Gandhi against the British rule as political activists. They realized how desperately they needed each other now.

Bhagwan had taken Jyoti along. Shaukat had come with Mullah Jaffar. He waited for Bhagwan to tell him what had made this a life-and-death meeting.

'Shaukat…'

Bhagwan unfolded Jyoti's plan. It was so fantastic, history had no precedent of such a community initiative.

'…A joint Hindu – Muslim funeral.'

'A joint Hindu-Muslim funeral?' Shaukat gasped. It took him a few minutes to grasp the meaning of it. 'The idea being…'

'The idea is to bring all together. The idea is no Calcutta of last year here. We agreed,' Bhagwan said.

Shaukat, although safe in the knowledge that the Muslims here were in a great majority, shook his head. The great triangle of the Sikh Sant, the Hindu RSS and his own Muslim AHAA boys in the middle had already turned the little town into a tinderbox.

'Too risky. It can destroy us all,' he finally said.

'Or save us all,' Jyoti said.

They met again soon after. This time at the police station, in full view of the town. With them were men of their parties. Out in the street stood six score men with unconcealed anger and concealed daggers. It was a touch-and-go moment. The two leaders embraced each other with visible warmth. Then, in a booming voice, the provisional new Police Chief Partap Singh read out a statement signed by them.

THERE WILL BE A JOINT FUNERAL LATER TODAY FOR OUR MARTYRED BROTHERS.

Everybody present feared for his life. But people were moved to see their leaders embrace, even if they thought it was for form's sake. They were touched by the statement. There was an uncanny lightness in the air. It was uncanny because people knew it was a trick.

It was a trick. Would it pay off?

Two thousand people turned up at the police station. The pall-bearers for Shambhu were Shera and Balla, to be relieved by the Prasad brothers. For Mam Din, it was Shaukat and the revered Mullah Jaffar, to be taken over by the other two pillars of their community. The Hindu cremation ground and the much larger Muslim cemetery lay next to each other on the outskirts of the old town. The march was more relaxed than funerary. Divided by the times and politics, many old friends were meeting after many months. Perhaps years. There were plenty of embraces – warm, sincere. Mohammed's sister's baby had arrived. A radiant boy, he told Jyoti. They were ready now for their departure, along with Aziz's family. There were speeches by the leaders, Shaukat and Bhagwan. The burial and the cremation took place simultaneously with the same question sitting on the tip of every tongue: would *it* last?

From a bush fifty yards away, Jyoti saw a tiny something fall to the ground, the shell of an unborn caterpillar. It stirred with life and opened up, to become a little butterfly with bright red wings, a thing of beauty. It struggled for a moment, then it took to flight – a fascinating sight. At the same time, a small brown bird with a yellow beak darted out of another bush towards it.

'Train at dawn tomorrow, if it comes tonight,' said

Mohammed. There hadn't been a train for days.

'If the butterfly escapes, Mohammed will get on that train,' Jyoti said to himself. Exactly ten yards from the spot of its birth and exactly seven seconds later, the bird swooped on the butterfly, missing it by the skin of its semi-transparent wings.

Jyoti was reminded of something – the four annas he owed to Mam Din. The influx of refugees had unleashed an army of beggars into the Puranapur streets. On his way back home with Bhagwan, he changed his five-rupee note and stopped four of them one after the other. He gave each one of them a rupee note, raising their eyebrows and those of his brother's: this was extravagant alms-giving.

'What's come over you, Jyoti?'

'I had a debt to repay.'

More vulnerable for being surrounded, the Hindu-Sikh enclave was patrolled at night by vigilantes – well-chosen tall and sturdy RSS men. In twos and threes, they walked up and down the streets. The .303 Rifles from the First World War slung from their shoulders. They carried spears and shouted:

Jagtey Raho, Khabar Dar!

Their words of reassurance reverberated from the walls. They banged the blunt ends of their spears on the brick street, as they warned in loud voices the people asleep on rooftops. The *cadre* did this until dawn. Heavily indoctrinated, the ultra-nationalist group with a majoritarian worldview were determined to protect the Hindus. The RSS men were tough. They wanted to make sure that those sleeping in the street and on rooftops could wake in the morning unharmed by the Muslim militants.

Following the extraordinary events of the day, many RSS men had decided to rest their weapons and take the night off. Hadn't Hindu, Sikhs and Muslims sworn eternal friendship over the dead bodies of the poet Mam Din and Shambhu?

Chauri Galli always turned in early and slept soundly. As the Badami Mosque's minaret clock struck ten, Rakhi, a light sleeper, stirred. She had heard another sound. It was not the warning from the street below. Nor was it the muffled roar of a distant mob Rakhi had learnt to tell. She tugged at Jyoti.

'What do you hear tonight, Lady JPji?'

'Listen, ji…'

'Jyoti Prasad… Jyoti Prasad…'

Somebody was down there. Not in the street, but in their backyard. Jyoti leaped from his bed.

'Mohammed?' What was the fool doing there at this godforsaken hour? Good thing that the RSS patrol was off tonight; otherwise he might have been shot. Slipping into his shoes, Jyoti ran downstairs and let Mohammed in. In the dim sixty-watt naked light of his courtyard, he saw his friend's face had turned yellowish in fear.

'Anyone after you? What's happened?'

'My son…'

'Maqbool?' Jyoti knew – the boy had been murdered.

'…Snake bit him. A cobra. He's dying.'

'Doctor?'

'Doctor Alam can't help. Hasn't got the serum, and the hospital is shut. Only a snake-bite healer can.'

'Sham Sapera?' The ace snake charmer was also a renowned snake-bite healer.

'He won't come to my house in the Muslim area, being a Hindu. Says we'll cut his throat.'

'O, the fool. I'll get him.'

Rakhi had come rushing down. She begged Jyoti not to go to a Muslim area at this unearthly hour. She laid down on the floor between her lord and master in this life and the front door.

'Don't, Nathji. Don't. Think of us all.'

'Little Sister Rakhiji, one thousand and one apologies. Promise to bring him back safe and sound in half an hour. Swear on my dying son's head.'

Rakhi felt devastated to hear about Mohammed's son. Of Vishnu's age, she had known him since he was a toddler. When things were normal and Puranapur had not yet turned into a ghost town, the boy often came to Chauri Galli to play with Vishnu and Shashi.

Jyoti took Mohammed to Sham Sapera's house first.

'No, Prasadji. No.' Sham Sapera refused to go to the Muslim area at this time of night.

It took Jyoti a while to charm the snake-charmer. Sham Sapera took his craft's basket and bag, and accompanied the men to Moti Bagh, the affluent part of the city.

The boy lay on a charpoy in the common grass patch surrounded by nameless wild bushes. Some fifteen men sat around the snake-bitten boy on charpoys – the family elders and neighbours. Several women in veil stood around, weeping silently. Sham Sapera intently examined the ankle where the boy had been bitten. Then, he asked where exactly the boy had been stung, at what spot in the grounds. He was pointed to the widespread bushy growth. This was of interest to Sham Sapera. The layout and something inside him told him that the serpent was still around, in the wasteland. He took out his equipment from his bag and sat down cross-legged on the grass next to the boy's charpoy. He told everybody to get out of sight. Nobody knew why or for what reason. But they obeyed, knowing that the snake charmers, ever effective, were a mysterious lot. They went away and stationed themselves in doorways and windows.

'Breathe not a breath,' Sham Sapera whispered loudly.

Nobody did.

Then, with Jyoti and Mohammed helping, he laid the boy down on the grass and shooed them away to Mohammed's back door. All set, Sham Sapera took out a long bulbous *been* from his basket and started playing on it a hauntingly captivating tune. People watched from doorways and windows. He went on and on and on. Surprising everybody, slowly and stealthily in the waning moon, a glistening line, some six feet long, slithered in through the grass. It advanced and stopped at the boy's right foot. It put its mouth to the boy's heel as Sham Sapera played on and on. Minutes later, the night glistened with that line no more and Sham Sapera's magic flute fell silent. The creature of the wild had gone back into the bushes. And now Sham Sapera began chanting mantras in the serpent language only he knew, having learnt it as a boy from his father who had learnt it from his father. At the same time, the snake man started sweeping a small broomstick up and down the dying boy, up and down… to sweep all death and disease away, to put harm to the night breeze, which had suddenly started blowing.

'Lord Shiva's obedient agent came and killed his own poison,' the snake charmer slowly said. 'The boy will run like a hare in two days.' Exhausted, the man fell silent. His incredulous but immeasurably grateful audience gaped in awe.

All those present sighed loudly; a few wiped tears. Salma, the boy's mother, half-removed her veil, took off her gold locket and held it out to Sham Sapera.

'No, sister,' he nodded his head. 'Sham Sapera didn't come here for gold or silver. He came here to save your son's life.'

They were leaving.

'Brother Jyoti.' Salma removed her veil completely, giving Jyoti his first ever glimpse of her face. It was an honour.

Does tragedy have to strike before we pull down age-old barriers? Jyoti wondered.

'Brother Jyoti, give this to his wife from me,' Salma said, giving Jyoti the necklace. Then she pulled off two gold bangles from her left wrist. 'And these to my sister Rakhi.'

Mohammed and a few other men walked the two through the Muslim area to the safety of a Hindu street. He hugged Jyoti in farewell.

At home, Rakhi stood in the doorway, crying. 'My Nath! My Nath!' She couldn't stop crying.

'Told you I would be back safe and sound. And here I am, my Lady JPji. Now give me a smile.'

Jyoti handed Rakhi the bangles, and she cried again and wrapped herself around him.

'What times are we living through, O Krishna!'

The train had come to Puranapur earlier. At dawn, Jyoti heard its shrill whistle. The cry of the steam engine saddened him. He was glad to hear it.

The rains had come this year with a vengeance. Jyoti had not seen in recent years so much water from the heavens. In the distance, the great rivers of the Punjab leaped into floods. Roads disappeared. Railroads were washed away. Bridges crumbled and hundreds of villages were submerged under water. The rural areas were cut off from the rest of the world. People in Puranapur remained marooned for days together. The Ravi Canal, a short distance away, was level with the fields, the russet-painted bridge over it presented a bizarre sight presiding over a vast lake in isolation. In the town itself, people were grateful that they had hoarded foodstuff and other commodities over the past two weeks. Though their reasons for doing so were totally different, they were thankful that they had now enough to survive until the floods receded.

Jyoti's calendar had reached its very last leaf. It said ONE.

It was 14 August 1947, Pakistan's first day of Independence. Jinnah in Karachi shared a state car with Mountbatten for the inauguration ceremony. The vehicle flew a flag fashioned by him – a green field with a white crescent moon and a five-pointed star. The Governor General beamed with just pride to see it flutter vigorously in the breeze from the Arabian Sea.

The same night in Delhi, a thousand miles east and to the blaring of conch shells, Nehru ushered in India's Independence as an English clock in the National Assembly chimed 12:

'Long years ago, we made a tryst with destiny, and now the time comes when we shall redeem our pledge, not wholly or in full measure, but very substantially. At the stroke of the midnight hour, when the world sleeps, India will wake to life and freedom. A moment comes, which comes but rarely in history, when we step out from the old to the new, when an age ends, and when the soul of a nation, long suppressed, finds utterance.'

All India Radio relayed Nehru's speech to the new nation. But only a handful of Hindus and Sikhs in Puranapur heard it. For the town throughout that day was without power. Dr Gupta had a battery-operated set, the only one around. He had moved it to his clinic; people were surprised to see the doctor's clinic open well past the usual evening hours. In pelting rain, the Prasad brothers had gone there to listen to the first Prime Minister. A small group had already collected – about fifty Hindus and Sikhs – with intent looks to know what freedom would mean for them. The old Harrovian spoke in English. Not everybody in the group could follow him well. As ever, he spoke movingly. Speaking in a deep, resonant voice about a people waking for a *tryst with destiny*, Nehru laid bare an outline of the India he was going to lead. It gave goose pimples to the listeners. They embraced each other and held hands like children, tears streaming down their cheeks.

India was free after a long spell of foreign domination. That it was really free, no longer the colony of a European power was hard to imagine. These men did not know what freedom meant. It was a strange moment, a baffling moment, a moment of a kind of joy they could not name. It was also a moment of sighs, beautiful sighs.

'OK. Independence has come. But which way does our dear little Puranapur go?' Jyoti asked the question uppermost on every mind.

Puranapur was free. But where was it, in which free state? Radcliffe had completed his job and departed. He had handed over the new map of the subcontinent to the Viceroy to be announced in three days. There had been no mention of the line of division in the leaders' speeches in Delhi or Karachi, for the real fear of bloodshed.

People shuffled away uneasily in groups of three or four or more in the hauntingly unlit streets that had become little rivers of rain. They knew that despite what Bhagwan and Shaukat had said publicly, the Hindu lives and those of their loved ones hung by a very thin thread; they simply did not trust the Muslims, a gut thing. The thread would snap if Puranapur went to Pakistan. It reduced INDEPENDENCE to a meaningless word, a dangerous word. As soon as the two brothers reached home, they did something planned long time ago. In the dim light of a kerosene lamp, watched by their mother and wives, they dug two deep holes on either side of the of the jasmine bush now in full bloom, its fragrance casting a magic spell in spite of the rain. In the two holes, they buried their wives' gold, already packed in two damp-proof bags. They were ready to fly at a moment's notice.

The rain fell noisily.

Just then, a miracle – the power came back. A wondrous omen, a divine moment – the coming of light at the moment of Mother India's liberty!

'Ma, it means Puranapur will go to India,' Jyoti said loudly and went and placed his forehead at his mother's feet. Bhagwan did the same after him. Then, the brothers embraced each other. Rakhi and Maya did the same, first bowing to Dadima's feet, then embracing each other.

Next morning, Day Zero, the rain stopped and the sun shone fiercely for the next two days. On Day Three of Independence, there appeared something rare in the sky above Puranapur – an aeroplane. The children ran up to their roofs to greet it.

'Aeroplane. Aeroplane…' they shouted gleefully.

In normal times, they would have taken to the streets and chased the noisy machine high up in the sky and shouted aloud. But the times were not normal. Elders in Chauri Galli were terrified. They were afraid that it might be a Pakistani plane.

'Come to drop bombs on our heads.'

The flying machine in the blue sky was painted yellow, a single-seater. The children could see the pilot. He waved to them, heightening their excitement. He entertained them to breathtaking acrobatics. He came low, low, low then shot up high, high, high. Coming down low again, he let a long white cloth banner out:

JAI HIND

Jyoti stood by a large pit of muddy water in his backyard. He brought out what he carried in his pocket at all times – a tiny bottle Dr Gupta had given him. It contained pills for Dadima, Rakhi, Maya, Meenakshi and Mona. They were to be given these if captured by the Allah Army. He emptied the bottle in the muddy pit and threw it after the pills. At the same time, there was much commotion in his street. People poured out of their homes. With their arms around each other and tears oozing out of their eyes, they started shouting:

JAI HIND, LONG LIVE INDIA

Vishnu, watching from their quaint wooden balcony, jumped in the air like a gazelle, and put his arms around his mother who stood next to him.

'We've gone to India, Ma. Free India.'

Rakhi hugged her son tight and pressed his face against her belly and Vishnu saw something he was not prepared for – his mother first hiccupped and then tears oozed out her eyes.

'Ma!!!' Vishnu tightened his clasp. He understood. 'I love you, Mummy. From here to the end of the world.'

'What did you say?' Rakhi wanted to hear that again.

'I said I love you from here to London and back.'

Rakhi beamed a deep smile as Vishnu wiped tears off his mother's lovely face. Now, he too started crying. That set Shashi off. The two boys held hands and ran out of the house to announce the news to the rest of the world. They were not allowed to wander far from Chauri Galli, but they fearlessly went, as they did almost every day, to all the five approachable corners of Puranapur. Their friends joined them, and shouting and laughing, they roamed the streets until Mohammed Chacha's factory where they saw two men with a Brownie camera like the one that had come with Uncle Aziz's stuff, but which, sadly, didn't work. They were taking photographs of the factory and the empty street. At the same time, the boys saw their headmaster coming their way from the other end of the street. Fearing his *medicine* of a few slaps for being out and about when they shouldn't be, they raced back home.

'Look – Uncle Bhagwan.'

Bhagwan had been out of the house since early morning. He was with his deputy Desraj. The two men carried a basket each. They were full of laddus. Each time someone passed, Bhagwan dipped a hand in one of the baskets and handed out a laddu. Then he hugged them.

'Rejoice, Bharjai. Rejoice,' Bhagwan shouted at his sister-in-law on the quaint balcony, adjusting his Gandhi cap. Maya, Meenakshi, Mona, Mindi and other children joined Rakhi. They were jubilant to see Bhagwan and rushed downstairs.

'Rejoice, Maya.' Bhagwan hurried into the house and handed out laddus to everyone. Jyoti too joined them, followed by several neighbours. The house filled up with much noise, boisterous banters and laughter after a long spell of gnawing suspense and fear. Yet, everybody looked as if they had known all along that their beloved Puranapur would be on India's new map. Then, Dadima held up a hand – *shush*. She broke into a popular song, just four lines, tears rolling down her guava-pale, semi-translucent cheeks:

Now this land is ours, ours, ours alone,
Upon it will now rule our own, our own, our own
Say not our head wears a topi white or brown
For now, it wears the golden crown.

This mesmerized all present, especially the Prasad children. They had never seen their grandmother cry, nor ever heard her sing. They sang the couplet in one voice, wiping their eyes and noses with their sleeves.

'Oye, what is this nonsense?' Vishnu shouted at them. 'We are supposed to celebrate, not cry. So, sing and dance, you fools. We are in India.'

'Were we in Japan before?' Dadima asked mischievously.

Jyoti sat by Bhagwan on the divan. Jyoti was tired. He had a sleepless night, thinking. He felt completely drained – a sense of surreal relief had brought on this sudden exhaustion. He glanced at Bhagwan and knew that he too felt like him.

'Bhagwan, you look tired.' Jyoti pressed his brother's hand. It was quite warm; Bhagwan ran a mild temperature.

'Dog tired.' Bhagwan also had a sleepless night, thinking. And because of another infernal power cut, the two had to get up early to go to Dr Gupta's to listen to the news on his radio; the Radcliffe Boundary Award was being broadcast. After that came the news of the instant horrors the announcement had wrought upon the now divided Punjab. Their Puranapur was unharmed, but an orgy of mayhem had begun in the rest of the province.

'I feel dog tired,' Bhagwan said again.

'Why don't you have a short nap, ji?' Maya said.

'Why don't you, Bhagwan?' Jyoti said and shooed the children away.

Bhagwan dozed off straight away.

Sometime later, he heard someone shout for him from

the street; it was the spy Hirdey. He knew why. *Shaukat wants to see me.* It had been always Bhagwan asking for a meeting. Never Shaukat. Now it was the other way round.

'So, you got your Puranapur. But what about us?'

'Shaukat, you wanted Partition. Not us. Congress never made any distinction between Indians. Only the League did.'

'So much hatred. So much madness.'

'We asked for it! All of us. And the Angrez let us have it.'

'I don't know. I know nothing anymore. I am tired.'

'Me too. Finished. How's the back?'

'Bad. And this time, I've really got something up my arse. Your RSS and your mad Sant. We are trapped.' Shaukat broke down, a moving sight, a grown man weeping.

'Okay, yaar. What do you want?'

'Nothing. Just let us go. That's all. The Ravi Canal is the border. Only two or three miles away. Let my people go, as someone said.'

'Why don't they?'

'How can they? The mad Sant and his Nihangi vultures are waiting. They want our heads, our gold, and our women. The moment we set foot in the fields, they'll…'

'Mountbatten has created a Boundary Force of fifty thousand. They'll escort you to the border. Naturally.'

'Bhagwan, you know and I know that no army-sharmy is coming to this dunghill. Even God has abandoned us now.'

Bhagwan clasped Shaukat's hand and broke down himself.

'Was it worth it, Shaukat?'

'Only our Quaid seems to think so.'

'Papa!!!' Mona and Shashi cried.

'Chacha!!!' Meenakshi and Vishnu groaned.

'Bhagwanji!' Hirdey pleaded, shock and worry in his voice.

Bhagwan sat up, tears rolling down his cheeks. It was bewildering for his children to see him, the well-regarded leader of the area, cry like them.

'It's nothing,' Bhagwan said and wiped his tears with his sleeve like a little boy. 'Just a dream. But what news have you brought this time, Hirdey?'

'That Shaukat…'

'You don't mean…?'

'No, Janab. A major heart attack. The moment he saw the JAI HIND aeroplane he doubled up…'

'Where is he, at home or in hospital?'

'At home. The hospital is shut.'

'Has Dr Alam seen him?'

'The doctor left on his bicycle for Vatala with his compounder Ghulam last night to see his sick mother.'

'I must go and see him, Jyoti. NOW. What if Shaukat pops off? Then God knows what the AHAA might get up to. And that'll be the end of us all.'

'AHAA or HAHA, you are not going to the heart of the Muslim area, Bhagwan. Are you mad?' Jyoti said.

'You are certainly not going there, ji,' Maya pleaded. 'Think of your children. Think of me.'

'No, Papa, no,' the children cried collectively. 'We won't let you go.' They came and accosted him, hugging him, climbing to his shoulders, and sitting in his lap.

'Jyoti, you better explain to everybody how important it

is for us all that I go see Shaukat immediately. Good tactic. If I don't, things will get out of hand.'

'Then I'll go with you.'

'One of us has to stay behind. You understand?'

Jyoti did. He realized that Bhagwan had to go, and he had to go alone. The Muslims had seen the two leaders exchange embraces. It could work. The Muslims didn't trust Bhagwan or any other Hindu. But they had to this once and the last time for their own bloody sake. Jyoti knew that the beast AHAA was cornered, and the beast, too, knew it. And a cornered beast was more dangerous than a free one. If Shaukat Ali succumbed, there was no one to stop AHAA from burning Puranapur to cinders as a final suicidal act in the name of their religion. Jyoti let his younger brother go. It was dangerous and foolish. It was bold and brave. But it was necessary, a risk worth taking.

As Bhagwan cycled past by Dr Gupta's house at the main crossroads, a thought struck him. He stopped and knocked at the doctor's door.

'Doctor Sahib, please hear me out before you say no.'

The doctor heard him out.

'Now what made you think I would say no?' Dr Gupta went back inside to change into his working clothes, his white cotton suit, tie, and a khaki sola topi. He brought along his kit bag. The fierce afternoon sun beat down on them, but they hardly noticed it; they were on a life-or-death mission.

Shaukat Ali lived in the exclusive Moti Bagh, a few doors away from Mohammed's now locked-up *haveli*. The Congress leader and the doctor were not prepared for the reception they had in the multi-windowed Moti Bagh. Fifty young men in all-black, the colour of the Allah Hoo's Army, hung around idly in the street. They were flabbergasted to see the leader of the enemy camp along with the town's best-known doctor in their street. Anger and shock combined to raise a question mark: *how dare he?*

Yet, without thinking about it, they moved aside to line the narrow street, offering a sort of guard of honour. The reason for their visit had become clear; they had come to save the life of their leader. A slight shuffling took place in the crowd standing mournfully at Shaukat's door. They were mostly bearded men in white Pathani suits and a few women in black burqa. They stood around a charpoy outside the *haveli* in solemn silence. On the string cot, Shaukat lay sprawled, his head propped up by big fluffy pillows. An uneasy pause lingered after the greetings of *As-Salaam-Alaikum*. It was left to Bhagwan to break the ice. He addressed Mullah Jaffar:

'Poor Shaukat. We are deeply, deeply sorry.'

'So very good of you, Congress Secretary Sahib, to come and bring Dr Guptaji along. Our own Dr Alam is sadly out of station.'

'What happened?'

'On seeing the aeroplane, he complained of a pain in his left arm. It got worse. An hour later, he clutched his chest and staggered and slumped against a wall.'

Dr Gupta got busy immediately. Holding their breaths, people watched. Shaukat looked to be in severe pain and was in a daze. It became instantly clear to Bhagwan that any sort of conversation with him was out of the question. But his eyes were open. He acknowledged Bhagwan with the hint of a nod, signalling to his chest, which the doctor was checking with his stethoscope. That done, Dr Gupta looked into his ears with a miniscule torch, then his eyes. With all eyes on Shaukat, all this happened without a word being exchanged. All the while,

Shaukat gazed only at Bhagwan. Then he placed two fingers of his right hand on his pursed lips and looked at a man kneeling by him.

'Ali Sahib wants a cigarette.'

'NO, NO, NO!' Bhagwan cried.

'That's POISON for him,' Dr Gupta said. 'No more cigarettes for Shaukat.' Dr Gupta brought out a little aluminium bottle of spray. 'Open your mouth and raise your tongue.' Dr Gupta squirted a spray under the tongue and handed the spray bottle to Mullah Jaffar.

'Every two hours. And no more cigarettes. NONE.'

The doctor gave him an injection.

'This will regulate your heart and stop the pain.'

Shaukat nodded imperceptibly.

'And a pill from this small bottle tonight to make you sleep. I will be back tomorrow and every day.'

'Diet?'

'A cup of tea in a while. Dal-rice or khichdi later. And no exertion. COMPLETE REST and NO SMOKING AT ALL.'

Dr Gupta stood up to go. He was bemused to see dullah Jaffar holding out a five-rupee note. He waved him away.

'I came here not for a fee, but to save the life of an old friend.'

Bhagwan took the Mullah aside for a word in private. 'Jaffar Saab, I know it is a very delicate moment. But now, everything rests in your hands…'

'I know, and I repeat the promise Shaukat Saab made to you about our boys. Upon our holy book.'

'And I repeat mine on the Gita.'

FOUR

OVERNIGHT, GRAFFITI APPEARED in bold black letters in the two languages taught in the Punjab schools – Urdu and English. It said:

QUIT PURANAPUR

Overnight, looting of locked-up Muslim shops began. Looting seemed to have received a political sanction, making it socially acceptable. *Keep in Puranapur what belongs to Puranapur* – the masterminds behind the orgy seemed to be saying. To make things worse, at the Police Headquarters in Lahore, Ashraf, the police chief of the area, never came back to Puranapur; he had been transferred to another town in Pakistan. Partap Singh had now officially become the acting chief, though with a considerably reduced force. He rounded up a large number of volunteers – strong, able-bodied Hindu and Sikh youths – gave them khaki uniforms, guns and orders to shoot at sight the looters and arsonists. His words were precise: 'We are a bit short on ammo, so use it carefully.'

His men were so careful they never fired a single shot, helping themselves along with the looters.

Because of the location of Mohammed's furniture factory, not far from the Hanuman temple right in the middle of the Hindu-Sikh enclave, Jyoti worried. For a few locked-up Muslim businesses had begun to burn. Thus far, Mohammed's *karkhana* had been left untouched. But for how long? Whispers floated around.

Mohammed's factory was one of the most valuable businesses in Puranapur. Muslims didn't want it to go to Hindu hands. For Hindus, it was a rightful property for them to possess after Partition. There were good enough reasons for either side to…

'Any day,' the whispers said. 'Or night.'

Without appearing to hear, Jyoti heard. He kept a closer vigil over his friend's factory. It would be madness. It could lead to anything. Bhagwan had now gone back to his own house, but he came daily to Chauri Galli.

'Freedom came but sanity left us.' Bhagwan struck his forehead wondering at his brother's stupidity.

'Free country now, no? So, I can go to Sikandar Road whenever I want to, no? What use is Independence if a man can't take a walk in his own bloody town?' Jyoti remonstrated.

'Call that a walk? Walking to one's maker?' Dadima also slapped her forehead, in frustration.

'And three pieces of his own flesh and blood. Forgetting mother and wife,' Rakhi said.

But Jyoti laughed it off. He decided he had to be seen as the rightful new owner of the factory to keep miscreants away.

'They would take the legs of a chair away even if its seat is missing. Such thieves that they are.'

Without people knowing about it, Jyoti took to sleeping

there every other night. This was madness, sheer and total. Partap Singh sent his wife, Ravnit, to warn Rakhi. It had no effect. Then, he came himself.

'That AHAA! They'll happily blow themselves up if they can blow some of us at the same time, sister Rakhi.'

'But why, brother Partap?'

'They are desperate because they are away from the place they call their country.'

'What's the best course for us?'

'Just keep your husband in the house, sister Rakhi. I'm telling you.'

'Mohammed gave me his factory to look after, and look after it I will. I am telling you.' Jyoti sounded obstinate.

'Mohammed is gone, never to return,' Bhagwan said.

'Bhagwan, you disappoint me. A friend is a friend.'

'Talking to you is like talking to a brick wall.'

'Someone makes a brick wall. My husband is self-made.'

'Is that so, Lady JP?' Jyoti laughed.

'Fact is, Prasadji, you are losing both ways. Muslims think you are greedy, that you are after what is their property. Hindus and Sikhs think you are a traitor,' Partap Singh said twirling his moustache.

How could Jyoti explain that he had to do what he had to do? That if he didn't, he was betraying his friend. And friendship was above everything else.

The Muslim Puranapur began to empty itself fast. The first to leave were those who had flocked to it from their villages during the last few weeks. They were seen going in hordes, in long caravans of humanity trudging through fields. They went on foot and in bullock carts. They carried on their heads massive bundles of clothes and took with them sacks of grain and whatever utensils they had. Their cows, buffaloes, goats, and donkeys – loaded up with more bundles – walked by their sides. Though everybody accepted it – those who were going and those who watched – it was a strange sight, a nightmare. Nightmares are but dreams after all. But this was stark naked reality.

Those the Muslims were fleeing from watched, from the safety of their rooftops. But for the two-and-a-half miles, it could have been them as well. Had Radcliffe's line strayed from these couple of miles it would have been them. A gut-wrenching thought, horrific and incomprehensible.

With their hearts in their throats and feeling grateful for being where they were, the Hindus and Sikhs scanned these caravans – long trails of humanity, livestock, and woodwork – disappear into clouds of dust in yonder fields. Similar caravans coming from the opposite direction passed them, both seeking safety. Sometimes, they clashed, falling upon each other with knives and swords. When it rained, the bullock carts got stuck in the mud and mire. Many of these Pakistan-bound vehicles had to be abandoned with household stuff on them intact. The countryside was becoming a scattered graveyard of half-buried bullock carts.

There were ambushes at night, sometimes in broad daylight too, of the outgoing caravans. Not by the Sant's men – he had given Bhagwan his word – but by gangs of greedy goons, both Hindu and Sikh, whose aim was not only to loot but to snatch young women.

Knowing full well that after having been so defiled they would never be accepted back by their families, these women begged to be despatched to the next world. Sometimes, depending on their mood, the marauders obliged. Many women jumped into the wells that irrigated the fields. Others got the tips of their noses chipped off, the signature perversity effected by their abductors. They were then left to wander in the wilderness to 'seek their beloved Jinnah', the cause of their plight.

Early one evening, over a dozen such young women were herded into Puranapur. Flies had settled on their wounded noses. Their hair was shorn but not by scissors. Their soiled clothes in shreds. Expressionless, they seemed to sleep-walk. Two 'volunteer policemen' with lathis and a number of onlookers accompanied them. A handful of street urchins followed, laughing and jeering.

After being paraded through Saddar Bazaar, they were marched into Chauri Galli. Jyoti was having his evening bath under the hand pump. Vishnu and Mindi worked the handle by turn. Rakhi sat by Dadima on the *takht*. When they heard the noise from the street – an unusual, puzzling kind of hum – Rakhi rose and went to the door to take a look. The crowd had stopped a good fifty yards from Jyoti's house. A couple of street kids ran around looking for a dog's drinking vessel to give the unfortunate women a drink, for no family would give a bowl from the kitchen for them to drink from. That would pollute the bowl forever.

'Hai, my mother!' Rakhi wailed loudly in shock, pity and grief. 'Hai, hai, hai!'

It was an unbearable sight.

Hearing his wife cry, Jyoti leaped from under the pump and was by her side in seconds.

'Oh, God! Where are you?' Jyoti said in English.

Suddenly, there was an influx of more people.

The women were a mere fifteen feet from Jyoti. They smelled of old sweat, damp cloth and dried-up blood. Jyoti couldn't bear to take a second look at their faces. But he couldn't help it; he was spellbound. He thought he recognized one of them, of Rakhi's age. *Mohammed's wife?* But that was not possible. He turned to his son.

'Vishnu, go fetch Uncle Partap Singh. On double hop. Tell him to bring his rifle.'

The policeman, too, was having his evening bath. He picked up his rifle and ran with the boy, without his turban, wearing only his underwear and dripping.

'Why the rifle, Prasadji?'

'Partap Singh, clear the crowd. Tell them to go home.'

Partap Singh was taken aback. He saw nothing wrong with the crowd following the women. Jyoti read his thoughts. He tried to snatch the rifle from his hand.

'Fire a shot in the air to make them go.'

Partap Singh fired a shot.

'CLEAR OFF!' he shouted at the crowd.

'GO AWAY. BUGGER OFF. FATA-FAT, AT ONCE,' Jyoti shouted.

But nobody moved. The people were staggered, though. The women were Muslim. They had got what they deserved. It was common knowledge that whatever had been done to them was being done to Hindu and Sikh women all over Pakistan. So what was the matter with the usually gentle mill owner?

'Prasadji, Muslims are doing worse things to our sisters in Pakistan,' the RSS chief Dilbagh Rai said.

'Want to see what they are doing?' Singhara said to the growing crowd, waving a handful of photographs above his head for all to see.

'Aho, aho,' the crowd chanted.

'Don't vomit your guts out.'

A barrage of abuse hurled at Jinnah rent the evening sky

as the photographs went from hand to hand. They were of naked women. They were being whipped by bearded men in Muslim clothes. They were held down. Their mouths being fouled. Their breasts being carved off.

'Where you got them photos, Dilbagh Rai?' Partap Singh asked what everyone else wanted to know.

'That all you can say, chief? Nothing about our sisters being tortured by depraved Muzzies?'

'Enough. Full stop.' Partap Singh took the photographs and tore them up. 'That's Jinnah's Pakistan. This is Mahatma Gandhi's India, a civilized country. We have fear of God and love for humanity. We are not barbaric like them. NOW GO.'

Rakhi did something unexpected. She ran and got a bowl and two brass glasses from her kitchen, pulled water from the well herself and gave the dumbfounded women a drink. This shocked everyone – a Hindu wife doing that.

Looking at the women again, Jyoti felt sure he had seen one of them before.

Mohammed's wife? But…?

The woman's face was coated with dried-up blood. She was beyond recognition. Besides, Jyoti had seen Salma only that once, a brief glimpse in the light of a dying moon. Yet…

'Sister Salma, I am Jyoti. Mohammed's friend.'

The woman gave him an empty, glassy stare.

'Say you are Salma and come home. Rakhi will look after you.'

Partap Singh shuddered. The mill owner had gone totally mad. Did he realize the consequences if he took the woman in, whether or not she was who he thought she was, and especially if she turned out to be her?

'Prasadji, these are rustic peasant women. Can't you tell? Illiterate and slovenly. Leave them to the police.'

But Jyoti did not hear him.

'You are Salma. Say you are and come…'

'I am not her.' The woman turned her face away.

Partap Singh was relieved. 'I'll put them in the boys' school for the night. Take their names and addresses. Tomorrow, we send them to the Muslim area.'

'Waste of time if you ask me, chief,' said Hirdey watching it all from his window. 'First, they won't give their names and addresses. Then, who'll have them back?'

Baffled, Partap Singh took the women to the DAV School close by. Headmaster Rama Kant, who lived in his official residence on the school grounds, was not around. So he assumed command of the place and put them in the gymnasium. None of the women uttered a word when asked about their names, addresses… Exasperated, Partap Singh bolted the gym door from the outside and went away to arrange for food from the *langar* of the Sikh gurdwara. Then, he headed to the police station to file a report. Constable Ganesh stood under an arch of the yellow-painted 1920s station building.

'Why are you arranging for food for the women, chief?'

'Can't starve them. Can I?'

'Who says starve them? Just keep them hungry overnight. Maybe they'll talk on an empty stomach tomorrow.'

Partap Singh's own stomach turned when he opened the school gymnasium door next morning. He found all fourteen women hanging by their dupattas, by lengths of the school tug-of-war rope, badminton and volleyball nets. The veteran policeman had seen death in all its horror and brutality recently. But this…

'This is the price we are paying to make two countries out

of one. But what had these wretched women to do with all that?' The simple Sikh Policeman said to the English teacher Durgadas and another master who had turned up to witness this macabre spectacle in their school. They held handkerchiefs to their noses, and it seemed they would vomit any moment. 'Why did they have to pay the price? Religion?' Battle-hardened Partap Singh felt sick to the core.

'Tut, tut,' the men nodded in disgust, troubled by an uneasiness.

More men turned up from around town. Many boys too, Vishnu and Shashi among them. Finally, headmaster Rama Kant showed up.

Some of the onlookers were shocked by the gut-wrenching scene too. 'Good heavens!' They closed their eyes.

'Best thing they could do under the circumstances,' Rama Kant said, wagging a finger. 'Needs courage, though, to hang yourself. Even if you are a raped Muslim woman and your nose is cut.'

'You don't need courage. Only a length of rope,' someone from the crowd barked.

'You need both,' another voice piped.

'Just what I need,' Partap Singh said. The women were his responsibility. What was he going to write in his report? A report for what and for whom?

The bodies had to be disposed of quickly. The heat was rising with the morning. Soon, they would begin to give off a foul odour. Partap Singh sent for Jhandoo, the Untouchable who was in-charge of disposing of the town's unclaimed dead animals. He was in the service of the municipality. So was his twin brother, Bandhoo, the town crier. Bandhoo beat a big drum hung from his neck and thundered out public proclamations. Strong, dark, the twins had taken their jobs seriously.

Jhandoo arrived in the municipal cart pulled by a huge ox.

'Tch, tch!' Jhandoo muttered disgustedly arriving at the horror scene. He cut the hanging bodies down. He needed help to load them onto his cart. But everybody looked away. For the caste Hindus and Sikhs, it was a repulsive idea: they would get polluted if they touched the corpses. More so the bodies of raped Muslim women? *Ram, Ram, Ram!* A passport to perdition.

'I say, Vishnu, let's give Jhandoo a hand. Serve humanity,' someone said in an easy, friendly voice.

Gulshan!

Vishnu knew Gulshan by sight. The boy felt a flush creep into his cheeks. It was an honour to be spoken to by his future brother-in-law. He knew he had to comply even though he was aware who the women were and what had happened to them. He also knew he would get into trouble at home for doing the scavenger's work – touching corpses, dead Muslim women's bodies at that. But no one needed to know. Vishnu looked sideways at his shadow, Shashi. Together, they helped Gulshan and Jhandoo and felt proud of themselves after it was all over. They had served humanity. They signed a silent pact that neither would tell on the other at home.

The news of the collective suicide had reached Chauri Galli before Vishnu got home. He had a question for his mother who was deeply affected by it all.

'But why did they hang themselves, Mummy?'

'Because this world is full of mad and bad men.'

'To which I should add, it is full of some very irresponsible men too. Your own father for instance,' Dadima said, casting an accusatory glance at her son.

'Mother, Mohammed was like Bhagwan to me. I'll look after his factory till…'

'Till when?'

'Till everything settles down.'

'And then?'

'I will think of *then* when the time comes.'

Their conversation ceased abruptly. For Shera had turned up. He brought sensational news. It shook the brothers to the core even if it was not unexpected.

'That Shaukat. Is gone.'

The brothers looked at each other, the same thought resounding in their minds: 'Now what?'

Leaderless, with no one to keep it on a tight leash, how would the AHAA respond? With its newly acquired weapons, it was bound to go on a rampage as a parting gift before all the Muslims of Puranapur departed for Pakistan. However brave, the RSS did not have a matching arsenal. Nor was it likely to be the two groups battling it out between themselves like two armies in a battlefield. Now, all things pointed to whoever dared attack first... It was a question of stealth and timing.

Whichever way the brothers looked, disaster loomed large for Puranapur. It became imperative that they talked to Mullah Jaffar again, even though the good Mullah had confirmed Shaukat's promise to him and vice versa. At the same time, they would look in at the RSS for double reassurance.

Public meetings were banned. But the well-built, young RSS activists still met every evening and held their militia-type drills. They sang songs of heroic patriotism, hairs on their cheeks and forearms standing on end with high emotion. They did so boldly in the backyard of the Hanuman temple. Pandit Shri Ram left these Sevaks, in white shirts and khaki shorts, to their own devices and shut the temple gate. One evening, he let in two unexpected visitors.

'Prasadji? What a pleasure!' Dilbagh Rai did a namaste to Bhagwan, wondering about the purpose of the Congress leader's visit. It was well known that the RSS wildly opposed the Congress on certain issues of national importance. It considered the Congress to be too soft on Muslims.

'The pleasure is all ours, Dilbagh. Good evening, gentlemen,' Bhagwan said in English to the assembly of fifty odd volunteers. He carried a cloth bag the sort one took for shopping.

'Good evening, sir…'

'You are wondering why we are here?'

'You are always welcome, sir.'

'It is so heartening that you brave young men keep watch every night.'

'Our duty to serve you, sir.'

'But with bravery must go caution and restraint.'

'Of course, sir.'

'With the passing away of the League leader, things are going to change at the Toofan Mail speed. No one knows anything. But we little men can make a big difference.'

'We trust your judgment, Prasadji.'

'I have come here putting my total faith in you.'

'We will not start anything, Sirji.'

'And that's just what we've come here to hear.' Jyoti pulled out a book from the bag – the Bhagavad Gita. 'We want you to place your hand on the Gita and just say that.'

Dilbagh looked at Singhara, then at all the fifty men around. 'Do we…?'

'Yes, we do,' they said in one voice.

'Sir, we will not start anything, but by God if they touch a single hair on your head…'

The Toofan Mail was hurtling down at top speed to and from Pakistan, carrying wagons of dismembered bodies through clouds of smoke from burning villages. Strangely, the untimely death of Shaukat Ali had a certain calming effect on Puranapur, if anything. Things were quiet, or so they seemed. Foodstuff, vegetables and fruit from the countryside started arriving in town. Hundreds of Muslims, local and those who had flocked to Puranapur from the villages around it, left every day. Hindu families watched from their rooftops. Now and then at night, they saw a house or two burning in the Muslim area. Since the RSS had sworn peace upon the Gita, these incidents were not attributed to it. People ascribed them to criminal elements who only wanted to fish in troubled waters. The RSS men with volunteers patrolled the streets every night. Life around the 'Belly' was at a standstill. It was so for fear of the dreaded, but thus far inactive, Allah Hoo Army.

The scenario in the Muslim quarters was much more harrowing. Leaderless, people knew not which way to look. They just wanted to get the hell out of there. Yet, children played in the streets. As usual, Vishnu, Shashi and other boys roamed the streets out of sheer boredom. Sometimes, they witnessed a padlocked Muslim shop being looted in broad daylight. Of late, Muslims often came to the now all-Hindu Saddar Bazaar to buy staples and other essential things. The sun still showed no sign of relenting. Two days later, under a virulent sun, Vishnu, Shashi and others, wearing only vests, stopped a chickpea seller by the Haidar Furniture Factory to buy a paisa's worth of the appetising snack. Vishnu recognized the two men he had seen there before, or rather their camera. He couldn't tell whether they were Hindu or Muslim, but they had an odd look about them, as if they thought they were being watched. Looking at the factory, they nodded to each other, wagging a finger. They also bought the snack and then parted company, going in opposite directions.

'Tonight, then. At 10,' shouted one from a distance.

'Tonight, at 10,' said the other.

It was the nonchalance with which they talked disregarding the boys' presence that seemed odd to Vishnu. But he did not think much of it. Well, not until much later.

An hour after supper, Jyoti picked up the family's only weapon, an old rusty sword, and Mohammed's keys. Rakhi wasn't talking to him. Her forehead furrowed.

'Face, pretty Lady JP. Face.'

'Five dependents. Don't understand,' Rakhi spoke at last. But tonight, she didn't place herself between her husband and the door.

'Quite safe now, Begum. Why do you worry?'

'Who is worrying? Go and live there. Go, go, go.'

'Going, going, going.' Jyoti laughed as he went.

Sometime later, Rakhi ordered everyone to the roof. But it was too hot to sleep. There was not even a hint of a breeze nor a speck of cloud in sight. The blue-black sky was stupendously clear, a vast amphitheatre of teeming pinholes that were aglow. The kids could make out the solitary little railway station half a mile away in the fields. In between was the Muslim area. Mindi was counting the new fires. The nearest was about five hundred yards from them. Still, they could hear shouting and shrieking from there, frightening them in spite of the distance.

'That would have been us had Puranapur gone to Pakistan,' Vishnu said.

'I'm going to cut off that black tongue of yours, Vishnu,' Meenakshi said.

Mindi was terrified. 'What if the flames get to our house?' he said.

'Too far, silly boy,' Vishnu said.

'How dare you call him a silly boy? He is not,' Meenakshi said, hugging Mindi.

'I saw a half-dead Musalman in the pond by Mohammed Chacha's factory today. Half in and half out of water. When an elderly man passed, he shut his eyes and pretended to be dead. But when we passed, he opened them and said "Water, water". So we gave him a drink from his own *lota*.'

'That was well done. But what on earth were you doing there in the first place?'

'Watching men loot a Muslim shop.'

'Watching men loot a Muslim shop? Wait till Papa hears about it tomorrow.' Meenakshi gave Vishnu a slap on the head in feigned anger. Vishnu didn't even bother to duck.

This went on for an hour. Their mother turned up with Dadima and issued the order: 'Bed.'

But Meenakshi and Vishnu stayed on, looking at the fires. There were a couple in the Hindu area now.

'Worse than ever. Tonight,' Meenakshi said.

Vishnu swung around and caught her by the arm.

'Meenakshi!' Vishnu yelled in panic.

'What?' Meenakshi also panicked.

'Tonight! Those men said TONIGHT!'

'Which men?'

'Two men looking at Mohammed Chacha's factory.'

'What did they say?'

'They said tonight at 10…' Even before he could finish, Vishnu ran downstairs.

'Don't go out. Musalmans will catch you,' Rakhi screamed. But Vishnu ran. He ran through the pitch-dark streets he knew like the back of his hand. He tripped over the legs of two 'policemen' reclining against a wall, picked himself up, and ran on. He raced on and on and on until he came to Sikandar Road. Mohammed's factory was in flames. Smoke filled the street.

'Papa!' Vishnu screamed. Smoke engulfed him, and tears rolled down his eyes. 'Papa!'

He ran into two men with guns at the gate. They were the ones with the camera.

'Who are you?'

'Vishnu. Son of Jyoti Prasad. Nephew of Bhagwan Prasad. The factory is burning.'

'You've come to tell us that?' man number one said.

'My father is sleeping in it.'

'Why on earth is he sleeping there?'

The big factory gate was bolted from the inside. The men fired at the bolt. The gate opened.

It was an inferno inside. Great flames leaped out of mountains of furniture fully made or half made. Jyoti was trapped on the roof of the single storey office. Sword in hand, he stood by a charpoy, trapped. He was unharmed, but there were flames all around. If he jumped, he would land straight into the inferno. If he stood on… There was no way he could make it.

'Papa! Papa!' Vishnu screamed helplessly. His father was going to burn and die before his very eyes.

'Hold on, man,' the two men shouted.

There was a long ladder standing by a wall. They made a dash to it and carried it between them. They placed one end of it on the six-foot high wall and let the other drop on the ten-foot high office roof.

'Walk, man. Walk,' they yelled.

Jyoti couldn't – the ladder had caught fire. 'I can't.'

'Walk, Papa. WALK.'

It was his son's voice that did it. Jyoti did not walk across the horizontal ladder. He sprinted across it like a seasoned acrobat. His hair caught fire. Once clear of the flames, he jumped. The men rolled him on the grassy ground and beat the flames off his shirt. Most of Jyoti's hair and eyebrows were gone, but other than that he was all right. It was a miracle. Vishnu clung to his father and sobbed bitterly. Jyoti hugged his son tight and looked up at the sky in flames and said, 'THANK YOU, SIR. THANK YOU.' Father and son then looked back at the men. But the men had vanished in the night. One of them had left his own shirt for Jyoti.

The day broke. The word spread. People came – everybody. But before all of them had come Bhagwan and his family after the big fire last night. The men embraced Jyoti, the women Rakhi. But young Vishnu was the shining star; he had saved his father from being burnt alive. He was hugged and hugged and lavished with gifts of cash like a champion wrestler. Men thrust half-rupee coins and rupee notes into his shirt and shorts pockets. Ladies waved similar notes around his head three times before tucking them back into their bosom to place at the feet of Lord Hanuman in the temple.

Besides the universal congratulations, a mega question hung in the air: who were the arsonists who had saved Jyoti and left a shirt for him to wear?

Very much a part of the congratulatory assembly, Dilbagh wished he had been on duty with his deputy at Sikandar Road last night. He had spelt out what the RSS would do if they came across a single strand of Jyoti's hair, but whoever had started the fire hadn't left many on his head. Yet, it could not have been anyone from the RSS; its leader had taken an oath upon the Gita. And the esteemed Mullah Jaffar of the Badami Mosque, the only Muslim to attend this extraordinary celebration, if only for a few minutes because his community wouldn't like it to be longer, was ready to swear by the Quran that it was not one of the AHAA.

Then who? And why didn't they want to be known? Why did they set Mohammed's factory on fire? Any of the Sant's men? No. The Sant, a Sikh, had given Bhagwan his word. And a Sikh never went back on his word. Never. And how did Vishnu know his father was in danger? When he mentioned the two men with a camera, it only deepened the mystery.

All eyes were on Jyoti. He wore a Gandhi cap to hide his almost hairless scalp. He presented a pathetic sight with a pencil line for the eyebrows. He did not know what to say. He occasionally shook his head and struck his forehead; he felt bewildered beyond his ability to understand why. His entrails churned with wrenching shock. All he knew was that he was still alive. He felt himself from time to time to make sure he was. He wanted to be alive for Rakhi, for Meenakshi, for Vishnu, for Mindi, for… And he was.

The Mullah stood up to leave. But Bhagwan managed a word with him at the door, telling him to meet when needed to. He was pleased to get a nod from him. Inside, people were still congratulating Jyoti for his God-sanctioned escape, and hugging Vishnu.

As the venerable Mullah cycled off, Bhushan turned up to congratulate Jyoti and to convey messages of goodwill from the Sunar family.

'Gift to you from Independence, sister Rakhiji. Or should I say from Lord Mountbatten and Nehru?'

'Lady Mountbatten and Nehru I would say,' headmaster Rama Kant spelled out what was common knowledge about the two. Indians were laughing behind the back of their last Viceroy. Usually highly disapproving of this sort of thing – a married woman in liaison with another man, in this case a widower – they were more so especially of individuals in high places. But now, they were delighted. For there was a twinge of historic revenge in it: India's first Prime Minister receiving the favours of its last British ruler's wife.

'Caesars' wives! What do you expect from them in this day and age? But must hand it to Nehru, crafty old cock. Fifty-eight and still flying his kite. I like that. Don't you?' Rama Kant said in English, slapping his thigh.

There was an interruption.

'Wow!' the room cried at the sight of some mouth-watering delight.

Rakhi and Maya had turned up with a large brass wok, heaped with steaming hot halva. Nobody had seen this heavenly sight for weeks! Faces lit up. Smiles broke across faces as the popular sweet dish was served in little brass bowls, the cloying smell of ghee wafting around.

'Just the thing, I say,' the headmaster said. 'The whole country is starving, and we are hogging halva.'

The halva went down well and fast. Just when the last of the brass bowls was taken away for washing, there arrived at Jyoti's door another visitor, a total stranger. Large, unkempt and fierce-looking, he had come on a horse. A sword in a scabbard dangled by his side, and he carried a long spear. His clothes were rough, musty and weather-beaten. He had been travelling in the countryside.

'Name is Jawalla. Jawalla Mukhi. From Ambarsar.'

Ambarsar? Ambarsar was thirty miles away – thirty miles

of dagger and death and rotting corpses. How did the man manage to get here alive? And what brought him here at the risk of his own life?

'Messages. For those who will pay to know of their near ones and dear ones.'

'From my sisters Laaj and Kesari?' Rakhi's face lit up. But the good news wasn't for her. The man had come to tell the Prasad brothers that their younger sister, Kaki of Multan, and her family had made it to Amritsar. Multan had gone to Pakistan. Things there had been 'four times worse than what you could probably imagine'. Only 'God's chosen few' had escaped. Kaki and her family among them.

'Stuck in a refugee camp. Living four times worse than animals. The camp is full of the sick. They have puss-ridden wounds, diarrhoea, and diseases and flies.'

'Hare Ram. Hare Krishna…' Dadima folded her hands and raised them to her forehead in gratitude to God. Then she started to cry. She cried and cried, tears of joy.

All eyes now turned to the Prasad brothers. This was miracle number two in twelve hours. But it gave rise to a serious question: what were the Prasad brothers going to do about it?

'I'll go on my bike and bring them back in a tonga I'll hire,' Bhagwan said.

'Sheer suicide, Bhagwanji,' Partap Singh said.

'True. The countryside is teeming with Muslim marauders out for revenge…' Jawalla said, cutting his own throat with an imaginary knife. '…But a sister is a sister,' he said, implying that if he could get here, the brothers would get there too, in spite of the dangers.

'At least they are safe there,' Rakhi and Maya said, giving the man the last bowl of halva. They didn't want their husbands to go anywhere.

'I'll go. I know people at our headquarters in the holy city,' Bhagwan said.

'You can't go alone. I'll go with you on our bicycles. One and one make eleven,' Jyoti said.

As Jyoti said that, all the joy of the morning flew out of Vishnu's heart. It was a jolt. He saw his mother bite her lower lips, something she always did when she was about to burst into tears. He glanced at Meenakshi and saw her chin quiver; she too was about to cry. The happy morning became an hour of mourning. A long silence followed, spreading pain in the family's hearts. Others were thinking the same thing: 'The brothers will never get there. Or they will never get back.'

The silence howled. Dilbagh Rai finally broke it by clearing his throat. He nodded at Singhara. Singhara nodded back. 'We'll come with you, Prasadji. Four ones make one thousand one hundred and eleven. A real army. No one dare attack us,' Dilbagh said.

'We've got to go because we've got to go. Our sister. Why should you risk your lives, boys?' Jyoti said.

'Your sister is our sister, sir,' Singhara said.

'What about your parents?' Bhagwan asked. He was more than pleased about the strong young men going with them. Among other things, it meant that the RSS would not get up to any mischief in their absence.

'They would want us to go if it was our sister, right? They wouldn't stop us because it is yours, right?'

'Right,' the room chorused. Hearts were touched.

'I still think it is suicide,' said Partap Singh.

Dr Gupta said the same. Hirdey, Bhushan and even Rama Kant said the same. But the brothers were going. They would cycle by night and hide during the day.

'Only thirty miles. Two days going, two coming back.

Maximum. My HQ will help get a safe tonga,' Bhagwan said.

'Settled then? Tonight,' Dilbagh Rai said.

Vishnu shuddered. He had heard that word twice since yesterday. The last time it had nearly led to disaster. This time… he didn't want to think further.

Jyoti and Bhagwan took Jawalla aside to pay his fee. People went home. Bhagwan and family stayed on. The Prasads became a joint family again.

They waited for the evening. It came far too soon. When it was sufficiently dark, the two brothers and the two RSS men hopped on their bicycles. They had packed lots of parathas and mango pickle, and they were armed to the teeth. Dilbagh and Singhara had daggers and guns. The brothers only had swords. For Bhagwan, a follower of Gandhi, the apostle of non-violence, this was the most bizarre thing in all his life – carrying a sword. People came out to wish them godspeed. They were gone a mere thirty yards when a loud, crackling voice called them back.

'Bauji, you've forgotten something.'

It was a bad omen. You didn't call someone back like that if they were setting out on an important journey. It meant bad luck. And this journey was not only important, it was also dangerous. Death lurked behind every bush along the thirty-mile stretch. The cyclists stopped. They looked back at the one with the ugly mouth.

Shera!

'Shera! You idiot!' Rakhi and Maya cried.

It had been difficult for Shera to do what he had done. He had agonized over it all day. But he did not have the courage to speak to his master about it. And now, he was going. Shera couldn't let him go without saying what he had to say.

'Bauji, what if you get a puncture or two? Thirty long miles. Night time and rough, rough country.'

This hadn't occurred to anyone.

'So what do you suggest then, Sher Singh? Speak,' Jyoti said.

'That you take the best puncture man with you.'

'Arrey, Sher Singh, what thinking, oye!' Approval for Shera's suggestion was universal, as was the admiration.

'Go get your things then,' Jyoti said.

'Oh, no. Nobody is going anywhere tonight,' Rakhi announced. Shera had called them back. It only meant one thing – bad luck. And what was bad luck these days? Ask any Muslim gang roaming the countryside for Hindu victims. 'Not tonight. No way.'

'No way,' Dadima and Maya exclaimed.

The departure was postponed until the next night.

'But what if it rains tomorrow?' Jyoti said. Then they wouldn't be able to go tomorrow night either; the countryside would be deep in mud and mire.

'In that case…' Rakhi and Maya beamed. Suddenly, they were grateful to the idiot Shera. The sisters-in-law wanted to pray. They prayed – for rain.

The morning was pleasant, but the noon blazed with an empty blue sky. As the weary town lapsed into a siesta, the colours of the heavens above underwent a pleasant change. First came a welcome cool breeze, then a procession of darkening clouds, and finally a delightful downpour. It rained hard just as Rakhi had prayed for, for a good couple of hours. It was long enough to leave a healthy deposit of mud and mire everywhere. The children were jubilant; their fathers wouldn't be able to go tonight either. Rakhi shut herself in a room to thank Lord Krishna.

'Just what you wanted, no?' Jyoti said when she came out an hour later.

'What, mud and mire?' Rakhi was all smiles. And thankful to Krishna.

'Mud and mire bring a smile to your face? That's something.'

'And what would you do to bring smiles to my face?'

'Quite a lot.'

'But what in particular?'

'Anything you say, Boss.'

'Can't you ever think for yourself?'

'Oh, *that*? Now? You know what, Lady JP? Mohammed was right. How do we Indians manage with all those kid-kiddies and what have you got?'

'Four hundred million. We don't do too badly.'

'That's what Aziz said.'

'And what do you say, ji?'

'I say anything you say, Boss.'

'I say yes. Now.'

'But where? Haven't you any shame left in you?'

'None whatsoever.'

'Then where?'

By now, Jyoti felt as he had in the first weeks of their marriage. Rakhi too. Her cheeks burned and her body ached. An echo of yearning rose in her. She longed for him to take her in his arms and lay her down on a charpoy. Rakhi hadn't felt like this for a long time. She was surprised at herself. She was also surprised that she didn't feel ashamed of herself.

'Use your head, ji.' Rakhi was breathing a bit heavily.

Jyoti used his head and took her by the hand up to the roof. He bolted the door of the *barsati*. Taking her in his arms, he laid her down on the nearest charpoy. Rakhi surprised him. She kissed him on the mouth, and she kissed him with such fury and for so long, it left Jyoti breathless. Then she clung to his neck like Mindi had done, and she cried.

'I say. Boss. What's the meaning of this?'

Rakhi cried and cried. Then she laughed. She cried while she laughed. It was rain and sunshine at the same time.

Jyoti took matters in his hands. 'You wanted rain and mud and mire, and you got a lot. What more do you want, Boss?' Jyoti buried his face in her ivory white bosom – a divine moment.

'You.' Rakhi ran her hands over his hairless head. It felt warm and smooth, like her boys' when they were born. Only bigger and harder.

'What if I don't come back?' Jyoti said a while later.

'Then I'll perform sati.'

'My silly Sialkotni.' Jyoti pressed her to him, a galactic surge of tenderness engulfing him.

'Don't go, ji.'

'I have to. My sister. You would want me to go if it was Laaj or Kesari.'

'I wonder where they are. I hope they are safe.'

'Of course. Probably in a camp in Ambarsar itself. Which is less than twenty miles from Lahore.'

'Suppose something happened to them? Not a word from them for so long.'

'How could there be? It's worse than wartime.'

'And if you…' Rakhi couldn't finish the sentence.

She knew he was not going to come back. She knew they had made love for the last time. She began to cry again.

'…I'll commit sati. I'm telling you.'

'And I'm telling you, I'll be back in four days. Then we'll lock ourselves here again.'

But going depended on the weather. Would the sun

shine tomorrow and keep shining for four days? Rakhi and Maya cooked parathas once again. Once again, the street gathered outside Jyoti's house to see off the men, now five of them. Just before they got on their bikes, spy Hirdey showed up with a happy look on his usually harassed-looking face.

'Good news, ji. The Boundary Force is coming.'

'To protect us?' the women asked.

'No, to protect the Muslims, escort them to the border.'

'But it is our own army, so rejoice,' Jyoti said. 'We couldn't ask for a better omen than this.'

Rakhi looked at Maya and both of them folded their hands on their chests and murmured a little thank you to the square of the sky visible from a window.

It was time for them to leave.

'Vishnu, you are in charge now,' Bhagwan said to the eldest male member of the extended family. 'No more snake charming. Are you listening?'

'Yes, Chachaji.' Vishnu was listening to something else as well – a distant whistle. After the men had disappeared in the all-consuming darkness, and when the children were all up on the roof for the night, Vishnu jumped in the cool night air as he heard it again. 'Meenakshi, the train.'

'The train is coming. The train is coming,' they all shouted and ran downstairs to tell their mothers. They had forgotten the last time they had heard that whistle.

Dadima's leg was troubling her again. She would still churn the yogurt. To do that, she sat cross-legged. It was manageable. But she wouldn't milk Kunti today, since for that, she had to sit on her haunches like a gardener. That was painful. This morning, she churned the yogurt first. That done, she woke up Meenakshi. As ever, they had doubled up on charpoys last night. As always, Meenakshi and Mona liked that. They twittered away endlessly until they dropped off to wake together. So, when Dadima woke up Meenakshi today, Mona got up with her. They washed their faces and brushed their teeth with babul twigs. They had to be clean of hand and mouth to touch the cow. The cow was sacred and so, too, the ritual of milking her.

Dawn was just breaking. Vermillion and gold spread where mother earth met the Heavens. The girls walked barefoot on the grass strewn with pearls of dew. The tingling they felt under their feet was heavenly. They could have walked for miles. But the cow's enclosure was only fifty yards away. As they stepped out, Meenakshi shrank back in terror. There was someone there. The brass pitcher she clasped to her waist fell on her foot. She cried out in pain and the two girls turned around to run back to the house. Just then, the interloper showed up.

Gulshan.

'What, you again? Come to frighten us? Haven't you got any shame in you?' Mona took charge of the morning.

'I am loaded with it. But is that all you have to say to someone who cannot sleep, who walks the fields all night because he cannot sleep?' Gulshan said.

'Liar.'

'Do I look the lying type?'

'Oh, no. You and lies? Never. But why can't you sleep?'

'Fine question that. Don't ask me for the answer. Ask them,' Gulshan said in Urdu, pointing to Meenakshi. He had used the lovers' plural, like the great Urdu poets.

'So you have come to consult your sleep doctor about it, yeah? I know you're the idle type. I know your malady.'

'It's my heart, really. It's going, going…'

'It's not your heart. It's your head that is going.'

'You are as cruel as Jinnah, Madam Mona.'

'Enough of your clever talk. You impress no one.'

'Who said a thing?'

'All right. Consult your doctor. In that corner. A brief, brief consultation only. If my uncle came along, you would have to see a surgeon.' Mona moved aside.

'Liar,' Gulshan said. Obviously, he knew her uncle was cycling his way to Amritsar, or the daring young man wouldn't have come. He took a bewildered Meenakshi's hand and pulled her behind a mountain of hay. 'Liar, cousin Mona is.'

'Why did you come?' Meenakshi tried to hide her puzzlement.

'Because my heart aches. The more I think of you, the more it aches. And I think of you every moment of my life. So I cannot sleep. So I need my doctor.' Gulshan placed Meenakshi's hand on his chest and his own around her. Danger bells began ringing in Meenakshi's head.

'And I suppose your heart still aches.'

'Oh, much, much.'

'Really? Much, much?'

'But getting a little better. The closer to my doctor it gets, the better it feels. True.' Gulshan drew her closer. This was getting to be too dangerous. Meenakshi knew what to do. Run. But her eyes were closed. His too.

'True you can't sleep?'

'Totally true.'

'Why not?'

'Because I think of you all the time. Do you ever think of me?'

'Sometimes.'

'Only sometimes? See? I knew you don't care.'

'Don't say that.'

'Meenakshiji, I cannot live without you. I love you so utterly and totally.'

'Me too.'

'When do you think they'll marry us?'

'Does it matter?'

'Doesn't it to you?'

'No.'

'It more than matters to me. Because I am dying…'

Meenakshi could feel he was dying. Suddenly, she too began to die. Now was the moment to run. Run, girl, run. But she couldn't. His lips had found hers and…

'Shall we run away? Elope. Lovers' prerogative.'

'Funny boy.' Meenakshi laughed.

'Meenakshi mine, I am totally thine,' Gulshan said in English. 'Can I come every morning to tell you that?'

'No. How did you know you'd find me here with Mona?'

'I didn't. I came in answer to an inner voice.'

'What, have you become another Mahatma Gandhi listening to inner voices?'

'In the evenings, then?'

'No.'

'Pray, why not? Till your papa comes back.'

'Because…'

'I am head over heels for you.'

Mona coughed loudly. She was worried; they had been together too long. They would get discovered. Then?

'All right, Mr Patient. You are cured now. Off you go,' Mona said.

'One minute, Miss Cruelty.'

'Go quick, quick before my mother sees you. She'll break both my legs.' Meenakshi opened her eyes.

'Just another minute. Just want to say one more thing.' Gulshan held on to her hand.

'Say it quickly.'

'I am head over heels for you.'

'You've already said that. Go now.'

'Only one more thing. Can't wait to get married.'

'You'll just have to.'

'What if something happened before that?'

'But what? Hasn't everything happened already?'

'The AHAA. Rumour is they are planning to give a parting gift to Puranapur.'

'Uncle Hirdey says our army is coming.'

'I am fed up,' Mona half-shouted, reappearing. 'You've both gone mad. You more than him, Meenakshi, you fool. And you Mister Third Rate Patient, this is a respectable family. Get going. One double hop. One, two, three…'

'All right, all right, all right. One, two, three…'

Gulshan cleared the mud wall with one hop and jump.

The train had come from Pakistan via Amritsar. It brought hundreds of destitute Hindu and Sikh refugees, who slept the night out in the open under the stars on both sides of the railway line. The train's arrival caused much excitement in Puranapur; the world seemed to have rediscovered the *railgadi*. The bustle at the station grew all through the morning. To add to the return of the train there appeared in the town's main square an army truck removing fear and uncertainties from people's minds.

'Our army! Our army!' The chorus grew. Now everything was going to be all right.

The truck had come from Railway Road. It had twenty-five Gurkhas – fierce, light-skinned soldiers from Nepal. Holding their rifles, the faces shiny, smooth and expressionless, they looked around for possible trouble-makers. People lined up the streets to greet them. The truck ground to a halt in Chauri Galli, because there was an obstruction. The municipality's prize ox, Sarkari Saandh, the mighty black ship, blocked it. When the Sarkari Saandh stood like that – broadside, imperious and menacing – traffic came to a halt and a crowd gathered. The great hulk made no exception for the fabled soldiers of the Indian Army. It made for an amusing sight.

'See? The Boundary Force has come,' Hirdey said.

'How many Gurkhas you think they sent, Hirdeyji?' someone asked from the curious crowd of men and boys.

'Must be a hundred or two at least. Partap Singh has gone to the station for a meeting with their commander.'

'Is he an Angrez? Must be, if he is a commander.'

'No, he is as desi as you and me. Captain Kaul. More a boy than a man. Partap Singh has asked me to join them.'

'Can I come too, Hirdey Chacha, to see? I want to become an army commander when I grow up,' Vishnu said expectantly.

'Commander Wasp Balls, eh?' Shashi said and received a kick in his backside as Ravi and Vijay guffawed.

After a while, the massive beast condescended to let the army squeeze past. And the people went up to their roofs to see what the rest of the army was doing at the station.

They were disappointed. There was no army, only one little jeep. Hundreds of refugees sat on their haunches under the shed of the railway station warehouse. Lucky for them, there were two wells with drinking water in the adjacent fields. Hundreds more sat idly under shady trees all around, many of them cooking on improvised fires. Minutes later, the same army truck arrived. The Gurkhas jumped out of it, and with the help of scores of men, they started putting up tents. There were scrambles and scuffles as families tried to get into a tent as soon it was pitched up. There were only twenty or thirty tents, but scores of families. They drifted into town and knocked at every door for food and clothing. Living from hand to mouth because of what they were going through, the people of Puranapur still gave as much as they could. Some gave much more than they could spare.

In his father's absence, Vishnu did something he knew Papa himself would have done. Without his mother's permission, he took the mill keys and went to their flour mill with Balla and Judge. There was plenty of wheat, but only one sack of flour, that too only three-quarters full. Grandly, Vishnu doled it all out to whoever turned up. He felt mighty pleased with himself when he dished out the last half seer of the white powder gold to an old woman, enough for ten chapattis. He was bubbling with joy when he arrived at Chauri Galli. There was no one at home; the members of the two Prasad families seemed to have suddenly disappeared. Only his mother and Dadima were there, doing this and that in the kitchen.

'Mummy…' Proud and beaming, Vishnu told them of the great good deed he had done, his father's son.

'Hai, hai, hai, my mother!' wailed Rakhi. There was a mere two days of flour left in the mill owner's house! Then? Then famine. 'Hai, hai, hai,' Rakhi cried, aiming a barrage of slaps at him. She had never hit her son in anger before. Now she did.

'Ma?' Vishnu could not understand. 'What's the matter?' the boy was dumbfounded.

'Starvation. That's the matter.' With a hundred hammers already at work in her head, this was the last thing Rakhi had ever even imagined – starvation. Rakhi slapped the philanthropist right, left and centre.

'What came over you, silly stupid boy? What am I going

to give you all to fill your tummies?'

'Mummy, the refugees had nothing to eat. I did what Papa would have done.'

Ignited, with no idea when her Nath would return, Rakhi did not know how she was going to feed the family once the flour ran out. Yet, one half of her felt proud of what the stupid boy had done. The other half filled her with fury. How was she going to…? She raised her hand again, but Krishna intervened.

Maya and the children were at soap maker Phoolan Devi's a few doors away, because a travelling astrologer had dropped by. Having had their fortunes told, they all turned up just then. Vishnu was saved from more slaps.

'RAKHI! I have enough atta for a whole month at home,' Maya yelled.

Hundreds of refugees in rags scoured the streets for food and throw-away bits of cotton cloth. Strangely, though not locals, they somehow went only to the Hindu and Sikh neighbourhoods. Thousands of Muslims, meanwhile, had rushed to the station, clutching bundles in their arms and carrying more of them on their heads. They had been waiting for this day, for this moment. Deliverance was at hand. The train had come. It was here.

Being a 'refugee train', it was twice as long as the Puranapur train usually was. But it was still not big enough. Those who did not get seats, squatted on the floor, or decided to travel as straphangers. Hundreds more perched dangerously on the carriage roofs. No one knew when it would leave. It didn't matter for the moment. What mattered now was that they were out of the ghettos, on the train with their beloved ones. The steel reptile on rail would soon be on its way, taking them to a new life. It had to. They had waited so long for it. What difference would another hour or two make? They were Indian, or *Pakistani* – same thing – they knew how to wait. So what if the heat was rising? But what was the dumb stationmaster waiting for? Arms clasped behind his back and looking troubled as always, Nanda was waiting for word from 'advance'. He was waiting for 'clearance' from Vatala. But the telegraph was cut. So how could he get 'clearance' from 'advance'? Only he knew or did not know.

'Maybe the order will come by bicycle.'

As Nanda waited, tempers suddenly flared up. Arguments erupted. In a totally spontaneous move, those in the station warehouse and sitting under trees on either side of the rail track, and those on the train clashed. One of those spur-of-the-moment outbursts with no one to blame; it got out of hand. Many Muslims and some of the Hindu and Sikh refugees were armed. The Muslims had weapons of all sorts, including guns and grenades, which they began to put to use without any thought of consequences.

The hand grenades proved useless because they could travel only a short distance when thrown, which the refugees on the ground ran away from. But the refugees fired back with greater effect at people on the train's roof as sitting ducks. The result was many casualties, mostly among the Muslims, and absolute chaos. The RSS or the AHAA had nothing to do with this unpremeditated and unplanned battle. But it had been witnessed from rooftops and the news of Muslim casualties, hugely exaggerated, spread faster than the sound of gunshots.

In a flurry of activity at the station, the young army commander, boy-faced Captain Kaul, only twenty-three, a handsome Kashmiri Brahmin, gave an order to his men to open fire – not at the people, but well above their heads in the air. A machine gun began to rat-tat-tat, from the top of the single-storey station building.

In Chauri Galli, the Prasad children watched from their roof. It was exciting, the sound of guns firing and the rattle of the machinegun no one had ever heard before. But it lasted a mere few minutes. The young officer ordered Nanda to move the train five hundred yards out of the vicinity of the station. It was all quiet again and it being too fiercely hot on the Prasad roof, everyone came down to a cooler ground-floor room with Khus-Khus blinds and a ceiling fan overhead. Just as Vishnu and Shashi relaxed away from the sultry heat on the roof, Ravi turned up at the window, grinning broadly. He had come with hot news.

'More of those women in Saddar Bazaar. Come and see,' he said to the cousins.

'Which women?'

'You know?' Ravi whispered the R word. 'Come and see.'

Vishnu and Shashi leaped out of the window and ran with Ravi to Saddar Bazaar. A long procession of idle bazaar men and barefoot young boys was making its way up the usually bustling but now empty business centre, empty due to the afternoon heat. Twelve or fourteen women in tattered clothes walked at its head. They were heavily shrouded. People could still make out that their heads were shaven and that they had wounds on their faces blackened with soot or tar. It became instantly clear who they were. Partap Singh and Ganesh walked alongside, less like policemen and more like mourners. Oddly, there was no jeering.

For some reason, Sarkari Saandh happened to be there, idling away. He blocked the advancing procession. Inspector Partap Singh had to send for Jhandoo, the beast's handler. Everybody waited. Everybody talked of the same thing: what would Partap Singh do with these women after what the last lot had done? There were many suggestions.

'Put them on the train and send them to their Pisstan.'

'No room on the train even for an extra fly.'

'Who in *Pisstan* would have them back, anyway? No one.'

While they waited for Jhandoo to arrive, housewives leaned from their balconies on both sides of the bazaar to take a look. They held their earlobes in deeply felt pity, sorrow and consternation at what had been done to the desecrated and abandoned women.

'But why, brother Partap, does everyone look as if they are going to their own father's burial?' one woman, moved by the chilling sight, asked the policeman from her balcony.

In a melancholic whisper, the policeman explained the irony. 'These are not Muslim women.'

The shock of it! Raped Hindu and Sikh women in the heart of Puranapur? Hadn't the town had its share of the Indian tragedy? Hadn't it had enough?

'Why didn't these poor things do in Pakistan what those Muslim women had done in the DAV School here?' a street lout mumbled.

'Chief, what are we going to do with them?' Constable Ganesh asked his boss.

Ganesh's *Chief* was damned if he knew. The boy-faced Captain had ordered him to take the women away.

'Police responsibility, DSP Sahib. Not the Army's.' Captain Kaul had called him 'DSP' instead of 'Inspector'. Partap Singh had been flattered. He could not refuse. But now he wanted to kick himself.

Nearing the English Book Depot, they saw headmaster Rama Kant with an umbrella, coming their way on a bicycle. He saw. He guessed.

'Where are you taking them, Inspector Sahib?' he asked pedalling past. Without knowing it, he had answered his own question.

'Your school, Headmasterji.' Partap Singh hadn't really thought about it. But the school was as good a place as any, even if its record was not.

'And leave a long rope lying around,' a brute from the crowd remarked.

A few men laughed. The policeman's nostrils flared in anger. He had recognized the voice. 'Judge!'

Judge stood arm in arm with Balla by the open sewer lining one side of the bazaar. 'What if your own mother were among them?'

That was not fair either, for Judge's mother had died when he was five. He was brought up by an aunt. Whether it was fair or not fair, Partap Singh gave him a kick up his backside all the same for good measure. It was also to set an example.

Jhandoo arrived, riding pillion on someone's bike. He carried his whip. When Sarkari Saandh saw it, a visible shiver ran through his shining black coat. He began to lick Jhandoo's hand with his pink, sandpaper-like tongue and followed him like a puppy.

Partap Singh took all the keys from the school chowkidar. He selected a few boys, Vishnu and Shashi among them.

'Lads, go get food. Beg, borrow or steal. Good food.'

The boys were overjoyed to be given such an important task. They ran. Partap Singh ushered the women into the school hall and locked its two doors, but there were windows. He couldn't do anything about that. As the crowd began to call it a day, he called Balla and Judge back.

'Judge, race your arse to the Widows' Ashram. Ask boss woman there to send help. Come right back with helpers.' He posted Balla and Ganesh at the hall's entrances.

The Widows' Ashram was a high-walled enclosure of some fifteen mud huts. It was built in response to Gandhiji's *padayatra* across the region a few years ago. For the frail man in loincloth, such tours of a place on foot was a powerful way of communicating with the people, setting off reforms. The Ashram housed Hindu and Sikh widows and their children.

'No one goes out, no one comes in,' the policeman firmly said, staring at the remaining onlookers.

He went away to do something he should have done the last time – inspect the school. He double-locked the science room, which had jars with POISON written on them. He put padlocks on the notorious gymnasium entrance and exit. After rendering the rest of the building harmless, he came and sat down on the school's elegant veranda with pillars and arches. Before this architectural marvel, there spread out a picturesque garden – rows of flower plants, vines and creepers. The mild breeze carried the fragrance from the flowering shrubs and bushes. In stark contrast was the foul-smelling *ganda nala* going past the school boundary wall like a moat.

'We were better off under the Angrez,' the policeman muttered.

'What are you saying, Inspector Sahibji?' Balla sounded shocked.

'I am saying, why did Pakistan have to happen?'

'Best thing that ever happened to India. When gangrene sets in, you cut the foot to save the body.'

'But you don't cut the head off to remove the headache, do you?'

'Also true, Chief.'

'So, what do I do with this headache in the hall, Balla?' Partap Singh stared at Balla for a long while. A thought crossed his mind and a smile lit up his handsome bearded face. But it was so absurd it made him laugh.

Knowing who the food was for, housewives around Simla Hill gave generously. The boys collected more than enough. But the heavily shrouded women wouldn't look at the food. At his wits' end, Partap Sing urged them to help themselves. But no. He begged them to eat.

'Eat, sisters. Eat. The boys worked hard getting it.'

But nobody even looked at the stuff.

'Partap Singh, you know who you are? One hundred and one fools. That's why you went to the station to acquire this headache,' he cursed himself.

Judge arrived with four women from the Widows' Ashram. They all wore white, the colour of widowhood. Three of them were in homespun khadi clothes – kurta, salwar, the coarse white dupatta draped over the chest. They were all in their thirties. The fourth wore a white muslin sari. A little older, she was buxom and good looking. Her name was Sita. Everyone called her Mausi Sita, or Auntie Sita. The first thing she did was dismiss Partap Singh.

'You go. Men have done what they had to.' She sounded unduly angry.

The policeman was dumbfounded; usually he did the dismissing. But he couldn't believe his luck. He handed over the keys, twirled his moustache, and turned his back on the school. Ganesh, Balla, and Judge followed, like a defeated army with its general happy at his humiliation.

'You boys, come right back. You too, Judge. Hang around,' Mausi Sita was specific. It was an order. Mausi Sita took her assistants inside the hall and shut the door. Judge and the boys put their ears to the cracks in the wooden door.

'...A woman's self-respect is paramount for her. You've

lost that. You've lost everything…'

'How's she going to make the women eat with a lecture like that?' Shashi said.

'Shush,' Vishnu said.

'…Mother India, they say! What is Mother India? Who is Mother India, the ever suffering? I'll tell you who. You are. You have suffered what no living woman can even imagine. You are India's shame and sorrow. But Mother India is proud of you. You are her, alive…'

Vishnu was moved by those words. He rubbed his eyes.

'Didn't know wasps could be sissies,' Shashi whispered with a finger on his lips.

'Shut up, Cousins Wasp Balls. And listen,' snapped their sailor friend Ravi.

'…You have a choice. You either live or you die. You eat, and you live. You don't, and you die. Simple. No one cares for you. So, you have to care for yourselves.'

There was a long silence. Then the door opened partially. The boys peeped. The women were eating; only two of them weren't, one a girl. The boys felt glad. They felt rewarded. They hurried away. They saw someone coming through the trembling heat waves rising from the dusty white school hockey field, a little mirage. Mindi. He carried a cloth bag.

'What are you doing here in this heat?' Vishnu chided.

'Mummy has sent this bag of mangoes for the women.'

'Mindi *munda*, good *munda*,' Judge said, lifting him sky-high. 'The best.'

'Judge.' Mausi Sita appeared with an empty bucket. She ordered him to go and fill it up at the school hand pump.

'What's your name, boy?' Sita said to Vishnu when Judge returned.

'Wasp,' Shashi answered for his cousin.

'Wasp, go give everybody a drink inside.'

'Why me?'

'Because I say so.' Sita gave Vishnu a tin can.

Being close to these women bothered Vishnu, even if they didn't look at him. Vishnu had a morbid thought. It was too morbid for words. Suddenly, he thought that the women looked like his mother, each and every one of them, even if he couldn't see their faces. This worried him.

After giving the women water, Vishnu took Mindi's hand and they ran. Out on the veranda, Sita stood watching them, Judge in particular. As she looked, the same thought crossed her mind that had stirred Partap Singh while staring at Balla not so long ago. Only, she didn't dismiss it.

'Judge, go tell that foolish policeman to come right back. He shouldn't have gone away.'

'But Mausi, you yourself told him to go.'

'Don't talk back, man. Just do what you are told.'

Partap Singh was at lunch when Judge arrived with Sita's message. He took a long sip of *lassi* and belched loudly. He was annoyed. That woman! Who did she think she was? Lady Mountbatten? Not bad looking, but a proper red chilli in the arse. The provisional police chief of the place was not going to be ordered around like that. He waved Judge out of sight. He downed the rest of the yogurt drink in the tall brass glass polished to a glimmering shine, with ash from the hearth, by his wife, Ravnit. Burping another couple of times, he lay down for a couple of hours to beat the heat. He fell asleep immediately.

Judge came back two hours later. He told Ravnit Kaur that Mausi was furious. She had waited all day. Not wanting to disturb her husband's sleep, Ravnit had turned him away. Judge, the idiot, turned up for the third time. Partap Singh had just woken up.

'Mausi is boiling. Better send the Inspector Sahibji. Otherwise…'

'Otherwise what?'

'Otherwise she'll come here herself, the Chief Inspectoress that she thinks she is.'

Partap Singh put his police turban on and went.

Sita was indeed in a foul mood, her face red like a tomato. But the cop knew how to handle such women.

'Why waste anger on me, Madam. These women are no longer police responsibility. Anything else I can do, I will. Tonight, they sleep here.'

'And tomorrow and the day after? You are abandoning these unfortunate women. You are heartless.'

'Not my responsibility.'

'Full policeman, maybe. An inspector even. But you are not even half a man.'

'Tongue, Mausi, tongue. Don't take advantage of being a woman.'

'Don't Mausi, Mausi me. I am not a day older than you. And I am doing the talking. Not you. We've got a bad problem. I am talking of a solution. So be quiet and listen.'

Partap Singh was hypnotized. No woman had ever spoken to him like that. It was her voice – full of anger and steel. He dropped his gaze from her handsome face to his own police shoes. It made listening easier. Sita took him to a classroom. They talked there. It was a useful talk. It even became friendly as it went into the evening. They had found a solution.

'Just what I have been thinking about all day,' Partap Singh slapped her on her round bottom. 'Some woman. Some special woman, our Lady Sita.' He slapped her again. This time, he let his hand remain.

'And watch where you put your hand.'

'Oh where? Here? Ummm…'

'I'll pluck that beard off your face if you touch me again. Get that in your head.'

As the evening approached, a light cloud rolled over Puranapur's blue skies. Another, a shade darker, descended on Rakhi. While the cloud in the sky dissolved soon, the one hovering around her hemmed in. It had all started with that idiot Shera calling Jyoti back. Even though she had been grateful for it at the time, the net result had been the same – Jyoti had to go.

Rakhi busied herself with housework. It didn't help. Every other minute, she saw the silhouette of her husband in the dark of the jungle, wounded and crying, 'Why did you let me go?' She cried inside. But she knew he had to go. His only sister.

But what about her own sisters, Laaj and Kesari in Lahore? There hadn't been a word from them – no letter, not even a post card, though she had sent them three. But how could there have been, with post offices shut everywhere and letter boxes stuffed up?

Were they still alive? Yes, they were. They had to be. They must have escaped in time. Their husbands were men of the world. One was a government contractor, the other an engineer in the PWD, both well-to-do and well-connected. They too were probably stuck in a refugee camp in Ambarsar. In that case, why didn't they take the train last night? Maybe they didn't know about it. Maybe they are sick like the man Jawalla Mukhi said. Maybe her man would find them in the very camp his sister Kaki was in. Maybe they would be on the next train to come here. Whenever Rakhi thought about them, it was torture.

She was jolted out of her reverie by a shout from the veranda by Dadima. 'Rakhi *beta*, my legs. Send Vishnu.'

'Vishnooo,' Rakhi shouted in the air. 'Dadima's legs.'

Vishnu hated Dadima's legs. It was not that he hated her legs as such. He hated what he had to do to them every other evening. He had to massage them with *electricity oil*. This liquid was known to have a special healing capacity no other oil did. A pint bottle of it from an electrical transformer a friend gave Jyoti for Dadima's massages. This friend worked in the local power station.

Massage done, Vishnu had to walk on Dadima's legs and the rest of the body as she lay on a charpoy. He and Shashi had to do this often. They held a slim bamboo pole from their shipping company to steady themselves as they navigated Dadima. Dadima groaned every session. But that only meant she was loving it. As now.

It had been a strange day. The Gurkhas, the refugees, the gun battle, the machinegun *rat-tat-tat* and the women. The women in particular. What made Vishnu think they all looked like his own mother even though he hadn't seen anyone's face? Perhaps all heavily shrouded women of a certain age and size looked alike. Like Muslim women in burqa. Vishnu had seen them so often in Saddar Bazaar before the troubles began. Sometimes he had wondered how their families could tell who was who. The ten-year-olds were sure that the Muslims had an esoteric way of knowing who was behind the veil. However, that was before the two communities went off to live in their separate parts of Puranapur. Now, those women never came to Saddar Bazaar.

With the image of the shaven-headed women and a girl

hidden under shrouds in his school flashing again and again, a horrible thought struck Vishnu. It was so horrible he could have drowned himself in the smelly *ganda nala* for thinking about it.

While Shera's mother slept on the roof under the stars, Balla spread his charpoy in the street like every other family that did not have a roof. Every night in the summer, Chauri Galli became a clutter of charpoys stretching from one end to the other. Families slept only a few yards apart, within earshot of each other. Lots of stories and anecdotes flew around. There was no traffic after nightfall. Only bicycles walked by men could get through the narrow lanes cluttered with charpoys. Nobody really felt crowded. It felt good. It felt safe.

Just as Balla was about to doze off, Judge appeared from the darkness. He pulled him up and suggested a walk. There was nothing unusual about that. But for some reason, Balla felt something was off tonight. Maybe Judge wanted something.

'Independence came. But it brought no fun.'

'Meaning? Which hole are you speaking from?'

'Meaning we can't move an inch beyond the *ganda nala* since Shambhu went. Everybody is still scared shit of the Muzzies. Call that fun?'

'So what do you suggest?'

'Nothing. Only prove to ourselves we are not scared.'

'Judge *beta*, sometimes I don't understand you. Sometimes, I wonder which hole you talk from.'

'You would if you had what men call guts.'

'Back hole. Definitely, bloody fool.'

'Forgotten your grandmother? Forgotten Pandit Shambhu?' Then Judge said something in a whisper.

'No.' Balla was short for Balram. And Balram was the elder brother of Lord Krishna. Balla had never betrayed his name. He never lied, nor ever hurt anyone. 'No. No.'

But Balla was prevailed upon. When the street began to snore, Judge took him out to a mostly empty street. He took him to the back of a big house.

'You sure it's empty?'

'Sure as your gran is dead.'

The two climbed over the garden wall. Judge forced open a ground floor room and flashed a torch around.

Glass cases full of books and an accordion-type table lamp had a thin layer of dust on them. Other ground-floor rooms were equally done up with heavy expensive furniture.

'Rich people keep their valuables upstairs,' Judge said and led Balla up the stairs, a feeling of doom throbbing in his heart. They were about to be caught and shot.

Judge went to work on a window. It opened with a click and Judge said 'Jump'. The torch lit, and they landed in the room with a thud, coming face to face with an elderly woman. She stood on one side of the window, her hands raised above her head and an axe over Balla's head. Her mouth and eyes were wide open. She was hypnotized. She came alive when Judge flashed the torch in her face. The axe fell from her hands. Hurriedly, she undid the cord of her salwar. The garment fell in two neat circles on the floor next to the axe. Then the woman ran to the bed, the torchlight following her every move.

'Take me. Take me. But don't kill me,' she yelped, spreading herself on the sheets, facing the ceiling.

'Don't touch her, or I'll behead you.' Another voice.

Judge swirled his torch around, and they saw a man a little older than the woman. He held aloft a long, naked sword.

'You will?' Judge said. He advanced and simply took

the weapon away from the mesmerized old man as if it was a sugarcane stick.

Judge looked at Balla, and Balla looked at Judge. Next minute, they were back in the street, Judge laughing his lungs out and brandishing the naked sword as he made his way to Aunt Janki's house.

If that was funny, what was to come in the morning was not. A policeman came.

'Up, up, opium eater,' Judge's aunt woke him up. '*Odder* from Partap Singh. Wants to see you at once.'

'But?' How could the dreaded police have known they had gone looting? Knowing the bearded bastard, he shuddered.

Judge shuddered again as he came within sight of the source of the 'odder'. The spot where he had received the kick yesterday began to hurt again.

'Wasn't my idea, Inspector Sahibji,' he blurted out straight away.

'Never is. Always someone else's,' Partap Singh said.

'True, chief. Swear on my dead mother's head. That scoundrel Balla insisted.'

'We'll find out. We have our ways and means. Best advice, come clean.'

Judge knew the monster's ways and means. He came clean. The monster couldn't believe his luck. He twirled his moustache and cleared his throat.

'Very serious – looting. I can have you both shot…'

'But Sardarji, we took not a thing. Touched not a hair of anybody…'

'…Or put you inside for one year minimum.'

'…Not even a shirt button. Guru-knows-all truth.'

'Truth is, a guilty man would say anything to save his hide. But Judge boy, you don't have to say anything. I'll do all the saying. Point being to get you out of trouble. What friends are for. No?'

Now Judge was puzzled.

'A handsome young fellow like you should not languish in jail. He should be getting married. Making sons. No?'

'Problem is, nobody wants to give me their daughter. My aunt has tried. I'm ever a layabout like Shera and Balla.'

'But you would like a wife, though. You can have one.'

In one second, Judge knew. He panicked.

'Go pick one. Have first choice…' Partap Singh undid his left boot and placed it on the table in front.

Judge started to shiver.

'…Go choose, I said. GO, GO, GO.'

Terror struck. Judge did what was natural under the circumstances. He took flight. Partap Singh picked up his rifle and fired a shot in the air, scattering away a thousand little birds from a massive peepul tree, a common sight. Judge came running back.

'Gift from Pakistan. Write a thank-you letter to Jinnah in Karachi.'

'But Inspector Sahibji Maharaj, my aunt won't let me have a wife who's been raped.'

'Either that or a bullet or the jail. Tell her that.'

'Can I ask her to choose? I'm hopeless at this sort of thing, chief.'

The thousand plus little feathered angels flew around the school building a couple of times. Then swiftly, they swooped down on the same tree, like iron fillings attracted to a powerful magnet.

Judge was barely out of the school garden, leaping over the *ganda nala*, when Balla arrived. He came from the school gate where Ganesh stood guard. He didn't see Judge. It changed his life forever.

Partap Singh sweet-talked Balla for the first five minutes, fiddling with his boot on the table. Then he went to the point. Bewildered, Balla gasped for breath.

'Inspector Sahib, I can't take a wife who's been fucked by dirty Muzzies. I am a God-fearing Hindu. I'll become polluted for life, an untouchable like the Muzzies.'

'Of course you will. How can you demean yourself by marrying one of THESE women?' Partap Singh said gently, with great understanding. Then he roared. 'But you can rape a poor, old Muslim woman in her bed in front of her husband and then finish them both off!' Partap Singh glared, his mouth frothed – a mad dog in a barking fit – spittle flew on to Balla's face, which Balla did not have the courage to wipe off. This sudden burst of anger shocked Balla. Its genuineness frightened him.

'What you talking about, Chiefji?'

'Of rape and murder in a Muslim home last night.'

'Mistake somewhere, Inspectorji. You know me. Couldn't hurt a fly sitting or flying. Someone made a serious mistake.'

Partap Singh stood up. He picked up his boot and flung it at Balla with mighty force. Balla ducked.

'You made the mistake, Balla bastard. You. Boy from my own neighbourhood.'

'Swear, Sardarji. Swear by my dead gran. Swear by you.'

'Go choose, and I'll forget what you boys did. Wait till Shera hears about it when he gets back. He is going to get the red chilli of jealousy in his backside about you both getting wives just like that.'

'No one goes in. No one comes out,' Ganesh barked.

The school gate was closed. Ganesh stood there like a black cobra guarding a treasure chest. Vishnu had to think of another way. He walked away. Just then, he saw Balla coming out of the school gate.

'What are you doing here, Balla, so early, early?'

'Nothing.'

'Looks like you are coming from a funeral.'

'No. I'm going to one. My own.'

'Meaning?' Vishnu was sure someone had beaten up poor Balla. He liked Balla. Everybody liked Balla. Then who would have done that to him?

'Meaning? A gift from Pakistan.'

'You are talking in riddles, Balla. Tell me…'

Balla hurried away, and Vishnu didn't press him for an answer. Vishnu knew half a dozen ways of getting into his school undetected. He opted for one that was the surest but also the most hazardous – a leap across the *ganda nala*. He cleared the sewer in one jump.

Today, the school's prize Flower Garden didn't look its effervescent best. Monsoon foliage grew where it had never before. Long grass and unruly bushes dotted the front lawn. Several women sat under the shady trees. They sat singly or in twos or threes. They did not talk. They just stared vacantly.

Vishnu picked his way with great care. He couldn't afford to be seen. He was not seen. There was a large *langra* mango tree in a corner, headmaster Rama Kant's personal possession. Boys were not allowed even to be seen near it, for its fabulous fruit was the prerogative of the headmaster. It deterred no one, and only one-tenth of the crop ever reached the headmaster's house. Today, the tree was fruit-laden with just one ten-year- old around. Under this tree sat she who Vishnu had come to see in answer to that horrible thought that had troubled him so much. The girl with a shaven head and a face blackened beyond recognition. She was alone, contemplating her bare feet. Vishnu stole his way behind her. The element of surprise was all-important. If he was wrong, as Vishnu knew he was, the girl would not respond and he would leap back over the dirty moat and go home happy. If she did… Vishnu could not think beyond that point.

'Sharda…' Vishnu said in a whisper.

Startled like a doe, the girl swung around and saw Vishnu. Hurriedly, she adjusted her tattered scarf on her bosom and threw it around her head. Her chin quivered and large tears rolled down her cheeks.

'Sharda, don't cry.'

The girl cried and cried. As Vishnu came near her, she shot up and ran towards the school hall. Mausi Sita appeared, as if from nowhere, and caught Vishnu by his shirt collar. Vishnu tried to free himself. But Mausi was strong. She gave him a hefty slap on the face, bringing tears to his eyes.

'Peeping at these destroyed women from behind the bushes? Goonda lecher at your age?'

'Swear not. Swear by God.'

'Peeping Tom voyeur…' She gave Vishnu another slap.

Vishnu was overwhelmed physically. But being the wasp he was, he managed to fly away. Sita ran after him, causing much noise and commotion. The other women stood up and a ruckus started. Vishnu was over the three-foot school wall and about to leap across the *ganda nala*. He slipped and landed in shoulder-deep goo of human plus livestock excrement and domestic waste. He was coated with the stuff when he reached home, emitting clouds of revolting smells.

Vishnu knew what was coming and in which order. First the hullabaloo amidst jeering and laughter from every direction – north, south, east and the west of the extended family. Then, an angry lecture from his furious mother and a few half-hearted slaps. Lastly, a good long scrub by her under the hand pump and his clothes dumped in the garbage bin. In that order. Vishnu bore it bravely. Perhaps too bravely. That made Meenakshi suspicious. Something was wrong. When he was put in dry clothes, he took her aside and said, 'Auntie Laaj and Sharda are among the women in my school.'

'Silly, stupid boy. Have you no shame saying such things?'

'Saw them yesterday. Spoke to Sharda just now.'

'Silly, stupid, shameless boy.'

'Think for once, Meenakshi. Why would I say such an awful thing unless it's true? Think.'

'But how can it be? Lahore is a long way away.'

'I don't know. But it's them. Dead sure it's them.'

'What about auntie Kesari?'

There were too many questions. All too horrific. One question haunted them both: should they tell Mummy?

'Not till we are absolutely sure, Vishnu. Absolutely.'

'I am. Absolutely. But I'll make double, triple sure.'

It was difficult to leave home. Mummy was all eyes. 'Set one foot outside the house, and I'll tie up both your legs till your wedding day. Go have a nap,' Rakhi said after lunch when she saw him try to sneak out.

A treacherous shroud of languor hung in the suffocating air. The red-brick veranda was too hot to walk on barefoot. In the glare of the merciless sun, looking out the window hurt the eyes. All the children went to the front room on the ground floor for the daily siesta. Vishnu lay down next to Meenakshi. But he couldn't sleep. Nor could she. They tossed and turned in the room darkened by Khus-Khus blinds. Vishnu saw two tears trickle down Meenakshi's face. Slowly, they turned into a stream. Vishnu took her hand, unable to stop tears flowing out of his own eyes. Mindi and their cousins saw. They also started shedding tears silently. They were weeping for their fathers. Finally, the heat got into their limbs like a drug, like water and gravity, and sleep came. When Vishnu awoke, it was very dark. Evening had set in. Vishnu ran.

Once again, the school gate was out of the question. Along with constable Ganesh, another policeman was posted there. Vishnu did what he had done twice earlier in the day, once with humiliating results. He took a deep breath, a long start, and a leap over the smelly mucky trench that stood between his school and the rest of the world. He made it like a stag and looked to his right and left.

All clear.

All was clear, but all was not right. For something was going on around the grassy grounds of his school. Something strange and surreal. Many men were assembled there. Pandit Shri Ram among them.

Pandit Shri Ram of the Hanuman temple.

The priest sat cross-legged in front of a small fire leaping out of a steel bucket, chanting holy mantras. The fire had a sacred smell associated with religious ceremonies. On one side of the fire sat quietly fourteen rough looking men, Balla and Judge among them. On the other were fourteen women, whining. Partap Singh stood behind the men. Mausi and her enlarged team behind the women.

'Gift from Pakistan.'

The penny dropped. Ten-year-old Vishnu dashed straight into the ceremony. The women cried out. The men stood up. The priest shut up.

'Wasp? You again?' Mausi shrieked.

'Uncle Partap…' Vishnu dragged the policeman by the hand. Breathlessly behind a bush, he told him…

This was too fantastic for words. Even for war, peace or Partition, this belied all credibility. How could it happen? How did it happen? The only thing Partap Singh knew was that he had to do something about it and now.

'Vishnu, son, open your mouth to no one till Prasadji returns. Not even to your mother. Especially her, you hear? Now go, run,' he said and went back. After a quick word in Sita's ear, he quietly dismissed two men and led two women to a classroom.

Not to risk jumping over the *ganda nala* with the stinking leap of the day, Vishnu ran to the school gate. Outside it, he collided with constable Ganesh. The two fell.

'Left your eyes at home?'

It was not Ganesh.

'Vishnu? What are you doing here?' It was Gulshan.

Vishnu knew not how to apologize enough. It was all too obvious how he felt. 'Don't worry, Vishnu. My fault. I was not looking. Next time I leave home, I shall take my eyes with me.' Gulshan laughed. 'But what are you doing here at this time? What's going on in your school? Certainly not classes?'

Vishnu thought fast. *If I can't tell my very own brother-in-law, who else in the world can I tell?* Vishnu could not stop himself. Nor the flood of tears that accompanied this extraordinary tale.

Now it was Gulshan's turn to think fast. 'First, let's find out what is going on.'

Taking Vishnu's hand, he led him back to the school veranda. There, among the arches hid Rama Kant and master Durgadas behind a pillar. Unknown to them, Gulshan and Vishnu shielded themselves behind another column to watch. Then the priest's voice came over, an incomprehensible mumbo jumbo, the Sanskrit mantras. He chanted them mechanically like a gramophone with a cracked record. Trees and bushes leaped to life as violent shadows each time he poured a ladleful of ghee into the fire. Flames flickered, shadows lurched, Vishnu's heartbeat pounded.

'There it is. History unfolding itself in the flesh,' Rama Kant said to Durgadas.

'Meaning what, sir?'

'Meaning these women are the body of India – defiled, violated, mutilated.'

'At least they have a future now, sir.'

'Yes, a future of a sort in the hands of men hastily rounded up by an incompetent bully, men who happened to be around, like India's leaders.'

'For once, Partap Singh is doing a fine job, Sirji.'

'Like that *Mouthbatten*. Handing it over to those available in a hurry.'

'Don't agree, Janab. Our leaders are great men – Nehru, Patel, Maulana Azad…'

'Like that Pandit, that Sita woman, that fool of a policeman, those sad yobs. Doing through conscience or coercion, thinking they are doing the right thing.'

'Where do these women fit in this equation, Sirji?'

'The women are like India herself. Accepting what is done to them.'

'History, sir, history.'

'History is living itself out before us,' Rama Kant went on, wretchedly.

'Too much philosophy, sir.'

'This is what happens when people having lived together for thousands of years decide to part ways, let a total stranger draw a border within the country. That border is actually a line of blood. These women are the outposts of that line, pointing out that if you scratch earth for a new border real blood is spilled. The Mahatma knew that, he opposed Partition. The last Viceroy and the first Prime Minister should not have accepted it. They'll be gone soon, but India will suffer forever like these wretched women.'

'Philosophy, sir. Must write a book about it.'

'Oh, shut up, Durgadas. Just watch.'

What his teachers said was mumbo jumbo to young Vishnu, though not to Gulshan, who was struck by the truth of the headmaster's observations. But the two were spellbound by what was taking place around the sacred fire. The ceremony continued. The two men turned away and literally sprinted through the school flower beds to leap over the foul-smelling ditch lest the foul-tempered tyrant call them back.

Gulshan took Vishnu's hand and led him out of his school. In Vishnu's face, he saw Meenakshi's, tears streaming down her comely cheeks. He would have given anything in the world to be with her if only for a moment. He put an arm around Vishnu and led him away from his school, his chest throbbing with a deep longing to see Meenakshi. He had to see her. But how? Just when his beloved needed him the most, he couldn't be by her side.

They came to a street hand-pump. Gulshan made Vishnu have a quick wash to cleanse his tear-soaked face.

'Listen, Vishnu. Hurry back home to be with Meenakshiji. Don't let her know you've cried. Promise?'

'Promise.'

At home, his mother sat cross-legged on the floor, praying to the colour pictures of the gods – Shiva, Rama, Krishna, Hanuman and Guru Nanak. She didn't chant any mantras this evening, though she knew a few. Her favourite was the Gayatri mantra, an all-time, all-purpose hymn. Rakhi had learnt it as a child, even before she had learnt the alphabet. She had been told to chant it at all times – when she felt troubled, when she couldn't sleep, when she wanted something desperately. The mantra always worked.

Usually, Rakhi murmured the mantra to herself, only her lips moving. She didn't do that this evening. Nor did she pray in any of the languages she knew – Punjabi, Hindi or Urdu. Punjabi was her mother tongue, but she always prayed in Hindi. Punjabi seemed too common, vulgar even. Urdu, patronized by the courts of Muslim nawabs, could not be the right medium for prayer. Hindi, derived largely from Sanskrit, the language in which the ancient texts were written, was her preferred language.

Rakhi looked at the gods with pleading eyes. She left it to them to deduce why she was looking at them like that. They had given her a body. The body needed to breathe to survive. With begging eyes, Rakhi pleaded. Finally, she spoke:

'Just this one thing and never again shall I ask for another. Send him back to me.'

Rakhi closed her eyes. She could still see the gods. Sometime later, when she opened them, she saw Meenakshi sitting behind her. Around them sat Dadima, Maya, Mona, their hands clasped on their chests like Rakhi's. Then, all the children came and settled down around them, and Dadima began the evening prayer: *Om Jai Jagdish Hare*.

The Prasad brothers were not at all religious. Their families never sang the evening prayer. But today, it happened just like that. Today, it was more than a prayer. It was a conversation with the gods, a physical need. They felt less lonely, less forlorn and more hopeful.

Just as everybody rose, Vishnu arrived. His usually round face looked long. His forehead was creased like his mother's when she was distraught. One look and Meenakshi had guessed. Her chin quivered and tears nearly beat her resolve not cry. Yet, all she wanted to do was hug her mother and cry and cry. She did just that, puzzling everyone and no one.

Balla and Judge walked side by side. Their wives walked three paces behind them.

'Shera is going to get the chilli of jealousy up his backside about us getting wives just like that,' Judge hissed and wished he had not said that. It was flippant of him, and he hadn't meant that.

Balla didn't answer. He knew Judge was right. If there was anything in this world Shera wanted it was a woman. Balla would have given anything for him to have been around and got married instead of him.

'What are you going to do?' Judge whispered.

'Don't know.'

'Funny. God gives you a wife after all, and you don't know what to do?'

A hitherto unknown kind of excitement bubbled in the young men's bodies in spite of the bizarre circumstance of their *marriage*, one of history's most unusual. Neither of them had yet seen his wife's face; the she-wolf of a Mausi had done the choosing. She had turned Judge's aunt away for being 'too choosy', saying it was either that or a year inside for her nephew.

'Will you?' Judge nudged Balla.

'Will I what?'

The two friends looked back. Their wives, even though their faces were covered, looked young – twenty or so – and firm of figure. They arrived at Simla Hill. They would have to part their ways here.

'Won't you?' Judge didn't wait for an answer and walked away, followed by his wife. Balla dropped back to be close to his.

Their silence irked him. It made him feel foolish. Balla must say something. He was the man. But say what? Balla had never held a conversation with a young woman. He did not know what to say to her. Nor had he ever been so close to one, almost touching her. It was exciting, despite everything. It was also frightening. He wished it were Shera, not him.

There was a bit of rock jutting out of the dust track that led to Chauri Galli. Balla tripped on it and fell flat on his face, hurting himself. He felt very, very foolish as he stood up on his feet again. His wife had stopped a few feet behind him.

'We've been married good and proper by Panditji around the holy fire. It was God's decision; that's why Partition happened. I'll be a good husband, wife,' Balla said to hide his embarrassment. He was surprised at himself for being able to say anything at all. Calling her *wife* seemed strange. So far, he had thought of her as 'she' or 'her'. But it sounded better. It reduced some of the vast distance that existed between them. Balla went on.

'We are God-fearing Hindus. It was our destiny. They killed my grandmother too, you know?' Balla didn't even know why he said that. What did she care? Or maybe she did. Now, he couldn't stop talking. He told her where they were going. About his gran. About Shambhu, about Shera and his mother. Balla had consulted Chandri about this 'marriage', and she had given him her blessings. And when they arrived, Balla had a high-voltage shock. His wife did a strange thing. She put her arms around Chandri and broke into sobs, making his heart leap to his throat.

'Ma, Ma…' she wailed.

It was devastating. Balla was dashed. He was revolted with himself. He wished he had not married her after all and run away at the last moment. He cursed Partap Singh for trapping him into it. He cursed the old Muslim couple for not taking the train with other people of their street. He cursed Jinnah for

Pakistan, Mountbatten for Independence, and Judge for last night's stupidity. Above all, he cursed himself for agreeing to it.

'Ma, Ma…'

'Balla, go see a friend for an hour,' Chandri said.

Balla did not want to see anyone. He went and sat out a couple of hours on Simla Hill. Fed up, he walked back to Chandri's house. Her door and the two windows were shut. But there was light inside. Balla could see through the cracks in the wood. And hear.

'When it happened? Where it happened?'

'Many nights ago. The train from Lahore was stopped at a river crossing. They dragged everybody out. They cut everybody to pieces. Everyone except girls.'

'One man?'

'No. Four, five, six? I fought. I bit. They beat me, Ma. You don' know how they beat me. Ma, look…' the girl started to cry. 'They stuffed my mouth. They tied my hands. One man sat on my face and… Oh Ma! Send me somewhere to die. I beg you.'

The girl spoke very clearly. She was educated. Balla felt ashamed of himself.

'Why didn't they kill you?'

'They did. Thinking I was dead, they threw me in the river. Why I didn't drown? I don't know. A dhobi found me next morning washed up on the bank. He handed me to an army truck with many women like me. They put us in a small camp for women, at the Attari border. After a few days, we were sent to a very large camp in Amritsar, where there was no place for women. Then we were put on this train.'

'Have you got the belly?'

'No. I was in my monthly.'

Balla looked through the crack. His wife was his age and good looking. She had mango-shaped breasts. He had to admit the she-wolf had chosen well.

'Listen girl, what's your name?' Chandri finally said.

'Sarla.'

'Sarla, nothing was done to you. You did not want it. So, nothing was done to you. Understand?'

'What are you saying, Ma?' The girl was aghast.

'Balla is alone in this world. He is an innocent boy. His innocence will purify you.'

'What are you saying, Maji?'

'I know what I am saying. You did not will it. You did not want it to happen. So, nothing was done to you. Nothing. God knows it. I know it. Balla will too. Make him a good wife.'

After Dadima had milked Kunti early next morning, Meenakshi, Mona – she had to be taken into confidence – and Gulshan met in the cowshed. Mona kept watch.

'You know our shame now.'

'There is no shame. It's a tragedy.'

'What will happen now? What to do?'

'Do nothing till your papa comes back.'

'What then?'

'God who inflicts wounds also heals them,' Gulshan said.

'Some wounds kill. People die of them.'

'We will survive them. Your aunt and cousin will survive them. In time, all this will be forgotten. We and India will be strong again. The future is before us. It has just begun.'

'What a beginning!'

'Yes. What a beginning, indeed. When your papa and uncle return, they will take matters in their hands. They are men of the world. Important men, both.'

A thought that could not be dressed in words crossed both their minds at the same time. It was an ugly and deeply painful thought. What if they did not return?

Meenakshi crushed an end of her dupatta and bit it to stop tears trickling out of her eyes. Gulshan longed to take her in his arms and press her to his heart and take away all the sadness from her and quell the great storm in her bosom. Meenakshi too longed to be in her lover's arms. As if being there would give her the strength she needed.

'Do you still want to marry me?' she whispered.

'Meenakshi, the breath of my life. Why do you say that?'

'I don't know. Partition. It has come into our home. Between you and me too.'

'But how? Meenakshi, my Meenakshi. If it was yesterday, I would have lured you into my arms with silken words to kiss you and tell you how I adore you. But today, there is nothing I want, only to be here, with you.'

'Be with me.'

'I am. Totally.'

'Be with me more. Forever.'

'I am and will be. Forever.'

The Prasad brothers came back early that evening. With their bicycles, they came by train, a refugee train. Inspector Partap Singh was on the platform to oversee the arrival of refugees. The brothers noticed that he didn't look his usual warm, friendly self and seemed to avoid eye-contact. By him stood the smart and open-faced Captain Kaul – the only army officer for miles around – looking a little bewildered to be the centre of attraction of so many people. A station porter was sent to find a tonga for the Prasads. Their heroic guards – Dilbagh, Singhara and Shera – cycled off home straight away. After embracing the Prasad brothers and still avoiding eye-contact, the Police Inspector did the introductions.

'Leading pillars. Mr Bhagwan Prasad, our Congress Secretary. Elder statesman Mr Jyoti Prasad, the brain behind the successful joint funeral initiative I told you about, Captain. They lit the flame of peace in Puranapur.'

'I guess we'll be seeing a lot of each other,' Captain Kaul said in English over the handshakes.

'I look forward to that, Captain. Come and see me any time you like,' the Congress leader said.

The introductions had to be brief, because the brothers had to take their sister and her family of four exhausted children home. The two-hour journey had been tiring; the train absolutely jam-packed and suffocating.

The train had brought more refugees, hundreds of them. The Prasad family could have come a night earlier. But the extra-long train specially created for the Puranapur line had to be sent west across the new border to fetch the Hindu and Sikh refugees. Hundreds of thousands of them were stranded in the new country, as hundreds of thousands of Muslims were interned in similar camps this side of the new border. Disillusioned and ravaged, the camp-dwellers had begun calling the new countries *Piss-stan* and *Hindu-shit-stan*. One in three wouldn't make it.

The arrival of the brothers, their sister Kaki, and her four children – her husband, a bank officer, had gone on to the head office in Delhi – created quite a furore. Before leaving Amritsar, Jyoti had bought something special to take home. Two big baskets of laddus, from a famed sweetshop outside the gleaming Golden Temple. Four laddus were sent to every house in Chauri Galli the moment they arrived. Jyoti himself took one hundred and one rupees to the Hanuman temple for thanksgiving.

The evening thus advanced in a flood of tremulous joy with Jyoti changing into fresh clothes after a quick bath under the hand pump. Bhagwan followed. A convivial mood set in, marking the relief at the return of the men from a difficult outing. A lively evening of laughter and warmth. Still Dadima cried hugging her only daughter. She cried uncontrollably holding her grandchildren. Then everybody hugged everybody else and laughed. Everybody except Meenakshi and Vishnu. Their hearts were crying. Their minds numb. The same question assailed them: *Do Gulshan and Partap Singh know our father is back? If they do, what next?*

Vishnu was sure they did. In fact, the whole of the town knew that the Prasad brothers were safely back, as people had come from every street to congratulate them. Later in the evening, just as Partap Singh was getting into his civilian kurta-pyjama, Gulshan came to see him, looking grim.

'What are we going to do, Inspector Sahib?'

'I was just about to go see Jyotiji. But don't think it's a good idea.'

'You are quite right, sir.'

'I think I'll wait till the morning. Let them sleep well tonight after such a terrible trip, son.'

When morning dawned, Rakhi announced she was going on a fast to thank Lord Krishna. She bathed early and dressed with care. She put on the sari she had worn on her wedding night. Her bridal sari was made of shimmering scarlet silk with flowers embroidered all over it in gold thread. Rakhi wore it on very special days. On her face, she rubbed Afghan Snow; the summer cream gave her fair complexion a new glow, emitting a soothing fragrance. Her boys wanted to kiss her cheeks. She wore lipstick and a red bindi in the middle of her forehead. Then, she put a little vermillion powder in the parting of her hair and pinned a small gold brooch to her hair over her forehead. She looked so beautiful, Mindi proposed to her.

'Mummy, I want to marry you when I grow up.'

On another day, Vishnu would have said, 'Me first. I'm older. My right.' But today, it hurt him to see his mother adorn herself and make herself so impossibly beautiful not knowing what a blow was waiting round the corner. He knew that Meenakshi was being equally tortured. Obviously, there was nothing that Gulshan could do. What the sister and brother were thinking of was what Partap Singh would do. Everything was in his hands now.

Last night, Partap Singh had suggested waiting until morning. But when the new day came, courage left him. He did not think Jyoti's house was the right place for this horrendous revelation. Nor did he feel that Jyoti was the one he should first speak to. Who then?

'Bhagwan,' Ravnit Kaur suggested.

Gingerly, Partap Singh sent for Bhagwan. It was an imperious request, the policeman asking the Congress leader to come to see him. Bhagwan was puzzled. But he went, thinking it must have something to do with the AHAA.

'Don't know how to put it, Bhagwanji…' Partap Singh said when the leader arrived and tried to drag words out of his own mouth. 'I really don't know how to put it, Bhagwanji…' But he managed.

It was unbelievable. Bhagwan had never heard of anything stranger in all his life.

'What to do? How to tell Bharjai Rakhi?' Bhagwan was

completely stupefied.

'And who will tell her? Has to be my brother himself. I'll ask my son to go find Vishnu. He can quietly bring Jyoti here.'

There was no need to send for Vishnu. He stood outside the open window, listening. He had followed his uncle. He did what he was told.

On seeing his brother in the policeman's house, Jyoti knew instantly that something was very wrong and that it had nothing to do with the Allah Army. Yet, it was something bad, and it had something to do with him, Jyoti. After making small talk about the trip to Amritsar, the policeman went straight to the point. A deep, revolting shock clouded Jyoti's face and distorted his features. The absence of eyebrows had made it a little fairer. But now, it became ash-white and sickly grey. Partition had entered the very walls of his home. It had already destroyed Rakhi's sisters' lives. Now it was about to rack hers and his.

'Bhagwan…' That was all Jyoti could say. Uttering his brother's name fortified him. It was an admission of total helplessness. It was also a plea. *What to do?*

'…Bhagwan, let's go and bring them home.'

'But?' the policeman and the politician said, implying a question. It was a sinister question, an ugly question. *But what about the world? What about the Prasads' name and standing?* They would become instant outcasts.

'No but-shut. Let's go.'

'Think, Prasadji. Think.' Partap Singh had a brainwave.

'Think of what?'

'Think of it like this. Nobody knows what really happened. Nobody needs to know. Not even sister Rakhi herself. Not for the moment at least.'

'Tell her what, then?' Jyoti could see her all done up like a beautiful bride, surrounded by her young admirers.

'That they have just arrived on an army truck. That they were separated from their families and that nothing else happened to them.'

'You are mad. People will see. They'll know. Rakhi will know.'

'People will see, yes. But they won't know. They don't have to. Leave it to me. I'll requisition Tota's tonga and drive it myself. Who will know?'

They went to Vishnu's school. Laaj was unrecognizable. Once the epitome of feminine beauty, grace and glamour, she now presented a piteous spectacle with a half-blackened face, shorn hair and clothes in tatters. She put her arms around her daughter and the two sobbed uncontrollably. It was awful. This mutilation, the disfigurement of beauty. The two brothers broke down loudly in a series of hiccups. Standing behind them, Vishnu wept silently. Even the diehard police inspector couldn't stop the tears rolling down his bearded cheeks.

'All right, all right, Sister Laaj. Let's put behind what's happened. Lord Krishna will give you the strength to do so,' Jyoti said, taking charge.

In reply, Laaj started slapping her own face violently. Jyoti and Bhagwan held her hands to stop her from injuring herself further.

'Come home now and bathe and put on clean clothes.'

'No. I can't show my face to my sister now. Send us to another town to die. Why did they send us here?' Laaj sobbed.

It had happened by chance. After the train from Lahore had faced the wrath of the rioters, and after the assailants had killed their victims and subjected the younger women to the most barbaric violation before abandoning them, they were picked up by a detachment of the so-called Boundary Force. The army handed them to the Indian police at the Attari border post. The police shunted them from camp to camp and finally put them on this train that came to Puranapur. It had happened all by chance.

'All thinking done, Sister Laaj. Meaning, nobody knows. Nobody need to know. And I have a tonga outside.' The policeman's voice was reassuring.

They went. Partap Sigh did a clever thing. To make the world think they were coming from where the Boundary Force was, he drove Tota's tonga to the station first. And when the horse-driven carriage arrived in Chauri Galli, that's just what the world thought – refugees from the train last night. It had a shock, though, when the vehicle stopped outside the mill owner's house and its passengers went inside. The house issued a loud burst of wailing: 'Hai, hai, hai! Oh God… Oh, God. No, no…'

'Looks like someone dead arrived,' people said.

'Or worse than dead,' Tota said. He knew it all. But he kept his mouth shut at Partap Singh's orders. Just then, the man himself came out and explained in a mournful whisper.

'Families of Rakhiji's two sisters. Murdered at a river bridge before Attari. All of them. Only one sister and one niece escaped by hiding under corpses. Just come in a special army truck from Ambarsar.'

'Hai, hai, hai!' the crowd lamented in a collective wail. 'Hai, hai, hai!'

'Oh, God, what has happened to you?' cried neighbour Phoolan. 'Where is your heart?'

'*Doston*, go home. Leave the poor family to grieve in peace and quiet,' Partap said with utmost gentleness.

But nobody moved. People could feel the Prasads' pain.

They were hugging each other and crying. Faces were anguished. More people came and many of them went inside the house to offer their condolences. Lastly came someone special – Dulari. She came with her sister and brother. The onlookers in the street made way for the important widows. Dulari and Piyari sat down cross-legged on a rug, with the women on the covered veranda at the back. They started doing what the other women were – beating their chests and weeping. They stretched their hands, touching the shoulders of those sitting in front, and kept beating their chests. Children watching were deeply moved. Although Vishnu had witnessed this ritual of collective mourning before, he was more than touched. He was bewildered.

Bhushan sat with the men in a room out of sight of the women. The men just sat there in silence, as if they were waiting for something to happen. Custom demanded that they sit there long enough to convey their sympathy. Custom also demanded that they do not stay there too long. Especially the Sunars. For as yet, their boy was only betrothed to a daughter of this house. An hour later, they left. And Vishnu noticed that although the sisters had wept a lot, their eyes were dry. Both of them kept handkerchiefs to their noses as they stepped into the street. Vishnu saw Dulari's handkerchief drop from her hand. It was shock that did it: there was not a single soul outside! The crowd that had nodded on her arrival an hour ago had simply vanished. Tota, waiting in his tonga for the Sunars to come out, had not been able to keep his mouth shut for long. The Sunars did not know. They were puzzled why people had gone away.

'I know. Fear of what AHAA might do after their losses at the station,' Bhushan said. 'What do you say, Tota?'

Tota told them. The Sunars were dumbfounded. As they settled down in the tonga for their ride home, it became clear to Dulari that they had to take an important decision and take it quickly. Now. Piyari fully agreed. Only their brother did not agree.

'Nothing to do with our Gulshan and Meenakshi. Whatever has happened has happened,' the brother said.

'That's exactly why,' the sisters said.

It had been the longest day in the life of the Prasad family, and the most painful. Evening came at last. It came abruptly. Jyoti felt suffocated in the hushed darkness hastened by the Khus-Khus blinds of his house. It became oppressive. Jyoti needed to escape from it, however momentarily. But he did not know how to. It would look odd, even heartless, to get up and walk away. This grief had to be borne collectively. What made it unbearable was the colossal lie that went with it – a shameful farce. How long before the world found out?

Unable to remain there any longer, Jyoti rose from Bhagwan's side and went out for a breath of fresh air. From his plot of land, he looked at the cause of the sudden coming of the evening – a darkening horizon. The sky, usually agreeable at this hour, had a menacing look – grey and yellow-green. From beyond the horizon, a darker shade of grey was advancing unseen. Jyoti feared he knew what it was. It made him aware of what was going on in his chest. But that feeling had been there all day long. It became a shattering commotion when he caught sight of a figure cutting across from behind his house towards him.

Hansraj, the Sunars' servant!

The man walked apologetically, as if he was ashamed of himself. He carried something in his arms, a bundle. He held it to his chest with care, as if it were a sleeping baby. Jyoti had hoped never to see that bundle again, for he knew well what it contained – his gifts to the Sunars, marking his daughter's betrothal to their son.

No words passed between them as the servant returned the engagement gifts to Jyoti. Then he bowed his head and stood on. Jyoti understood. Jyoti crushed the bundle in his hands and walked calmly back to his house. The courtyard, the veranda, and the rooms rang darkly with silence. The house was exhausted by the day's tears. Jyoti went to his personal almirah and hid everything there. The diamond ring Dulari had given to his daughter was kept on a tuft of cotton wool in a silver box to be officially put on her finger at the fire ceremony. The turmoil in Jyoti's heart turned into an ache as he held it. He went out and gave it to the man.

No one saw this exchange. Nor did Jyoti tell anyone, not even Bhagwan. Jyoti did not believe what had happened was real. The only real thing was the sudden emptiness, a void of pain. How can a void be real? Yes, it can, like that of the sky. For Jyoti felt it. He wanted to conceal it from himself, but couldn't. Therefore, it was real. He felt too close to the world. The wounded animal he was, he needed to be alone with his pain. He had to rush to a dark corner of the jungle to lick his wounds. But Jyoti did not want to go far from the house; that would make the situation worse. He knew where to go – to the roof of the house cradling a cherished memory. The darkening horizon looked a good deal different from there. The sky appeared to be in panic, like the homing birds flying crazily around, as if they were lost. Just how Jyoti felt – panic stricken and lost.

What was he to do? How would he face tomorrow, the day after…? He must tell at least his own mother. What was he trying to prove by hiding from his own family what the whole world perhaps knew by now? Maybe he should go downstairs, take Bhagwan aside, and tell him after all. The brothers had never held back anything from each other. His mother neither. How would she feel about it? Above all, how would Meenakshi feel about it when she was told?

Anger swelled up Jyoti's chest. It was not just for the

Sunars. It was for the world, for the earth and sky and the coming storm and the Hindus and Muslims and the old India and the new India. It was for yesterday, today and tomorrow. It was a faceless anger, which burned his insides, and he did not know what to do about it. What if he took a step over the roof wall? Would it extinguish the fire that raged inside his ribcage? No, he had to live for the sake of his gem.

There was a movement behind Jyoti. He turned his head. Meenakshi stood a few feet away.

'Meenakshi *beti*...?' What was she doing there?

'Came up to be with you, Papa.' A tear rolled down her cheek as she spoke. Jyoti wiped it gently with his hand. Then he put an arm around her and pressed her to him. Jyoti felt confused because he had never held his daughter like that since she was a little girl. Father and daughter stood there like that for a few moments, Jyoti scanning the grey-yellow menace far away.

'An *aandhi* is coming to hit Puranapur. This dust-storm is going to be a black, black one,' Jyoti said. He felt better for saying it – the spoken word was comforting. 'Let's go downstairs and tell everyone. But before that let's see a...'

'See what, Papa?'

'...A smile on that sad moon face.'

Meenakshi couldn't smile, though she tried. She couldn't – and she still kept trying – yet she looked more than beautiful. It broke her father's heart.

'Try harder,' Jyoti said, smiling.

Meenakshi tried. She succeeded.

Our great Hindu society is essentially very sick. It has passed a judgement on her, Jyoti thought. *It has cast her aside like an old shoe. What has she done to deserve it?* Jyoti looked at the sad horizon, then at the dark horizon of his own mind. *Our great leaders did not know what they were doing. The hurt they are inflicting on millions for their vanity… they are little men indeed.* He pushed back the lump in his throat.

Dadima and Bhagwan came up, looking for him.

'Where are you, Jyoti?' Dadima said.

'What do you mean where I am? I am here, Ma.' Jyoti had decided. He would send Meenakshi downstairs and tell them.

'Boys, take everyone away from this house of mourning. Bhagwan, take them to your house. Make a fresh start; tomorrow is a new day,' Dadima said.

'No, Ma. We all stay here together. I cannot bear to let anyone go anywhere else,' Jyoti said.

Jyoti did not send Meenakshi away. Instead, he put one arm around her shoulder and the other around his mother and led them down the stairs. His arms around his mother and daughter seemed to soothe his scalded soul. But he still faced the torturous questions: *What to do? When to tell my mother and brother? And how?*

His mother's words rang out in his head: 'Tomorrow is a new day.'

There were two gates to the Sunar *haveli*. One said IN and the other said OUT in English. Gulshan stood by the IN column. Hansraj took the OUT gate, avoiding Gulshan.

'Hansraj, come here,' he called. He wanted to know why he was avoiding him.

With the look of a thief caught red-handed, Hansraj went to the IN gate.

'Where have you been? What's the matter? You hiding something from me?'

Hansraj hadn't been anywhere. Nothing was the matter.

Nor was Hansraj hiding anything. But someone had to tell Gulshan. It better be him.

'Gulshan *babu*...' Hansraj loved the boy. He told him.

The transformation in Gulshan was terrifying. He snatched the box with the diamond ring from his servant and ran to where his mother sat – with her brother and sister at a large round table with a tea service.

'Mother, what have you done?' Gulshan said, holding the diamond ring under her nose ring.

'None of your business.'

'Whose then?'

'It wasn't easy. But we had to do it. Ask your auntie. Ask your uncle.'

'But, Mother...'

'How could I take a niece of an *achchut* woman from a family now become *achchut*, tainted, untouchable?'

Gulshan was lost for words. Anger, pain and total helplessness assailed him all at once.

'Mother, go tell them you made a mistake,' he said.

'What nonsense are you talking, boy?'

'Go tell them you made a mistake and take the ring back with you. I beg you.'

'You've gone mad, boy.'

Then, Gulshan did go mad.

'I haven't, you have. YOU HAVE,' Gulshan shouted, pulling the table cloth off with a fast flick of his hand. All crockery fell on the brick floor and broke. But the teapot remained on the table as if a magician had pulled the cloth from under it. Gulshan picked it up and dashed it against a wall.

'Hai, hai, hai. You are not my son. You are a demon. You have gone MAD.'

'Go take the ring back, Mother. Go apologize. Go say

you made a mistake.' Gulshan picked up a chair and smashed it against another wall.

'GULSHAN!' Bhushan yelled. He came and caught his arm. But the boy was strong and suddenly possessed of a much greater strength. He freed himself with a powerful jerk, throwing his uncle on the floor in the process.

'May snakes bite me and worms feed on my corpse for begetting you,' Dulari wailed, beating her chest with her hands.

'Go now, Mother. Otherwise…'

'Otherwise, what?'

'Otherwise, I am leaving this house.'

'Had your father been alive, he would have broken every bone in your body for speaking to me like this and for doing what you have done.'

'Take the ring back, or I am going.'

'Go, go, go. Go sit on the Belly of Puranapur till your own belly howls with hunger. Then you'll come running back with your tail between your legs.'

'I will not. I am my mother's son.'

'We will see.'

Numb, Gulshan went and sat on the Belly of Puranapur.

Puranapur, lying in flat low country, induced massive dust-storms. They would come a couple of times every summer, turning the town upside down, as if it were an old umbrella. Furious winds with hints of rain lashed at the parched land of the Punjab doab, whipping up a dense shroud of dust. If they came during the day, they 'put the sun to shame', so went the saying. They made 'night out of day'. Not surprisingly, they were called *kali aandhi*, or black dust squalls, followed sometimes by lashing rain. Everybody grew up hearing tales of the mighty *aandhi*s flying away a couple of people. One such tale was being told on Jyoti's large roof at the moment where Meenakshi and Mona shared a charpoy. Like the others, they too were subdued. But chirpy Mona still had enough talk left in her.

'Our friend Shanti says her granduncle flew from one end of Puranapur to the other in one such dust storm.' Mona watched her cousin closely. 'She says he landed on Simla Hill,' Mona said.

'Why didn't he take her grandaunt along? Flying grandparents – she could have boasted about them,' Meenakshi flicked a smile.

'I wish we could fly from here, Meenakshi. I really, really do.'

'You'll have the wind behind you all right tonight, Mona.'

'You really think people can fly in these winds, Meenakshi?'

'Silly, billy Mona, not even a bird can fly in these dust storms. How would a man?'

'Just asking.'

'A silly, billy question.'

People could swear a distant so-and-so of theirs had flown in one such *kali aandhi*. They were exaggerated accounts of people getting lost in them. Mercifully, those windblasts never lasted for more than half an hour or so. Rain came in their wake, cleaning the sky and everything below.

Exhausted, like the rest of the family, by the events of the day, the cousins fell asleep in no time. The others too.

People elsewhere in Puranapur were also sound asleep. But as soon as the storm unleashed itself, those sleeping on rooftops or in the streets, woke up hurriedly. They rolled their beddings, picked up their charpoys, and ran indoors.

While all the others on Jyoti's roof scrambled down the stairs, Rakhi remained there a little longer. She had heard a strange boom through the shrieking winds. Finally, she too came down to where the women slept. But there was no charpoy for her and she hadn't brought one from the roof. She took a cushion and lay down on the floor, staring at the dark wall and listening to the winds howling. Rakhi couldn't sleep. Nor could she think. What the day had revealed had impaired her capacity to think. She stared and listened. Eventually, sleep came, and with it, came hell itself.

Shaukat Ali's premature death left HMS Muslim League of Puranapur rudderless. The Allah Hoo Akbar Army had given him its word not to start anything. It was annulled now. Now, there was nothing to hold its braves back. Yet, it had suddenly begun to seem pointless, even to think of doing anything. To what end? The Muslims simply had to leave Puranapur, and sooner the better. The most sensible thing to do now was to ensure they left without inviting serious trouble. The elders knew that awesome retribution would inevitably follow were these impetuous young men to instigate some action. For once, common sense prevailed and these AHAA members too came to form the same opinion.

But even though the train had left Puranapur soon after the incident, the news of the high toll of the morning's violence at the station kept spreading. This had inflicted a deep wound on the hotheads. Only ten all together, they called themselves the True Ten.

'Death is only a way of going to paradise,' these boys proudly said.

Death for Allah was everyone's 'BRIDE'.

The day advanced in a hazy light though the sun glared relentlessly.

The True Ten met secretly in the desolate thorny Jungle. Arm in arm in a close-knit circle, they pricked their index fingers with a needle and joined their blood. Then, they took an oath: 'No one must know of our decision, the decision of the True Ten. It's to be a total surprise for our own army and for our enemy.'

They had stolen what they needed. When the day was nearly done, an omen appeared – signs of the approaching black *aandhi* – happily sanctioning what they were setting out to achieve. It could be realized only through the removal of as many of those whose kith and kin had caused the carnage of their kith and kin on board the train.

The True Ten could not very well go to the railway station to wreak havoc on the sleeping, squatting, or sitting-duck Hindu and Sikh refugees. For that would pit them against machinegun fire from the Indian Army. They chose instead a soft but sure target. They went for streets around Simla Hill made mainly of wood, such as Chauri Galli, even though it was well-guarded by gun-carrying RSS vigilantes. The True Ten struck when the black *aandhi* unleashed itself on a sleeping Puranapur. As their devices went off, the heavenly winds fanned the fires from house to house. Strangely, only six of them aged between sixteen and eighteen fell to the vigilantes' bullets. It made those four who hadn't weep. They wept not at their comrades' deaths, but at not 'getting married' along with them.

The half hour of the storm proved long enough for the fire bombs to take maximum toll in Chauri Galli and the streets around Simla Hill. Come morning, streets that last night exuded all the glorious smells of life from frying garlic and spices to the fragrance of jasmine, now smelled of charred wood and death. Smoking rubble and heaps of white ash filled squares and rectangles, which, until a few hours ago, were rooms in which people talked and laughed, cooked and quarrelled, made love and slept.

Puranapur was numbed. The sight of many of its homes and hearths reduced to rubble and ash was stunning. It was a more horrific blow than anything that had happened before; the earthquake of fifteen years ago clearly was no match. But that had been an act of God. This wasn't. This was an act of revenge in the name of God. Consequences? Punishment? Nothing mattered now. His servants had had their half hour of glory. They didn't want gold, and they were too young for women. They wanted to kill for their God and die for Him. They were well rewarded.

People wept and wailed. Then shock took over. It stilled their cries. At times, some of them clung to each other's neck. There was this collective need to weep together at the sight of what they saw.

The great umbrella of smoke over Puranapur announced its fate to the surrounding countryside. Today, no prayers were said from the tall marble tower. By the time the raucous crows, kites, parrots, peacocks and the rest had taken to the mango, jamun and tahli trees, people in the villages knew. Just after noon, the Sant with his second-in-command Gautam galloped into town at the head of two hundred heavily armed Sikh horsemen. They were in full ceremonial regalia as designed by their Tenth Guru, Gobind Singh ji, in the late 17th century – high blue turbans with black bands, flowing yellow kurtas and white churidars, colourful and fearsome. The expressions on their bushy, bearded faces were louder than the colours they wore.

The spectacle of Puranapur turned into a vast cremation ground shook the fiercest of the Sant's warriors. They rode through near-burnt-out Chauri Galli in throbbing silence.

Dumbfounded, homeless people followed. The Sant held up a hand outside Jyoti's house, its once beautiful balcony burnt to cinders and its doors and windows badly charred.

'Where is my brother Jyoti Prasad?' he asked no one in particular.

No one answered.

'Has he turned into ash too?'

People around his mount shook their heads.

'And his family?'

'Unharmed,' someone said.

'Guru be thanked. And my brother Bhagwan?'

'Alive. But burnt.'

'Take me to my brother then, you good people.'

People led the Sant to Dr Gupta's clinic in Saddar Bazaar. The usually bustling bazaar was smouldering. The doctor's clinic had, by some miracle, escaped the arsonists' attention. Two score charpoys cluttered the street outside it. On them lay men, women and children with blood-stained bandages.

People moved about among groans and cries. Dilbagh Rai, Singhara and many of their armed comrades were attending to them. The Sant and Gautam dismounted to enter the clinic. Its interior was clogged with more makeshift beds of the injured. Jyoti Prasad sat on the edge of one such charpoy occupied by a heavily bandaged figure, Bhagwan Prasad. Around it stood or sat on the floor all the women and the children of the joint family with pained, puzzled and tear-soaked faces. The doctor was nowhere to be seen. Nor was anyone else present concerned about the Prasad family. They all had their own wounds, visible and invisible, to look after. There was just one outsider among the Prasads – Gulshan, his arms around Vishnu and little Mindi. Due to another power cut, the overhead fan was not moving. The heat inside the room was stifling.

Jyoti's quaint-looking balcony had been the first to catch fire as a fire bomb landed on it. The women had all hurried down with the children. They had herded them out safely through the back veranda to his plot by the cow shed. To make sure no one was left inside the house, Bhagwan had dashed back inside. By then, a hand grenade on the balcony had exploded; the impact was so severe that the glass almirah containing expensive crockery and other valuables fell on the unfortunate Congress leader, a man of peace. Dilbagh and Singhara were guarding Chauri Galli. They saw the two attackers attempting to throw another fire bomb at the Prasad house. Seeing the vigilantes, the teenage marauders went for their guns. But before the volunteers could take aim, they fired at them, missing. The next moment, Dilbagh and Singhara shot them down.

Dead silence descended on the room when the Sant and Gautam entered. Jyoti stood up and Bhagwan stirred.

'Who comes?' Bhagwan said through the bandage on his face, his voice faint, his eyes shut.

Jyoti and Sant embraced. It was the embrace of mourners. The Sant did not like the mill owner much because of what he had said to him at their last meeting. But seeing his friend Bhagwan in the state he was, and after hearing about the attack on the Prasad home, his heart went out to him.

'What have they done to my brother, Jyotiji?' he said, his face fuming with anger, his chest heaving.

'You can see with your own eyes what they've done to him, Sant,' Gautam said.

'I will make them pay for this. By the Guru, I will.'

'You shouldn't have started it that night, Santji, burning Mohammed's factory,' Bhagwan said with half a voice.

'It was not me, my brother. I swear to you. I'll do anything to prove it.'

'Will you? You call me your brother, so do just one thing for me then.'

Bhagwan sat up, surprising everyone. The Sant bent down and kissed his bandaged head.

'Anything. Name it. Say it.'

'Do you swear?'

'I do.' The Sant and Gautam knew what Bhagwan was going to say: *wipe out those who turned much of the town's core to ash.* This was exactly what the Sant was going to do in any case. One half of Bhagwan desperately wanted the Sikh warrior to do just that. But his other half, the ardent devotee and committed disciple of the Mahatma was strictly against it.

'Return with your lions to your villages. Let the Muslims of Puranapur go to their Pakistan,' Bhagwan managed to say in a loud whisper.

'WHAT!'

The Sant had seen it all. The badly burned Congressman was a very sick man, sick in the body and now, suddenly sick in the head. He stood up straight, ready to leave. He bowed to touch Dadima's feet and made respectful obeisance to the other women. Smiling, the Sant affectionately patted Vishnu and Shashi. He wanted a word with Jyoti and made a sign to him to come outside.

'I don't understand my brother Bhagwan. Hasn't the Congress done enough for the Muslims, given in to all their demands?'

'This is not giving in to any demands, Santji.'

'It's worse. They firebombed our homes, killed our parents and children and very nearly the Congress leader himself, who now tells me to let them go? Is he mad? What does he think I am? A gutless coward?'

'Bhagwan has the highest regard for you.'

'Bhagwan told me he had Shaukat Ali's word Allah's army wouldn't start anything.'

'Why they did it, we really don't know, Santji.'

'But I do. Hate. Others will learn about it later.'

'What do you want to do then, Santji?'

'I want them to shiver and shit in their pyjamas tonight.'

'Perhaps they already are, Santji.'

'Whether they are or not, I have to do what I have to do. Send them to hell. I'll return tonight. *Rabb rakha*. God bless.'

Without another word, the Sikh warrior left. He took his men to the railway station. He was told that the army there was conferring with the police. A couple of hundred men and boys followed. At the station, he chose to stop where the railway line ended a hundred yards on. The men and boys thronged the platform, watching. From the other side of the track, the refugees too watched the Sant and his colourful men from their tents, now quite a colony of them. In between were the Gurkhas, a mere handful of them, the rest were helping out in the half-burnt town, and their youthful commander Captain Kaul with clear-cut handsome looks. He had been told on the wireless that another Gurkha unit was on its way later today. Feeling deeply relieved, he was discussing this with Partap Singh on the station porch. Earlier, he had inspected Puranapur, and his heart had been torn apart by what he had seen. It had shattered his belief in the natural goodness of human nature. The young man barely out of teens had uttered just one word to his escort of four Gurkhas accompanying him that summed it all up.

'Madness.'

'No, Saa. It's evil in man,' replied one of the equally shattered Gurkhas.

Yet, as he surveyed the disturbing scene before him with the policeman and his Gurkhas, the young officer was as self-assured as he had been trained to be, fully aware of the gravity of the situation. He did not like the look of horsemen. They meant mischief, and they carried an air of danger about them. Captain Kaul could see trouble ahead. The Sikh police chief Partap Singh fully agreed. The captain ordered the horsemen to move on: 'Go back to your villages.' After some hesitation, the Sant and his men moved. There stood grandly near an ancient peepul tree by a pond a hundred yards away. The horsemen defiantly stopped under it. They answered the boy captain in a loud shout:

Khoon Ka Badla Khoon
Khoon Ka Badla Khoon!

This was what the people on the station platform had come to hear. They took no notice of Partap Singh when he told them to disperse.

'DSP Sahib,' the youthful officer called the policeman and talked to him for a minute. Partap Singh wrote it down in his notebook. He tore out the page and gave it to Bandhoo, municipal town crier who shadowed him. He had come with his drum suspended from his neck, resting on his rotund belly. He beat it with two cane sticks and, in a loud and clear voice, he read out twice what was written on the paper – once for the horsemen and the second time for the others:

BY THE ODDER OF KAPTAAN KAUL SAHIB OF THE INDIAN ARMY, AN IMMEDIATE CURFEW IS HEREBY IMPOSED ON THE TOWN OF PURANAPUR. GO HOME AT ONCE. ANYONE SEEN IN THE STREETS AFTER THREE O'CLOCK WILL BE SHOT.

Nobody moved. It was a 'bogus odder'. What about the people

whose homes had become charcoal and ash? Where were they to go? Anyway, there weren't enough policemen and soldiers to enforce the curfew anywhere. Besides, would a Hindu or a Sikh policeman shoot a Hindu or a Sikh? Would even a Gurkha? This was the railway station of Puranapur in 1947, not the Jallianwala Bagh of Amritsar in 1919. Back then, a detachment of soldiers had, at the orders of the English General Dyer, shot at an assembly of twenty thousand Hindus, Sikhs and Muslims in an enclosed park with a narrow entrance, peacefully protesting against the oppressive new British laws.

'Our Captain has gone nuts,' people said in the tents, a few of whom had been present at the Amritsar massacre. People on the platform stood on with wait-and-see faces, and stationmaster Nanda peeped through the bars of the ticket-counter window. What would the horsemen do next? What would the army captain do?

The horsemen did nothing. They coughed and laughed. They wanted the young officer to know they thought he was joking. They expected him to go inside the little red brick station house and call it a day.

Captain Kaul began to look worried. His order had not been obeyed. He was being laughed at by these blue-turbaned goons with murder in the eyes. Captain Kaul had to do something. And do it quickly. Otherwise…

'Lal Bahadur…' he called out his Havildar, a round-faced Gurkha twice his age, who had nearly tasted the bullet many times in the African desert and Sicilian vineyards with the Eighth Army a few years earlier.

'…The jeep.'

'Yes, Saa.'

Captain Kaul took a light machine gun from another Gurkha and walked briskly to the roofless jeep, setting his officer's cap squarely on his head under a glaring sun. Lal Bahadur walked by his side. The captain drove the jeep himself. He stopped it fifty yards from the pond and stood up, resting the barrel of the LMG on top of the windscreen. It was pointing at the horsemen.

'As commander of the Army of free India in Puranapur, I order you to leave here.' The captain spoke in crystal-cut Urdu, the way all officers spoke.

Several men guffawed. The titch-button of a boy was bluffing. What did he think they were? Wankers?

'I repeat my order. Get out of Puranapur. NOW,' Captain Kaul shouted this time. His hand holding the LMG shook and his boot resting on edge of the jeep's open door twitched. Lal Bahadur had never seen his captain like this. Only he knew what it meant. It meant that Captain Kaul would discharge the magazine of the LMG if not obeyed immediately. He knew this officer. He too stood up. Captain Kaul said something to him.

'Yes, Saa…'

Lal Bahadur saluted and called up his men, a dozen of them, on the station platform. They raced up to the jeep, flinging them flat on the burning earth, and pointing their .303 rifles at the ready at the horsemen.

Some horsemen laughed, nervously this time. It was a sight too strange for words. Their own army commander training a machine gun at them. They were angry.

'All right, all right, Kaptaan Sahib. No need to spend too much anger on us. We are brothers after all. You and I and our men. No?' the Sant said.

'Only came to see what they had done to our lovely Puranapur. All that smoke, Kaptaan Sahib,' Gautam said.

'You've seen. Now kindly go.'

'But what was our Army doing when Allah Hoo Army was burning our houses and our people?'

'As usual, our Army was sleeping,' the Sant said.

'They should have kept you a few years longer at school, Kaptaan Sahib,' Gautam laughed.

There was a short, sharp burst of fire from Captain Kaul's LMG. The horse whined loudly, shuffling.

'All right, all right. We will go if you insist.'

'I insist. And no mischief as you go.'

'Mischief? What mischief? Do we look the type?'

The Sant and his men cantered away in the haze of the scorched wilderness. Half a mile on, they stopped in a mango and jamun grove.

'That boy will be a proper general one day,' the Sant said.

'You stopped to tell us that, Sant?' Gautam said.

'And that we've left something behind.'

'What?'

'Some unfinished business. But day time bad time for our unfinished business.'

'So?' said many, exultantly.

So, a decision was taken, a time fixed, and embraces exchanged. Then, the horsemen galloped off to the villages they had come from.

Back at the station, the young army commander breathed out a long sigh as he handed back the LMG to his Havildar. It was not a sigh of relief. For he knew Puranapur had not seen the last of the mad blue turbans. To confirm this hunch, a sign suddenly appeared – a twitch in his left eye. He had learnt as a boy from his mother that this was a bad sign. Now it meant that the Sant would massacre the Muslims. And there was nothing the well-meaning young man could do to stop him. His youth began to tell on him. He felt lonely, desolate. There was only one somebody who could at least offer advice, if nothing else. This somebody was much older and was living through the tragedy of last night himself. Besides, Captain Kaul hardly knew the Congress leader; he had met him only once and that too just for a minute.

'Lal Bahadur. The jeep.'

The jeep tore through the half-burnt Saddar Bazaar to Dr Gupta's clinic. The well brought-up and impeccably-mannered army officer was crushed by embarrassment to encroach upon Mr Bhagwan Prasad's privacy, made all the more acute when he saw him so bandaged and surrounded by his entire family. But he could talk to his brother Jyoti Prasad, just as much a Congressman himself. The Captain had heard all about him from the police inspector. Partap Singh had told him how close the brothers were, how sometimes, it was the elder of the two who decided. Bhagwan signalled to Captain Kaul to talk to his brother.

Allah Army's dastardly attack had changed everything; all vows and promises had gone up in last night's smoke. The entire Muslim population of the locality was trapped and exposed. *Does Mr Jyoti Prasad have any idea how to avoid their destruction? Yes, Mr Jyoti Prasad does.* After what Bhagwan had said to the Sant when the mad man was leaving, an idea struck him. It was a plan as absurd as it was novel. However, it could succeed depending on how well the Muslim elders responded to it.

In the little room Dr Gupta's compounder used in the clinic, a meeting of great importance took place. Lying on the stretcher, Bhagwan chaired the meeting. Around him were his hairless brother in white khadi wearing a Gandhi cap, and the troubled young officer in perfectly ironed army khaki. Unable to talk, Bhagwan let his brother do all the talking, urging the very young officer to listen to his every word.

'Captain Kaul, you have to go to the Muslim area and talk to the Muslim elders,' Jyoti said.

'And say what, Mr Prasad?'

'Make them understand and agree with our plan for their escape. It is for their own good, considering what their murderous Army did last night.'

'What if they don't even want to hear about your plan, Mr Prasad?'

'Some among the bloody fools are bound to have some fucking sense in their heads clogged with hate,' Jyoti shouted uncharacteristically. 'They can't all be that mad? Or stupid?'

'I hope not, sir.'

'Or do they want the equally hateful Sant to blow up their homes and let his Nihangis gallop away with their daughters to gang-rape them?'

The soldier was moved by the mill owner's passion.

'If they want life and liberty, they must follow our plan to the letter, Captain Kaul.' Then Jyoti revealed his plan. Its simplicity amazed the soldier.

The Muslims received Captain Kaul, a Hindu and a Brahmin, with a warmth that surprised the young man. He was shocked to learn that the attack last night was the work of a secret and an unknown faction of ten young men.

Captain Kaul had visited the Muslim area regularly since his arrival in Puranapur five days ago. He was always well-received. But today was special. Today, he was their Prince Charming, their possible saviour. There was a persistent fear; they knew what was coming. Their only hope was this repugnant young Brahmin who spoke in Urdu, as if he had been brought up in a nawab's palace in princely Lucknow.

But what he said troubled them as much as what they feared was coming. It was that not the young Hindu officer, but, shame upon shame, the badly burnt Congress leader who would be their saviour. Or rather and equally shamefully, his brother.

Captain Kaul, his left eye still twitching, stunned his audience of the Muslim elders, including Mullah Jaffar, further by demanding that the remaining four men who had lobbed all those bombs, killing so many and burning a large number of homes, be handed over to the Army.

'In due course, they'll be tried in a court of law. Only that can save you, gentlemen, from what is coming from the Sant and his men.'

Was the pretty boy joking? Had he taken leave of his senses to expect them to give up their errant, but beloved sons just like that? Things had gone too far, didn't he know? Then what was he talking about?

Mullah Jaffar and the elders knew what the serious-looking boy-officer was talking about. So they didn't ask. They merely shook their heads; they were not giving up their boys come what may.

The man in uniform had expected that. He stunned his aged audience even further. He told them what the Congressman Bhagwan Prasad's brother had instructed him to tell them.

'You must leave Puranapur as soon as possible. All ten thousand plus of you. This instant. My few men cannot do anything for you anymore.'

'Kill him. Kill him,' came shouts from some AHAA soldiers watching and listening. 'KILL the Hindu dog.'

'You may do that. I am alone with my driver. But that will not save you.'

The elders nodded. Captain Kaul went on.

'I urge you go now. NOW. Fly. The mad Sant is on his way to fire-bomb you.'

'KILL THE MAN. KILL THE HINDU DOG.'

'Foul language will not save you. Fly now. NOW. And save your souls. My few men and I will, of course, escort you till the canal bridge. It's my duty as an Indian Army officer. There, your boys must blow it up after crossing it.' Captain Kaul saluted and went to his jeep.

Panic struck. It roared in as his jeep roared out. The dazed Muslim elders knew well what their *heroes* had done. What nobody knew was the extent of the damage caused. The usual gathering place was the vast maidan around the Badami Mosque with the marble minaret. The Muslims remaining in Puranapur – the very few families that had cars had left long ago – thousands of them, thronged there to sit out the last hours in the place of their birth and that of their forefathers. They waited for the heat to abate. When the sun went down on Puranapur, its skyline still murky with atoms of last night's bonfire, they took the mud road to the canal under three miles away. To an eagle or a vulture doing some late flying, returning to its nest for the night, it would have looked like a mile-long snake of man, woman, child, horse, donkey, dog, mule, goat and, of course, the bullock cart. At its head rode Captain Kaul's jeep with three non-military men. And his Gurkhas now in two army trucks, one behind the jeep at the head of the snake, the other at its tail. The snake moved sluggishly towards life and freedom across the Ravi Canal – a three-hour walk.

The Muslims of Puranapur left in the town their precious dwellings to save their souls. These would become homes tomorrow to Hindu and Sikh refugees ousted in a similar manner from their houses in what now had become Pakistan.

The Sant returned at night, with twice as many men as had

accompanied him during the day. In the black ink of the hour, they swooped down on Muslim Puranapur, uttering deafeningly the Sikh battle cry.

But a wall of humiliation echoed it back. For there were no sweet-sounding screams of women and children the horsemen had expected, nor the sound of gunfire from the Allah Hoo Army. The place was empty. Only owls and bats and shadows inhabited it now.

'We've been made donkeys of. Double donkeys. What now, Sant?' barked Gautam, slapping his forehead in disgust at his leader's brilliant 'leadery' and planning.

'They can't be far off, thousands and thousands of them. How far can they get to by walking? They are on their way to the canal. We'll catch them. My guarantee,' the Sant said.

'O you and your guarantees, Sant.' Gautam was heart-broken.

'Let's go and meet them there. They are waiting for us. Must not keep those waiting who are waiting. It's bad manners.'

'You and your fucking good manners, Sant!'

The Sant, his talisman in hand, turned his charger around. He and his followers galloped away to catch the retreating Muzzies. Twenty minutes or so later, they found them trudging along the bank of the Ravi Canal, it was swollen bank to bank with the monsoon of recent weeks. But they were on the other side, where Pakistan began, on the side of freedom, of life. The great snake had crossed over. The Muslims were safe. Their boys had blown up the bridge only minutes ago.

WAHE GURU JI KA KHALSA!
WAHE GURU JI KI FATEH!

Four hundred angry throats thundered, their battle cry now

making no sense. With smoke bringing tears to their eyes and the pungent smell of cordite filling their flaring nostrils, the Sant's men were gutted. Their wolf-mouths were still dribbling at the sight of so many women they couldn't lay their hands on. *What a waste, O, what a waste, Guruji in heaven! Not fair, this. Is it?*

More bitterly disappointed was the Sant himself. A mere thirty minutes separated him from the fulfilment of his life's dream. He would have turned this wide ditch of water crimson, and his boys would have got their just reward – all those beauties.

'I wish that Congress traitor Bhagwan Prasad were here even in his bandages at this moment with his stupid brother. I would give them both the ducking of their lives and leave them at the bottom of raging waters.'

The bandaged Congressman was there at that moment. He had insisted on coming along despite his open burn-wounds. Maya had tried to stop him by lying down on the floor. His children had blocked his way to the clinic door. Even Dr Gupta had warned him that the wounds he had sewn up might reopen if Bhagwan didn't rest in his bed. But like his brother, Bhagwan never listened to anyone. He had to go and place himself before the Sant's horse to stop him from what the bearded madman with a gold-tipped arrow had promised to do. Bhagwan went with them, one arm around his brother's shoulder and the other around Gulshan's.

They were exactly four hundred yards away in Captain Kaul's jeep now racing back home.

ACKNOWLEDGEMENTS

I wish to say a big Thank You to Laura Morris for making this book happen and everything else. I am equally thankful to Rani and Kaushaliya whose support and affection sustained me through the course of writing about what was essentially a part of my life.

My express thanks go to Bhaskar Roy of Palimpsest and his supremely gifted team for working their editorial magic on *Line Of Blood.* It was a pleasure working with them.

London
2 March 2017

Balraj Khanna